Ovidia Yu is one of Singapore's best-known and most acclaimed writers. She has had over thirty plays produced and is the author of a number of comic mysteries published in Singapore, India, Japan, America and the United Kingdom.

She received a Fulbright Scholarship to the University of Iowa's International Writers Program, has been a writing fellow at the National University of Singapore and was inducted into the Singapore Women's Hall of Fame.

Also by Ovidia Yu

The Frangipani Tree Mystery
The Betel Nut Tree Mystery
The Paper Bark Tree Mystery
The Mimosa Tree Mystery
The Cannonball Tree Mystery
The Mushroom Tree Mystery
The Yellow Rambutan Tree Mystery
The Angsana Tree Mystery

The Rose Apple Tree Mystery

Ovidia Yu

CONSTABLE

CONSTABLE

First published in Great Britain in 2025 by Constable

1 3 5 7 9 10 8 6 4 2

Copyright © Ovidia Yu, 2025

The moral right of the author has been asserted.

A CIP catalogue record for this book
is available from the British Library.

ISBN: 978-1-40871-702-8

Typeset in Contenu by SX Composing DTP, Rayleigh, Essex
Printed and bound in Great Britain by Clays Ltd, Elcograf S.p.A.

Papers used by Constable are from well-managed forests
and other responsible sources.

MIX
Paper | Supporting
responsible forestry
FSC® C104740

Constable
An imprint of
Little, Brown Book Group
Carmelite House
50 Victoria Embankment
London EC4Y 0DZ

The authorised representative
in the EEA is
Hachette Ireland
8 Castlecourt Centre, Dublin 15,
D15 XTP3, Ireland
(email: info@hbgi.ie)

An Hachette UK Company
www.hachette.co.uk

www.littlebrown.co.uk

This book is dedicated with love and gratitude to Krystyna Green who made Su Lin and Le Froy's adventures possible. Thank you, Krystyna!

Disclaimer

———◆———

Though I've taken artistic licence with regard to the geography of the Cameron Highlands, in other respects I have tried to make it as factually correct as possible.

Rose apples are now available in markets but I believe taste less sweet than when eaten straight off the tree.

Prologue: Tea Ceremony

———◆———

My left knee hurt, but the familiar pain was almost comforting. I was kneeling, head bowed, holding a cup of tea in both hands. Le Froy, on my right, was in the same position. If I was crazy enough to be in love with this man, at least he was crazy enough to be in love with me too...

'Only *goondus* go around looking for trouble,' my grandmother grumbled, resplendent in her intricately embroidered *sarong kebaya*. *Goondu*, from a mix of Tamil and Malay, means 'idiot' in Singlish. '*Aiyoh!* Why are you two so *goondu*?'

Aiyoh expresses all the annoyance and exasperation of a sigh, but with more force. Which sums up my grandmother's approach to life: even if you don't like what you have to do, you must do it with all the energy you can summon.

Not exactly typical wedding good wishes.

'Please drink some tea, Ah Ma,' I said, offering her the tiny cup with both hands.

My grandmother accepted it. The tea had been brewed in the proper traditional manner with red dates (for good luck), rock sugar (for a sweet union) and dried longans (for male rather than female offspring) but, from my grandmother's expression, you'd think I'd handed her kitchen swill in one of her best, reserved-for-special-occasions porcelain teacups.

'When people are fighting and getting murdered, any normal person would run far away,' Ah Ma muttered, 'not run towards – like asking to get killed faster!'

A sharp tongue click made us all jump. It came from Gan Jie, the black-and-white amah who'd supervised the tea-ceremony preparations. It was the same warning she used, with an even sharper pinch if you didn't jump to respond, when servant girls or house boys behaved badly. I saw them grinning. With the rest of the Chen Mansion household, they were standing in a row behind my grandmother and Uncle Chen as part of our wedding ceremony – which was as much for show as for luck and blessings.

Gan Jie was probably the only person my grandmother was afraid of. Ah Ma might be the head of the Chen family, but Gan Jie ran Chen Mansion.

My grandmother plastered a smile on her face, 'Congratulations. Please try to stay alive.'

This wasn't how I'd expected my wedding to be. I'd never been the kind of girl who dreamed of a fancy one, but I'd certainly not anticipated everything happening so fast.

Traditionally, the tea ceremony should have been carried out using my mother's wedding dowry tea set, which would then be passed to me, as the eldest daughter, to bring to my new family as part of my dowry. That there had been neither a tea set nor any dowry underlined how good my grandmother had been to take me in and bring me up.

After disgracing the Chen family by eloping, my father and his Japanese wife had died while I was still a baby. Their deaths, added to the polio that had crippled my hip and one of my legs, was why neighbours and fortune-tellers had strongly suggested that the best thing Chen Tai could do to cancel the bad luck I'd carried into the household was put me down a well. Instead my grandmother had not only raised me as her grand-daughter but sent me to learn to read and write English at the school set up by the ladies at the Mission Centre.

'If you can't get married, at least if you know English you can earn your living,' she'd explained. But learning to read and write, as well as speak, English, had opened up a world of possibilities for me. And not only that: attending the Mission Centre school had led me to Le Froy and this moment.

It was the best thing she could have done for me and I wondered if Ah Ma realised and regretted that.

'Chen Tai, please drink some tea,' Le Froy said, in Hokkien. He proffered his cup of tea as Ah Ma handed mine, now empty, to Gan Jie.

'Congratulations.' Ah Ma managed a smile for him without being prompted. 'After this, you can call me Ah Ma.'

'Thank you, Chen Tai,' Le Froy said.

That brought another genuine smile from my grandmother. 'Thank you for being part of our family. Please look after my granddaughter. You must make her behave herself and try to keep her out of trouble.'

'Don't ask for the impossible,' Uncle Chen muttered.

'I will try my best, Chen Tai.'

Another nod and a smile. Women found Le Froy charming and even my grandmother wasn't immune from it. Another reason why our marriage wasn't going to help my popularity in local circles.

When I'd first met him, Le Froy had been out east so long that he was tanned dark enough to pass for a local – which he'd done when he'd gone undercover as a drain inspector to expose gambling dens – although probably not as often as the stories suggested.

Since his imprisonment by the Japanese he'd lost a foot and most of his colour. There was no mistaking him for a local now. But though his skin was paler than it had been, he still looked tough and wiry, like an invasive root that's been unearthed but cannot be pulled out. The dark hair he'd had when we first met was streaked with silver now but was still thick. And still lovely. As far as I was concerned, he looked better now than ever before.

That was one blessing the war granted us: the ability to see how incredibly beautiful a person was just by virtue of being alive.

Best of all, Le Froy and I were married.

From Murder to Marriage

◆

Of course I'd not expected Ah Ma to be happy about such a rushed marriage. But I believed – or hoped – she would put a good face on it. It *was* my wedding day. And, after all that Le Froy had done for me and my family before and during the war, she could hardly disapprove of him. I suspected she felt that if she could delay our marriage long enough, that day might never come. I might yet agree to be matched with a nice young Chinese man from a respectable Chinese family or Le Froy might leave the island to marry an *ang moh*.

'How do I look?'

To sign my marriage contract, I was wearing a Western-style cotton frock with pink and blue flowers on a cream background. There hadn't been time to find a bridal dress or a traditional ceremonial gown.

'You look okay,' Little Ling said.

'Is Ah Ma ready yet?' I looked out of the front window hoping to spot Le Froy's car. The driveway outside Chen

Mansion was long enough that you could see automobiles before you heard them. 'Do you want to come in Le Froy's car with me, or wait and come with Ah Ma and your pa?'

We were going to be early for our ten-thirty appointment at the Registry of Marriages, but both Le Froy and I preferred to wait than to be waited for when it came to something so important.

'Ah Ma's not going,' Little Ling said. 'My pa also said he's not going.'

It wasn't a big deal, of course, just an appearance at the registrar's office to sign the marriage certificate before witnesses. But it was the only wedding I would have, and I'd hoped to have my family with me to share it.

'I'll talk to her,' I said. I started for the corridor to Ah Ma's room. 'It won't take long. We can go somewhere to eat afterwards.'

It felt almost more important to me that my grandmother should share a meal with Le Froy and me once we were legally married rather than when we were signing the register. That was my Chinese side speaking: sharing a meal would mark it as a special occasion and eating together as a family would bond the relationship between Le Froy and my grandmother. I was thinking we might go to Wing Choon Yuen, the banquet restaurant we'd gone to for my uncle's fiftieth-birthday celebration.

'No! Stop!' Little Ling grabbed my arm. 'Please don't, Su-jie! You mustn't. Ah Ma doesn't want to see you!'

'What?' I realised I hadn't seen – or heard – my grandmother all morning. At home she was usually bustling around giving the servants instructions, telling me and Uncle Chen about something she'd heard on the radio or from a neighbour, or asking Little Ling what she wanted to eat. I'd been too wrapped up in my plans and packing to notice. 'I only want to go and tell her I'm leaving now.'

Little Ling shook her head. 'Ah Ma doesn't want to see you,' she repeated. 'She told me to tell you she and Pa both don't want to see you.'

Part of me wanted to bang on Ah Ma's door until she let me in, even if she was angry and yelled at me. All my life my grandmother had told me exactly what she thought of me, but she had never turned me away.

I couldn't deal with that now, though. I could hear Le Froy's tyres grinding along the gravel outside.

'Would you like to come?' I asked Little Ling. 'We can go for ice cream afterwards, if you like.' I didn't like ice cream, but I really wanted someone from my family to be at my wedding.

'I need to stay here to talk to Ah Ma,' my cousin said. 'You go now. But you must come straight back here for lunch afterwards. Promise! You and Le Froy must come here. Don't go anywhere else first.'

There was no way Little Ling could talk our grandmother out of her sulk by lunchtime, but I was touched that she meant to try. And if I was wrong, so much the better.

'I promise,' I said.

Little Ling gave me a quick hug as I left.

'Everything okay?' Le Froy asked, as I got into his car.

'Everything's good,' I said. And I meant it.

I'd known for a long time that Thomas Francis Le Froy was the only man I ever wanted to marry. Unfortunately I wasn't alone there. Chief Inspector Le Froy of the Criminal Intelligence Department had been a legend in Singapore and the rest of the Crown Colonies before the war, and finding him a wife had been a principal pastime of expatriate ladies. I'd heard them compare him (favourably) to the film stars Rudolph Valentino, Douglas Fairbanks and John Barrymore.

He was still good-looking. I don't think anyone could have noticed that he walked, hiked and even played a little badminton on a prosthetic foot, unless they already knew. We were a matching pair of cripples, given my polio-damaged hip and leg.

'Everything is perfect.' I smiled at my husband-to-be.

It was only three days previously that Le Froy had proposed to me, if you could call it that. And it had only come about because of the Emerald Estate Murders.

The Emerald Estate was the rubber plantation up north in Perak, Malaya, where two white planters and their families had been murdered. According to the *Malayan Tribune*, brothers Jonathan and Samuel Walker, with Jonathan's wife Brenda and Samuel's wife Melinda, had been found dead by their estate manager on his return from a night in town.

There had been rumours of Japanese soldiers hiding in the jungle after the Allied forces' victory. According to the stories, they refused to believe Japan had surrendered or would ever surrender. Their orders were to terrorise the people until the Imperial Army returned and, if defeat seemed inevitable, to take as many of the enemy with them in a glorious suicide.

To be honest, I'd never met anyone who'd encountered one of those hold-out soldiers. In fact, all the Japanese military I'd met seemed as exhausted and fed-up with the business of war as we were.

Some locals said the workers were angry with the Walkers because they were laid off at the start of the monsoon season and told to leave. Most boss planters let the tappers stay on the property even if they are not yet hired for the following season. But the Walkers made them all leave. A lot of them had come from India or Indonesia and were desperate, but even many locals had nowhere else to go.

All of the victims had been shot, as well as stabbed. According to the local authorities, *Evidence shows the killers used both imported and local weapons, pointing to Communist vigilantes hiding in the jungle surrounding the rubber plantation.*

I'd also heard rumours that the vengeful spirits of local girls assaulted and driven to suicide by the Walker men had been seen around the plantation: they had driven the Walker brothers mad so they'd killed their wives and each other.

That wasn't surprising – the stories, I mean, not the murders. *Ang moh* men had a reputation for forcing themselves on local women, which made the British authorities and local parents wary of European–Asian relationships like ours.

'The governor had me over for drinks this afternoon,' was how Le Froy began. We were sitting on the porch after dinner at Chen Mansion. 'He's worried about the situation upcountry.'

'He's trying to call you out of retirement?' I guessed.

It had become increasingly clear that the British were having trouble in reimposing order on their colonies. It was hard to distinguish fighters for Asian independence and members of the newly illegal Communist party from petty criminals and troublemakers. Given that Le Froy had set up and run Singapore's criminal-intelligence network and pretty much wiped out gang activity, it had been only a matter of time before the struggling British administration turned to him for help.

'What did the governor offer you? And what did you say? You'll haggle with him before you accept, right? You can't just go back at the same salary – think of inflation! You're in Singapore so you must bargain.'

Le Froy's reluctance to do so was one of his only faults. Like many British, he didn't understand that bargaining was a game and a challenge. It was about balancing the social currency of supply and demand and getting the best deal for all involved. Every local child knows that if you see someone selling rose apples from his roadside tree, you'll be asked to pay a lot because *jambu*, or rose apples, are almost impossible to buy commercially: they decay too quickly to transport. On the other hand, if you offer to hawk the fruit to passing traffic or chase off marauding birds and squirrels, you might get a share of the money you collect, while eating as much as you like of the fruit.

'He wants me to look into the murders at the Emerald Estate.'

'The governor wants you to go up to Perak? In this weather?' It was never a good idea to travel during the monsoon season. 'But that's old news. They've already caught the Communist vigilantes who did it, haven't they? What do they expect you to do?'

'The new estate owner is getting death threats,' Le Froy said, 'from the same people, it seems.'

'What?' If the new owner of the estate was being threatened, the authorities had either arrested the wrong men or more of them were still at large. And since the murderers had no qualms about killing white men, they wouldn't balk at bumping off an *ang moh* police investigator.

'The monsoon is bad this year. Roads may be washed away. It'll be difficult to get there and you may not be able to get back until after the rainy season.'

Le Froy nodded, clearly distracted. I suspected he was already thinking about the case.

'When do you start?'

'I'll be officially reinstated once I sign the contract. But he mentioned that some people have issues with my violating some of the conduct clauses.'

'You? Like what?'

'In particular, the one that prohibits associating with undesirable elements of society . . .'

'He was talking about my family.'

I knew the Chen family had a not entirely undeserved reputation for running the local black-market. My late father had been the notorious Big Boss Chen, who united the local *tong*s and convinced them to work with instead of against each other. That was why Uncle Chen, despite his size, was known as 'Small Boss Chen' even twenty years after his brother's death.

But it was Ah Ma rather than Uncle Chen who managed the family businesses and property rentals, though she always referred to it as 'helping neighbours'.

'Those conduct rules were drawn up with gambling, opium and prostitution in mind. Family members, however questionable, are exempt.'

I couldn't process what he was saying. Was Le Froy telling me this was goodbye? I'd never considered such a possibility until now. I turned to him and saw he wasn't looking at me. Instead, he was fumbling clumsily in his pocket. Fumbling? This man who could whip off his prosthetic foot mid-stride and throw it like a precision weapon? He finally pulled out a little crime-scene-evidence canister. It looked like one of those used to collect bullet casings and tooth fragments.

'Something that belonged to my mother,' he said.

'You're not carrying your mother's—' I was trying to decide whether teeth or kidney stones would be worse, when I saw what he was holding out to me.

'Green and blue sapphires set around white diamonds,' Le Froy said. 'She wore it till the day she died. Will it do?'

'Will it do what?' I took the ring automatically, but my mind was blank.

'For a wedding ring,' Le Froy said. 'My mother asked me to give it to the woman I married, with her love. See if it fits.'

It did.

'I know it's not new—'

'I like that,' I said quickly. 'I like knowing that it belonged to your mother. But tell me what this is for. You just said you can't see me any more.' I've never been good at romantic moments.

'Family members are exempt from the clauses. I have the right to consort with my wife's family,' Le Froy said. 'It's the perfect solution. What do you think? Will you marry me?'

I thought it was a brilliant solution. Would I marry him? Ever since I'd learned Le Froy felt for me as I did for him, I'd dreamed we would, someday, somehow, be married and live happily ever after. But, given our circumstances and the British administration, I'd not been able to see how this could happen.

'Of course I'll marry you!' I wasn't ladylike but I was honest. 'When?'

'As soon as possible. I want us to leave together for Perak. We can get on the Sunday-morning train. By the way, I love you.'

'I love you too.'

And that settled it.

'If you want to change your mind this is the time,' Le Froy said. 'When we come out of there,' he gestured at the Registry of Marriages, 'it'll be too late.'

I realised we'd arrived and parked in one of the slanting lots in front of the offices.

So, here I was on my wedding day. I would have worn a white dress for a Western-style wedding or a red outfit for a Chinese ceremony, but I was getting married at a government office in an almost-new cotton frock.

'I don't want to change my mind.' I climbed out of the car and smoothed my dress.

I knew I was doing the right thing. I just wished my family could have accepted it.

The Surprise

It wasn't the kind of wedding most girls dream of. Still, I believe it's better to marry the right man in the worst circumstances than to marry the wrong one in the best. The look on Le Froy's face as we stepped back into the sunlight after the brief ceremony showed me his thoughts were running along much the same lines.

He held out his arms and I moved into them, surprised by how comfortable, familiar and right it felt. Even though we had embraced before, this felt like coming home.

'A celebratory lunch in the Farquhar Hotel for my bride?' Le Froy suggested.

'I promised Little Ling we would go straight home for lunch after signing,' I said. 'I would like to. I hope you don't mind.'

I didn't know if there would be any lunch for us at home. But with Ah Ma's disapproval still hanging heavy over me, I didn't feel up to facing the judgemental looks we'd attract. Wealthy locals in their Western finery would whisper about sarong party girls as any Westerners pretended, with pitying disdain, not to recognise Le Froy.

I wasn't imagining things. I'd seen all these reactions when my best friend Parshanti was out with Leasky, her Scottish doctor husband.

And that was yet another drawback to getting married at such short notice: Parshanti and her parents were spending three months on Langkawi Island, where Dr Shankar, her father, and Dr Leask were studying the medicinal properties of various roots, bark and sap used by locals in traditional healing. This had started as a passion of Leasky's but Dr Shankar was now just as enthusiastic. I was sure they would have come back to witness my wedding if they could have made it in time, and I knew they would be happy for me when they got back, but it wasn't the same.

'I think Little Ling is trying to persuade my grandmother to say something nice to us before we leave, but I don't think she'll manage it.'

On the way back to Chen Mansion, I told Le Froy about Ah Ma refusing to see me, and hoped she'd have got over it, but I had to prepare him in case she hadn't. To his credit, he didn't tell me she would come round or that everything would be all right. He knew Ah Ma – and me – better than that.

'I would like to pay my respects to your grandmother,' he said, 'and invite her, with your uncle and Little Ling, to join us for wedding-day *laksa* – crab meat as well as prawns. What do you think?'

'Wedding-day *laksa*?' I laughed. 'I've never heard of such a thing!'

'Because it only exists on this one day. From next year onwards it will be known as anniversary-day *laksa*.'

It was wonderfully ridiculous, and I felt instantly more cheerful. It's almost impossible to feel sad when eating – or even thinking about eating – *laksa lemak*. There's something about the rich savoury sauce and slippery white noodles that transports you to a place where life is safe, luxurious and full of delicious surprises, like cockles in the bottom of your bowl. So, I was feeling positive as we drove eastwards along Mountbatten Road. Even if Ah Ma and Uncle Chen couldn't be persuaded to join us – highly likely, given they'd refused even to see me that morning – there was a chance they would come round in time.

All of that was driven out of my mind when Le Froy had to stop because the driveway to Chen Mansion was blocked by three huge lorries trying to turn out onto the main road. What was happening? You saw those fourteen-foot canopied lorries only when they were transporting funeral-wake equipment or seizing confiscated property. Were they here to seize our furniture? My grandmother wouldn't move out of Chen Mansion – she had always said she would die in the house where her husband had died. What could have happened since I'd left that morning? Was Little Ling all right?

Even though the war was over, I still had nightmares of Japanese soldiers breaking in and rounding us up to be shot.

'What's going on?' Le Froy looked tense as he watched the vehicles negotiate the turn onto the main road. There wasn't room for them to complete the manoeuvre in one go and each had to reverse and adjust its position several times.

At least the lorries looked empty: if they had come to seize our furniture they'd been foiled.

'No idea. Drop me off and leave me here. I need to find out what's happening, but there's no reason for you to be involved.'

'If you're involved then so am I.'

'This isn't the time for romantic talk. If the governor's people sent them, you shouldn't be seen here.'

I opened my passenger door and started to get out, but Le Froy grabbed and held on to my arm. 'Much as I hate to refuse your first order as my wife, I suggest we—'

'Hello!' My door was pulled wide and Little Ling leaned in to hug me. 'Mr and Mrs Le Froy! You're back faster than we expected! Everything's almost ready!' She was breathless – she must have run all the way down the drive.

'What's almost ready?'

'Ah Ma got everything! Come and see! Quick!'

There were red and gold lanterns and banners along the stretch of driveway closest to the house and on both sides of the wide front steps, bearing the *shuang xi*, or double-happiness symbol, in gold. A red carpet with dragon and phoenix motifs lined the front steps, leading into the front room, which had been transformed into a wedding hall, ready for the tea ceremony.

'Ah Ma said that even if you can't have all twelve days for a proper wedding, you must at least do your Third Day Ceremony,' Little Ling said, 'It's the most important,' she explained to Le Froy, 'because that's when you get the wedding presents.'

'Twelve days.' Le Froy sounded dazed. 'I thought Chen Tai was against having the wedding.'

'I warned you, it's not easy marrying into a local family!' I was laughing and crying from relief. 'Thank you, Ling-Ling! But how did you manage to talk Ah Ma round so fast?'

'Ah Ma wasn't angry with you. She didn't want to let you get married without buying protection from the temples, so she and Papa had to leave early to get money and buy gold to pay for the special prayers at the Waterloo Street temple before your wedding. And she got them to adjust wedding clothes to fit you for the ceremony. But the surprise party was my idea!' Little Ling said proudly. 'It worked, didn't it? You're surprised, aren't you?'

Little Ling meant well, but she could have spared me a lot of stress.

'Very,' Le Froy said. He smiled, happy for me. I didn't want to think about how much Ah Ma must have spent to get the wedding feast and decorations set up so swiftly – not to mention how much she must have paid the temple for protection blessings. My grandmother didn't believe in leaving anything, not even luck, to chance.

And that was how we ended up going through the tea-ceremony ritual on our wedding day.

'Your father would never forgive me,' Uncle Chen's voice was thick with tears, 'for letting his daughter marry an *ang moh*. A police officer at that.'

'My father would thank you for looking after me so well. Le Froy is a good man.'

'Even if he is a good man, that doesn't mean he will make a good husband. Men!' Uncle Chen shook his head. 'No matter who they are, they drink, they gamble, they go to smoke opium ... Men are no good.'

Uncle Chen meant well. I managed not to point out there had been no guarantee that any of the men he'd tried to marry me off to previously wouldn't have ended up the same way.

'If he gives you any trouble, you come and tell me,' Uncle Chen said. 'Anything. If he gets drunk and beats you, you let me know and I will take care of it.'

'Don't worry. I'll be all right,' I said.

'You've got family,' Uncle Chen said. 'Anything wrong, you come back and tell your family. I will do what your father would want me to do.'

I knew he meant it. As the authorities were only too aware, my family has always preferred to handle any problems themselves, rather than depending on officials.

'You don't need to go with him to Perak, what,' Ah Ma said. 'Be a modern couple. Now is the 1950s already. Husband and wife don't have to be together all the time. He needs to go up to Perak to work, let him go. You can tell him you should stay in Singapore to help your old grandma here.'

My grandmother was such a force of energy that, most of the time, I didn't think about her strength or size. She had been 'old' as long as I could remember. But now, trying to persuade me to stay with her, she looked small and frail as well as old.

'Will you be all right, Ah Ma?'

She seemed to read my thoughts, 'Don't worry about me. Worry about yourself. Nowadays you young career women should be doing your own work, not following husband around!'

As Little Ling had foretold, there were wedding gifts.

Ah Ma gave me eight 100-gram gold bars. 'Portable currency. You can use it anywhere,' she said. 'No need to tell *him*. A woman should always have some private money of her own.'

The tiny gold bars were light and easy to carry if you were forced to leave your home country or trying to return to it.

She also handed me a small light green cloth package. By its weight I knew immediately that it was a *kris*, and when I folded back the cotton pocket I saw that it was the one she had slipped into my bag when I first went to work in Government House. 'Ah Ma, this is your *kris* – I can't take it.'

It was Ah Ma's talisman, inherited from the husband who had died and left her with two young sons.

'I was going to give it to you anyway,' Ah Ma said. 'This is a good time.'

'I don't need it,' I said. 'I'll be with Le Froy.' In case Ah Ma had any thoughts of my needing to use it on him.

'Just take it,' Ah Ma said. 'If you have it, you won't need it.'

A weapon and a spiritual object, the *kris* is as much a talisman as a weapon. It can also be a family heirloom, as mine was. It was a narrow, asymmetric dagger with a wide base. It had probably been made in Indonesia by an expert bladesmith, or *empu*. The iron and nickel alloy of its blade would have been heated to molten and folded with utmost precision up to a hundred times as chants infusing strength and protection were worked into it.

Not surprisingly, some people believe the *kris* possesses magical powers of protection. Did I believe that? Perhaps.

'Thank you, Ah Ma,' I said.

'I understand why you want to go,' Ah Ma said, 'so you should understand why I must help the tenants. Own people must help own people.'

I supposed I deserved that. I'd told my grandmother so many times that the tenants renting her business and residential properties took advantage of her. They were always asking for help (funds) to fix up the properties or unable to come up with rent because a son was sick or a daughter was getting married. Although Chen Tai presented a tough front, she was known for always helping her 'own people'.

It was totally different. The Chen business empire was all about hanging on to money and power. Helping Le Froy as his wife and partner? He was 'own people' to me now.

'You'd better come back,' Ah Ma said.

Uncle Chen presented Le Froy with a document stamped with the family seal. 'Su Lin will look after you as long as she is with you. If she is not, this should keep you safe.'

The document certified that Le Froy was under Chen family protection, to be treated with all the respect that a family member was entitled to. It was their way of accepting him into our family and Le Froy understood what it meant. I wouldn't have married a man who didn't.

'Why do you go to Perak?' Ah Ma shook her head. 'Don't let him take a job there. You mustn't stay there. I need you to help me here.'

The first time she'd said that it had been presented as an excuse I could use to stay in Singapore. This time it was a naked request.

I looked at my grandmother, She had raised me, so it was my duty to work for her for the rest of her life – or mine. That's how it is in Chinese families. Everyone works without pay, jostling for favour. After the big boss dies, the heirs fight over the spoils.

My own father had escaped, hadn't he? Then again, he and my mother had died in a cholera epidemic soon after marrying against Ah Ma's wishes. Maybe that was how Chinese gods punished unfilial children.

'What's up?' Le Froy came over to join us. 'Anything you know about Perak would be helpful.'

'Perak makes very good clay pots for cooking,' Ah Ma said, 'the *labu sayong* pots made from Perak River clay. You can use them on charcoal, on the stove or in the oven. Get some if you can.'

Ah Ma's eyes might be weakening, but her mind was still as sharp as the points of her *cucuk sanggul*, the fancy floral hairpins keeping her bun in place today. Between those and the pins on her *kerongsang* brooches, she was full of sharp points when she was dressed up. She'd told me once that the more beautifully you were dressed, the more defences you needed.

'Your pots are fine, Ah Ma,' I told her. 'You have too many as it is.'

'You will need them for your own kitchen,' my grandmother said. 'A complete set,' she added firmly. 'Some big pots for up to ten people. And small pots for children to learn how to make sticky rice cakes.'

'No need,' I said, realising which children she was thinking of.

23

'I've given you money to buy them. Why do you say you won't need them?'

I saw Le Froy following our exchange. He might not have grasped the significance of giving family cooking pots. But I suspect he understood what Ah Ma meant him to.

In the early morning, Uncle Chen drove us to the railway station. I was ready to start on the adventure of married life.

'Take care of yourself, Lin-Lin,' Uncle Chen said. He hadn't called me by my childhood nickname for years. 'Come home soon.'

'Please don't get married until we come back,' Le Froy said.

I looked at him in surprise, but Uncle Chen took it in his stride. 'I am never going to marry again,' he said. 'Too dangerous. Bad for the health.'

The Murder of the
Walker Brothers

———◆———

It wasn't the best time of year to travel. Rainfall is always
heaviest between October and February when the north-
east monsoon is in full force. It should have been almost
over but it had been a year of heavy rain, and many roads
were impassable.

To make things worse, several railway lines had been
devastated by the Japanese and our own people trying to slow
down their advance. Though efforts had been made to rebuild
them, many were still down. And several stretches of the
surviving north–south line were underwater due to the floods.

The further north we went, the worse it was. The weather
was largely responsible for the terrible flooding, but also this
was low-lying country. There were frequent landslides too. In
the old days, the trees on the hills would have protected the
valleys but they were gone in the crazy deforestation for rubber.

It wasn't an easy journey. Bus, train, Land Rover. But I found myself enjoying the trip. Or, rather, I found myself enjoying the forced leisure. When you are in a train, there is nothing you can do except wait for the time to pass as you watch the landscape. Nothing you do will change the direction or the speed. Sometimes our lives are like that. We just don't realise it. And we busy ourselves so we don't think about what we are moving towards.

Of course it was also good to be spending some time 'alone' with Le Froy.

I missed Singapore. Much as I loved the rustic tranquillity of wood-stilt villages and old trees, you couldn't beat tarmacadam roads and concrete bridges for holding up against the worst weather.

Perak was one of Malaya's northernmost states, sharing a border with Thailand, and the rains were even worse there than in Singapore. According to the lunar calendar the coming new moon would be a 'super moon', meaning the tides would be higher, and I was glad of the modern roads when we left the train at Ipoh station. On the way we passed groups fleeing the floods. In addition to rubber, Perak grew rice, and the *padi* fields were low-lying, suffering even more from the floods than other regions.

'You're evacuating because of the super moon?' I asked a man.

'It's not all Chinese superstition,' he said. 'Science backs it up. Because the moon is closer to the earth, the gravitational pull is stronger so tides rise higher and drop lower. The last super moon here, the floods came with the high tides even when it wasn't raining. You couldn't see the roads between the *padi* fields. It's already flooding now, after the weeks of rain we've had, and it'll get worse.'

I could understand the dread. What made it worse was that the waters swirling around us were so filthy with everything that had been flushed out of the drains and sewers. Household items and dead animals added to the chaos.

What a way to start our life together.

The Emerald Estate was on the outskirts of Kuala Kangsar, where the first rubber trees in Malaya had been planted. It was the royal town of the state of Perak and a collecting centre for the rice and rubber of the region, but we headed for Ipoh, where the nearest colonial office was. No one paid any attention to us. They were busy evacuating and sandbagging to protect what couldn't be moved.

'You don't look like our usual evacuees,' said a short but square-built man in a singlet and khaki shorts. He was carrying a shovel and two buckets. His greying hair was in sharp contrast to his dark skin, but he was probably much younger than Le Froy.

'My name's Le Froy. I'm looking for Brandon Sands?'

The man put down his equipment and held out a hand. 'I've been expecting you. I'm the local administrator, presently in charge of unclogging storm drains. Welcome to Ipoh, but you're not seeing it at it's best – or me.'

'You look like someone who gets into the trenches with his men. There's no better look.'

'I owe you a drink for that. But not right now. You're here about what happened on the plantation? Case closed. Once they rounded them up, the guys tried to fight their way out and got shot.'

'How many?' Le Froy asked.

'Five,' Brandon said.

'It sounds like they were desperate,' Le Froy said. 'Desperate men do crazy things.' He paused. 'I was told the new owner was having trouble with the same workers, though. But clearly this isn't a good time. Can you tell me where to find him?'

'Max Moreno was the original brains behind the Emerald Estate,' Brandon said. 'He went about tying up all the small plantations in the area to create this big deal he packaged as the future of Malayan rubber. He was going to build a rubber empire, everything from tapping and processing to exporting the latex. But he needed a British partner, and that was why Jonathan Walker was brought in. Then Max moved on to something else and Walker harnessed his brother. After the business went down, Max Moreno bought himself back in with Terry Cook as his British partner.'

'British partner?' I said.

'Moreno is South American.' Brandon Sands answered me as easily as he'd spoken to Le Froy and I gave him points for that. 'To qualify for government investment and rebuilding grants, you need a British partner.'

'The Walkers were shot as well as stabbed?' Le Froy said.

'Yes. It was a terrible business. That was how we knew discontented locals were responsible – they left some of their knives on the scene. Very distinctive knives. They were likely

28

trying to save bullets. After shooting the Walkers, they finished them off with the knives. To be honest, something like that was going to happen sooner or later. The pressure was building up. Protests and such.

'Japanese-run estates going to the British roused bad feeling around here. Locals had hoped for the return of their family smallholdings, which had been seized by the Japanese. Instead they were co-opted to form the industrial-sized plantation. They even had a lawyer to halt the sale long enough for them to have an official hearing on their claim, but it was deemed uneconomic and a step backwards to break up the giant estate into small farms. They were offered a concession: if the local farmers could match the price, they could buy the Emerald Estate and divide it up as they wished. Of course no local farmers could match the price – especially as they aren't eligible for the grants offered to European investors.'

'So you saw this coming.'

Le Froy's tone was matter-of-fact, but Brandon Sands bristled. 'British authority over the plantations is minimal. The white plantation owners rule their property like feudal land-lords. And you can't hold it against the local police. Obviously the British are trying to get things back to how they were before the war, but the Indian nationalists and Chinese Communists have got the locals all worked up about independence. And that Palin fellow isn't helping matters.'

'Harry Palin?' I asked. 'Is he here?'

Harry Palin, the son of a former governor, was an old friend.

Brandon Sands shook his head, 'He's been questioning the arrests and the shooting. Might shoot him myself if I saw him.'

'What's Palin done now?' Le Froy asked.

'He's been working pro bono for the Chinese Communists and jungle vigilantes. He made a big stink over the shooting. I swear he was more steamed up about the prisoners getting shot than the planters. And before the shooting he almost came to blows with Jonathan Walker. The police had to be called in.'

'Over what?' I could see Le Froy making a mental note to check on Harry.

'Palin claimed that the Walkers had no right to the Emerald Estate, that the property sale was illegal, that if the properties and factories seized from the Japanese wartime government were auctioned, the money should be given to the families the Japanese had seized them from, not fed into the British administration.'

'The man has a point,' Le Froy said.

Brandon Sands looked pained. 'It might seem that way. We explained that, since the Japanese hadn't left reliable records, it was impossible to locate the rightful owners. Did he expect us to hand over something so valuable to anyone who claimed their family squatted there?'

'What did he say to that?'

'Palin came back with testimonies from witnesses who lived there. Various unverifiable documents. He doesn't understand what he's dealing with. Breaking up the estate now would reduce its value to a fraction of what it's worth.'

'It's worth a lot?'

'The Emerald Estate is one of the largest rubber plantations in Perak. One of the largest on the peninsula. An estate this size with its own processing plant? Better than a gold mine.

And the world is hungry for all the rubber we can export, with the boom in American motor-cars using rubber tyres. It needs to be run efficiently.'

'But if Max Moreno is receiving threats,' I said, 'if someone is threatening the new owners, doesn't it show they arrested the wrong people?'

'That might be exactly why those notes were sent,' Brandon Sands said. I got the feeling he didn't think the threats were real. 'The Walkers didn't mention any threats. There were some protests and petitions but no threats were made. Most likely someone's trying to make us believe the wrong people were arrested and killed.

'The new owners are understandably worried. They've taken a house in the Cameron Highlands resort until the situation is resolved. It's the monsoon season anyway, so the plantations have shut down operations. Most of the colonials are on home leave. That's part of the reason why Civil Administration was so relieved to have Moreno step in. And they don't want to lose him.'

'Perhaps whoever was behind the murders was hoping that if a new buyer didn't show their hand, Civil Administration would decide to break up the estate and sell it in parts, rather than just allowing the rubber trees to decline. But the new buyers must have known about the murders, right? I mean, they knew what they were getting themselves into.'

'Not necessarily,' Brandon said. 'As far as they were concerned, they were in the right place at the right time to get a great deal. Until the threats started coming. That's what the police said, anyway.'

'I thought a police unit was assigned to the estate?' Le Froy said.

'Moreno hired private security – gangsters with guns – from the police ranks. I have the details somewhere – give me a moment. We're not evacuating, but everything's packed away from the waters.'

Brandon Sands clearly didn't approve and I agreed with him. My grandmother always said that if you needed armed guards it showed you had no real power. She liked to say she didn't need security because the people around her had more to lose if something happened to her. (She did have a driver, though, who doubled as a bodyguard, and Uncle Chen could have summoned up a small army in an hour if needed.)

'Three men.' Brandon Sands passed Le Froy a manila envelope. 'Carbon copies of the Walker reports and the lease agreement.'

'What do they expect three men to do against the hordes of Communist vigilantes they've been frightening people with?' Le Froy opened the envelope.

'They have to make a show of force. Even if they don't expect anything to happen, they have to ensure investors aren't frightened off. All they want is to get rubber production and exports going again.'

'What's this?' Le Froy flipped through the documents he pulled out of the envelope.

'The security team escorted Max Moreno and his party up to the Camerons. Knowing you were coming, I took it upon myself to book you a lodge there, too.'

'No!' Le Froy said.

'The Cameron Highlands?' I said involuntarily. 'Oh, gosh!'

Brandon Sands bestowed an unexpectedly sweet smile on me. 'I heard about your marriage. Congratulations to both of you. I booked a rental lodge in the Rose Apple Retreat, where Max and his partner are spending the monsoon season, but I'll be occupied here for obvious reasons. It's a perk of the job and would be a waste if no one takes advantage of the booking. I've heard the Cameron Highlands is considered an ideal honeymoon spot. A little bit of England in Malaya.'

On principle, Le Froy tried to avoid accepting anything that might be construed as a favour or a bribe. But this had been phrased as part of his assignment (and I knew he'd seen that the idea appealed to me). Still, he had to ask: 'Won't your wife and family mind giving up their time in that little bit of England?'

Brandon Sands looked at me, then back at Le Froy. 'My wife is related to John Archer, who became the first black mayor of London in 1913. My people settled in London in the early nineteenth century after fighting in the Napoleonic Wars. But in our bit of England, people still hold their noses or their babies tighter when we're around.' He picked up his buckets and reached for the shovel. 'Here we're just one more shade on the spectrum. I have to get on. People have been coming in all day. The worst affected areas around here are Kampung Pantai Tin, Kampung Tebuk Yan and Parit Marikan. Most of our evacuees are from those areas, but those further out are starting to come in. We currently have four relief centres housing the displaced, but we'll need more. If you decide to join them at the Cameron Highlands

Resort, I'll arrange for a car, but you should leave soon, before the roads are completely flooded.'

'The Cameron Highlands Resort.' Le Froy tested the words on his tongue. 'Where Japanese generals holed up during the occupation.'

'It's a resort on a plateau in the middle of the jungle, and in the rainy season, it's almost impossible to get through. It's not just inconvenient, it can be dangerous to get into and out of,' he said. 'Landslides, floods, roads blocked, bridges down. But if you've nothing special to get back to, it's not a bad place to hole up.'

Le Froy looked at me. I didn't try to hide my eagerness. He nodded. 'Thank you. I'll hang on to these?' He indicated the envelope and the documents.

'Be my guest.'

After the whirlwind courtship and marriage, I was getting a honeymoon in the Cameron Highlands!

Honeymoon in the Cameron s

———◆———

The roads were crowded with people flocking into town as we drove out in the opposite direction. This wasn't surprising, given more than a thousand people were being evacuated in Manjung district. The continuous rainfall since early October had led to reports of floodwaters as high as five feet in Sungai Batu and Padang Serai, the districts from which those people were fleeing.

But even when the monsoon season had passed, tensions would remain. Relations between the recently restored British administration and local people had been deteriorating for some time. Things were relatively calm in Singapore, but even there I had heard mutterings of discontent, which showed how bad it was.

Without discussion, Britain had imposed a new, centralised government, giving it precedence over the Malay state sultans, and people, royal and not, were understandably peeved. Even the occupying Japanese had made a show of paying respect to the sultans of each state, claiming to free them from the yoke of Western colonialism.

But I didn't want to think about that while I was enjoying the benefits of Western colonialism, snug and dry in the back seat of Brandon Sands's Humber Imperial. 'This is such a grand motor-car!'

'Brought in before the war and restored afterwards.' Ramesh Kumar, the Indian driver, seemed pleased by my enthusiasm and evidently didn't mind being pulled off drain-clearing duties to chauffeur us up to Moonlight Point in the Cameron Highlands.

'They don't make pre-war quality motors like this any more. Winston Churchill has one just like it. His has a partition behind the driver's seat and a giant ashtray in the back, but otherwise it's the same.'

'Parshanti's going to be so jealous!' I whispered to Le Froy.

He smiled, but said, 'I apologise that driving us up is adding to your workload.'

I was told it was a journey of just under sixty miles, but due to the crowds, the flooding and the winding, narrow roads of the ascent to the highlands, the drive would take us three to four hours.

Le Froy had tried to insist we could make our own way, that he would drive us if we could find a vehicle, but Brandon Sands had gently but firmly refused.

'It's not hard work. Mostly broken branches, soggy leaves and the occasional dead rat. But we've to keep at it or the floodwaters back up even worse,' Ramesh Kumar explained.

'Boss Sands has us all on shifts, but he's been working non-stop himself.'

It made me think even better of the man who'd just handed us a holiday that was probably a treasured bonus. 'I hope his wife won't mind missing out on their Camerons trip too much.'

'Mrs Sands is running the women's and children's relief centres,' our driver said. 'My wife and daughters are helping there too.' I'd barely registered a pang of guilt that I was doing nothing, before he added, 'They are good people. People have threatened them too, telling them to get out of Malaya or die.'

His eyes met Le Froy's in the rear-view mirror. 'Boss Sands says you are here to stop the threats. I hope you can.'

'You don't want independence for Malaya? Or for India?'

'I don't want people like Boss Sands and Mrs Sands to get hurt,' the driver said.

'Preferably nobody gets hurt,' Le Froy said. He turned to me. 'By the way, the security detail includes one Prakesh Pillay.'

'Prakesh is there? Since when?'

Le Froy laughed. 'He's one of the gangsters with guns Max Moreno hired.'

'I thought he'd taken a post in Kuala Kangsar in one of the new developments.'

I admit I'd been jealous of Ferdinand de Souza and Prakesh. They'd been awarded their captain's badges for accepting posts upcountry, a much faster promotion than if they'd stayed in Singapore. I, though, had lost my position as paid but unofficial translator when Le Froy retired.

But I was already looking forward to catching up with Prakesh Pillay. So far, married life was pretty good, even if I'd spent most of it cramped on trains and in cars, and my new husband was paying more attention to his papers than to me. Given the man I'd married – the only man I'd ever have married – this would be a dream honeymoon.

Prakesh Pillay and Ferdinand de Souza had been young corporals learning the ropes when I first went to work for Le Froy. We had made mistakes together, survived together and had become friends over the years. I missed our easy workplace camaraderie – especially as neither of them enjoyed letter-writing.

I only knew how Ferdie de Souza was doing – he had been posted to Pahang – because his sister Elizabeth was one of Little Ling's teachers at the Mission Centre school.

That was another sore point for me. I couldn't be employed as a full-time teacher there without a Teacher Training Certificate because I wasn't a 'native' English speaker. This, even though my English-language skills were just as good as – probably better than – Elizabeth de Souza's. But she was Eurasian and apparently the European blood in her veins qualified her to teach.

I had nothing personally against Lizzie de Souza, who always passed on news of her brother through Little Ling. She had even come over to help Ah Ma and Uncle Chen with some business letters after being asked to correct Little Ling's attempts. And, yes, I could have helped with those letters but I wasn't going to feel guilty about not having done so. I'd meant it when I told Ah Ma I didn't want to work in the family business, and I knew she was using Little Ling as the thin edge of the wedge.

That Uncle Chen was willing to accept help with English from a female outsider showed how much things had changed: in my childhood he'd railed against Ah Ma sending me to study English at school. He'd complained to her that I'd marry an *ang moh* and hadn't been wrong.

'If you need an English speaker in the business, you'd do much better learning English yourself than sending your daughter to school hoping that someday she'll come and work for you,' I'd heard Lizzie telling Uncle Chen. 'The best way to teach is by example. If you want her to learn, you should show her you will too.'

Things were certainly changing.

'Do you think we'll get a chance to see Harry on our way back?' I asked.

'Probably. If you like,' Le Froy said. 'But unofficially.'

'Why?'

'We're officially working on disbanding the Communist guerrilla forces and Palin's helping them file legal demands for back pay for the time they spent assisting British troops during the war.'

'That sounds fair enough,' I said. After all, the British forces had worked closely with the Malaysian Communist Party during the war. Harry, with Dr Leask and Parshanti, had survived several months in the jungle, thanks to the Communist guerrillas.

'But the war's over and the powers that be are worried the MCP is getting too popular. Now they're no longer needed, the official brief is to disarm and phase them out. Palin's use of legal channels to help their cause is making him even more of an undesirable element than anyone in your family right now.'

As we left the town the rain stopped and we could wind down the windows to let the moist post-deluge air blow in. Riding in a motor-car with the windows down and the wind in your face is one of the greatest luxuries of the modern world. On a bicycle, you're pedalling too hard to enjoy it, and in a bullock cart there's always such a strong smell of the animal.

Sometimes I think we get used to things too quickly. During the Japanese occupation, I'd believed that if only we could survive the war, we would all be at peace, and would live happily ever after. Now the Japanese were gone, but instead of being happy, people were picking fights with each other.

'Why are people still fighting?' I said aloud. 'Isn't it enough to be alive?'

'Be glad we're alive to complain about the small things,' Le Froy said. 'Some weren't as lucky.'

That's what he'd said to me earlier, in the train, when I'd grumbled about the broken springs in the seat digging into my back, and the uneven rail tracks that made every mile agony. I'd growled at him then, but it made sense now. What if the journey towards independence was like that one? We were still lucky to be alive. Even if the situation got worse before it got better. Once a journey's started, stopping on the wayside isn't an option.

'Here's to being alive!' I held up the flask of tea in a toast, then poured it. 'And to the Cameron Highlands!'

We were lucky. Though, of course, the old Chinese sages would have warned us to hold off celebrating till we saw what we'd encounter in the resort.

* * *

Heavier and heavier rain made the winding road feel like a fairground ride. Behind and below us we caught glimpses of the roads we'd travelled. We saw British-style houses and tea plantations, all looking scenic and unreal, and I began to feel slightly seasick.

'Maybe a Land Rover would have been safer,' Le Froy said. 'How much further to go?'

'We should be there within the hour,' Ramesh Kumar replied. 'Originally they made the trip up here in ox carts. Believe me, this is better.'

'Progress,' Le Froy said.

'When they built the resort, they used elephants to carry up their equipment,' the driver said. 'This is definitely progress.'

The Cameron Highlands Resort was built on a natural plateau in the Titiwangsa Range and named after William Cameron, the British colonial-government surveyor who discovered it while on a mapping expedition. At an altitude of more than six thousand feet above sea level, the temperature there was considerably lower than it was in the surrounding jungle.

The stories I'd heard about the Cameron Highlands painted it as something of a British oasis – a place where plantation owners and their families spent their days growing roses, eating strawberries and drinking English tea out of fine china cups in houses built in ye olde English style with real fireplaces. It was the closest you could get to being in England without leaving Malaya.

Growing up in a British colony, you were taught to believe in 'England' just as you believed in the Heaven that Mission workers talked about.

I felt as if I was going to step into the world of the books I'd grown up reading . . . house parties in landscaped gardens with fountains and roses, filled with people from the pages of Jane Austen, Anthony Trollope . . . and Agatha Christie. But I didn't want to think about murders in English villages.

'You don't really think there's any danger to the new owners, do you?' I asked Le Froy. I'd sensed he had doubts about the threats Max Moreno had reported.

'Don't worry about it,' Le Froy said.

'Almost there now,' Ramesh Kumar said. We'd reached a fork in the mountain road and he bore right towards a bridge.

'That bridge doesn't look very safe,' I said.

'The Moonlight Point is on the other side of the gully, the most isolated cluster of lodges,' the driver said, 'on the other side of this bridge. If you slide down that slope in front of the houses, you can walk over the golf course, but I won't be allowed to drive across it. There's a hiking trail down into the gully and up the other side. It would take at least a day to cross it in good weather. With torrential waters coming through, it's not safe.'

The gully below us was so thickly overgrown we couldn't even see the water we could hear gushing past. It was delight, as much as the chill, that made me shiver.

'We can always walk out across the golf course if we have to,' Le Froy said.

'No!' I said.

Maybe I shouldn't have.

Moonlight Point

———◆———

The Moonlight Point stood about half a mile after the gully bridge. The road looked as though it was on the edge of a lake, but the golf course had turned into a swamp. If you didn't know what it was supposed to be, it looked like a very pretty lake.

'The most private space in the Camerons,' Ramesh Kumar said, 'isolated from the rest of the resort by the golf course and bridge. Rumour has it the Japanese generals used to torture information out of victims here and throw their bodies into the gully when they were done.'

The golf course stretched out on our left all the way from the bridge. On our right the land sloped down to the primary forest. In front of us the three weathered lodges stood around a cul-de-sac island. The two larger buildings stood at right angles with the third, which looked more like a storehouse, a little further down.

I felt so happy to be there. Everything I'd heard about the Cameron Highlands being a little bit of England seemed true. The mock-Tudor buildings I was looking at might have sprung from a mystery story by Agatha Christie. There were even rose bushes by the front doors.

However, the tree that stood at the centre of the roundabout made very clear we were still in the tropics. It was a large old rose apple, heavy with fruit. As I watched, the birds, which had been startled by our motor-car, returned to their chirping and feasting. I felt instantly at home.

Rose apples were familiar to me from my childhood. There had been a tree outside the back fence of the Mission Centre school playground. Rose apples looked more like tiny pears than apples, and when they were in season, we feasted on them at break time, the tallest girls holding down branches on our side of the fence so we could pluck what we could reach.

This tree was an old one that must have been planted decades ago. It had a good thick reddish-brown trunk and the road around it was uneven where its roots spread and bulged through the tarmacadam. Its cheerful green leaves rustled and danced as the birds in it jostled for fruit. It was the kind of tree beneath which generations of grandparents would have sat, looking after children. To the trees, our change happens so much more slowly: today's grandmother might be the child who played under it fifty years ago, but the trees offer the same shelter.

It was a good reminder that some things remain the same wherever you go: trees bear fruit, making birds happy and benefiting the trees.

I intended to eat some rose apples, if I could find any the birds had left. Rose apples are small, with a crisp, sweet texture, a bit like a cross between watermelon and celery. There's a seed right in the middle, embedded in a cottony tasteless mulch, and if you spit it out, ants come and move it away, four or more of them working together to move their prize back to the nest. As children, we would scoop out the seeds from the bottom without damaging the fruit so the waxy pink rose apples looked like little bells.

As I climbed out of the motor-car it felt so good to stretch after the hours of sitting. I was going to have a wonderful fairy-tale romance-novel honeymoon.

'Shoo!'

I jumped, startled. A very large, very blonde woman in a floral frock shouted from the front steps of the Emerald Lodge.

'I hate those damned birds!'

I couldn't tell if she was pregnant or just heavy-set and told myself it was none of my business. She held an unlit cigarette in her fingers.

'Got a light? Someone pinched my lighter!'

Her raspy voice was directed at Ramesh Kumar, who had walked around to open the boot and get out our bags. He gave her a polite nod and said, 'No, ma'am.'

'Huh!'

If pregnant, I judged she had at least another three months to go, which was a good thing, given the forty miles of twisty road that had brought us up there.

Her attention switched to Le Froy as he came round from his side of the car. 'There you are! You didn't have to bring your servant with you,' she said. 'You must be Thomas Le Froy. We've been expecting you. Don't you know there's a full staff here? Or there would have been if Boss Max hadn't decided his people would do better!'

So much for my fairytale honeymoon: in the English-countryside world of the Cameron Highlands, I was still a skinny, limping Chinese local. I felt like getting back into the motor-car and heading down. I wanted to be anywhere but there. I was used to being dismissed by *ang mohs*, but I could tell the woman was using me to put down Le Froy. Or had Brandon Sands only pretended to be nice and phoned with his servant-girl information?

It brought home to me how much marrying me had jeopardised Le Froy's position among his own people. Would he set her straight? I wanted him to do that almost as much as I wanted him to pretend not to notice.

'Mr and Mrs Thomas Le Froy,' he said to her. His smile was cold, his voice excessively polite – dismissively polite. He would have been friendlier to a road sweeper, but there was nothing in what he said or did that she could have objected to. 'I believe we're expected?'

'Missus?' The woman laughed. The look she gave me made clear she didn't believe we were married. 'Hah! You don't have to make up anything for us. Nobody cares what you do up here. You can carry on however you like. Not that there's anything to do in this Godforsaken place.' She smiled, challenging him. 'For God's sake, give me a light. They've all gone off, leaving me alone, and someone's pinched my lighter. Again!'

Le Froy seemed not to hear her. As she stood waiting for an answer, he held out his arm for me. I slipped my hand through the crook and he walked me past the woman and into a courtyard space towards the rose-apple tree. He looked between the two larger mock-Tudor-style buildings. The sign in front of the larger one proclaimed 'The Emerald Lodge'.

'This was the Starlight Bungalow when I was last here,' Le Froy said, pointing at the larger of the two. 'And I believe this is where we'll be staying.' He indicated the one to its right. 'It was the Moonlight Lodge back then.'

'Still is,' the woman said, her smile gone now. 'Only this one's called the Emerald Lodge. Boss Max had the sign made.'

Emerald Lodge for the owner of the Emerald Estate. That made sense, I supposed. If you were obsessed with emeralds.

'You okay?' I felt rather than heard Le Froy's question.

Was I? I was looking forward to seeing Prakesh again – while remembering that he and Le Froy were on duty. I was looking forward to the cool weather, and I could certainly occupy myself happily.

'I'm fine.' I squeezed his arm in response and he smiled a genuine smile.

'The Emerald Lodge is where Boss Max, my husband and I are staying.' The blonde woman switched modes. 'You're in the Moonlight. Still called Moonlight, although after everything that happened there you'd have thought they'd change the name. That one back there,' she was pointing at the smallest, plainest building, 'that's where he put the estate manager and the servants.'

Her accent was English. At the risk of sounding snobbish, I could tell she'd been educated differently – or less – than the teachers who'd taught me at the Mission Centre school.

'We all eat in the big house because the cooks can only manage one full meal. They're locals, you see. From the plantation.

47

Boss Max brought them up with us because he doesn't trust strangers.'

'Then we shouldn't impose on you,' Le Froy said. He turned to Ramesh Kumar, who was standing by our two suitcases, 'Thank you for the ride up. But it looks like we may need you to drive us back to Ipoh town.'

'Oh, no!' the woman said. 'You mustn't think that's what I meant! You're expected, like I said. You didn't happen to see anyone on the road coming up, did you?'

'We passed a couple of vehicles on the way,' Le Froy said.

We'd had to pull over to allow them to pass.

'No, she would be on foot. But don't worry. She'd be long gone by now. Not that anyone knows how long she's been missing.'

'Who's missing?' Le Froy asked.

If the woman had meant to catch his attention, she had succeeded. If she hadn't done so intentionally, she was just naturally good at it.

'Mrs Max,' the woman said. 'She was here this morning but she wandered off. If you ask me, she probably just went for a walk and got lost. The men are searching the trails now.'

Le Froy walked across to the buildings to look around. I trailed in his wake as the woman and our driver stood and watched. Very likely we were only doing what all new arrivals did.

At the lodges, the descent into the forested valley started almost immediately behind and beyond the three buildings. It was as steep as the drop into the last gully we had crossed to get to Moonlight Point. It was as though we were perched on a promontory, but the water was too far below to see.

Two old women watched us with open curiosity from where they squatted, cleaning *kacang panjang*, long beans, by the drain that ran behind Rubber Tree Lodge before plunging downhill. They were wearing sarongs, with traditional head covering and clogs. I guessed they were the servants Boss Max had brought up with him.

Returning to the car, Le Froy looked out in the other direction. 'Those tyre tracks – they went across the golf course?'

'Max thought she must have tried to walk that way. If you go around by the road, the nearest other buildings are at least ten minutes away by car so it would be much faster to walk. Of course it's almost impossible at the moment when the ground is so soggy. But, Max being Max, he drove off to find her. My husband and Viktor took Viktor's jeep to see if she went down the road and the security people are checking the slopes, in case she went walking on the trails and fell.'

My ears pricked up. 'We know one of your security people,' I said. 'Prakesh Pillay? He's a friend from Singapore.'

She stared at me. 'I don't know the guards' names. For goodness' sake, girl. You shouldn't either.'

'Are there walking trails behind the buildings?' Le Froy said.

'Frida used to go out there, but it'll be difficult at the moment. That's where she probably is. Likely sprained her ankle or something. Maybe a day of being out in the rain will make that woman stop her tomfoolery and settle down.'

'Do you want to go after them?' I asked Le Froy.

'If you don't mind.' Le Froy looked around. An old van was parked half behind the store building.

'Viktor, the plantation manager, drove the servants up in that,' the woman said. 'Max keeps the keys to all the vehicles. Viktor's out in the jeep with the security people.'

'I'd like to make sure Moreno's all right. Here. Sands gave me the keys – I'm sure you can figure out which goes where.'

I took the keyring with its four keys – front door, back door, bedroom and study? 'You think someone took his wife to get to him?'

'No. I think she went for a walk and got lost. But I'll catch up with Max Moreno and find out what's happening. Ramesh, will you give me a ride to the main resort area?'

'No problem, sir.'

'I'll be back soon,' Le Froy said to me. 'Why don't you settle in and call home to let them know we got here in one piece?'

'I have bad news for you,' the woman said. 'A telephone pole's gone down, so the lines to our neck of the woods are out of commission. Have been since the day we got here.'

'Where's the nearest working phone?'

The woman shrugged, 'You can drive back down to the fork, continue to the resort village and try one of the lodges there.'

'About ten minutes, sir,' Ramesh Kumar said.

'Of course it'd be faster to cut across the golf course, but you can't risk that fancy motor of yours sinking in the muck.'

'I'll be back soon,' Le Froy said.

As we watched the Humber curve around the rose apple tree and head back the way we'd come, the woman said, 'Be glad you got here safely, though I don't know how glad you'll feel when you find you're trapped here.'

Getting to Know You

———◆———

Once I'd waved off Le Froy and the driver, I headed towards the Moonlight Lodge. There was an enclosed space next to it. I couldn't see through the barrier of yellow-green bamboo poles bound together with ropes. They looked weathered but still sturdy and the profusion of *ara jalar*, or creeping fig, showed they had been there for some time.

There didn't seem to be an entrance to the secret garden, but I looked forward to exploring it from the inside. I let myself into the Moonlight Lodge with the largest key on the ring. It was dark, a contrast to the quaint English exterior. The hall led into a lovely sitting room. It looked very comfortable and very English. There were thick tapestry curtains, armchairs and carpets. There were also dark wood tables, bookshelves, and paintings hanging on the walls.

At first glance it was opulent, but a closer look showed the effects of the equatorial damp and termites. We were in the Highlands, true, but we were also in the middle of the rainforest.

'Knock, knock.' The loud woman had followed me in. 'You don't have much luggage.'

She'd insisted on getting the servants – the two women I'd seen earlier – to carry our bags. I saw a third old woman watching, but we had only the two suitcases.

It had started raining again and I was grateful to be dry and indoors. I would also have preferred to be alone if I couldn't have Le Froy with me, but we don't always get what we want.

'I'm Mrs Terry Cook, but you can call me Daffy. Everybody does,' Daffy said. 'I've come to help you unpack.'

'Thank you,' I said, 'but I don't need any help.'

'Put them in the big bedroom,' Daffy told the servants, following them in and sitting on the bed, 'If it keeps raining like this it'll flood, which means we'll be cut off. God knows how long we'll be stuck up here.'

'I hope they find your friend soon,' I said.

I would have liked to kick off my shoes and stretch out on the bed, but since Daffy was sitting on it, I opened the closet and, finding lots of space and hangers, started shaking out our clothes before hanging them up.

'They won't, if she has anything to do with it,' Daffy said.

'What?'

Daffy shrugged. 'She can't have gone far. She's probably just hiding nearby. Trying to give Max a scare. They had a huge fight last night. Anyway, she likes walking around on her own. When we were staying at the plantation house, I'd get us a couple of gin and tonics so we could chat together while the men were out and she'd say she was going walking – in the jungle around the plantation. She's not from around here, doesn't even speak English very well. She was no fun. She didn't like dancing, wouldn't play cards, wouldn't even sit and chat . . .'

I got the feeling Daffy was lonely. She must have been desperate for someone to talk to if she was willing to talk to me. I wasn't putting myself down, just aware of where the social boundaries were drawn. Well, if she wanted to talk, I would talk to her.

'Tell me about the other people here,' I said. 'And tell me about the missing woman. Her name's Frida?'

'Elfrida,' Daffy said. 'But that's such a mouthful I call her Frida. Boss Max calls her "Woman". She wasn't his first wife so maybe he's afraid he'll slip up and get her name wrong. What's your name, by the way?'

'You can call me Su Lin,' I said, wanting to go by something less formal than 'Mrs Le Froy' or 'Madam Chen'.

'No, I can't. Why do you people all have such impossible names? I'm going to call you "Susie Linda".'

'What happened to Boss Max's first wife?' I asked. I wondered if she'd also disappeared.

'She's not even his second wife.' Daffy held up her hand with four fingers outstretched. 'She's his fourth! Can you believe it?' She shook her head. 'I don't blame them for leaving him, that's all I can say.'

'They all left him? They're all still alive?'

'These days, who knows? Half the world is dead.' Daffy didn't look surprised by my question. 'It's the rats that survive. You see them digging where the bombs came down? All that's alive down there is the rats.' There was a flash of raw pain on her face, and then it was gone. Almost as though she had wiped a streak off a mirror with a damp cloth. 'I'm not being cold-blooded, but I don't see why Max is making such a fuss. It seems to me she's gone off in a huff and she'll be back once she gets over it. She was staying here, you know. In that room on the right with the fenced-in garden. Max said she couldn't stand his snoring but I think she just wanted to get away from him for a bit.'

'Here in this house?' I remembered the 'secret' garden I'd seen from the outside and jumped up to explore it. But none of my keys unlocked the door to the room Mrs Max had been occupying.

'Max probably has it. He's obsessed with keeping everything locked. Don't worry, once they find her she'll move into the big lodge and you two lovebirds can have your privacy . . .'

'None of my keys fit this lock.' I gave the door one more – slightly harder than necessary – push and decided to leave it for now. 'How long has your husband been working with Max Moreno?'

'Boss Max and my husband Terry bought the Emerald Estate after the Walkers were murdered. No one else would touch it. The people around here are so superstitious.'

'What about the threats?' I asked.

'What threats? We were warned there might be flooding, but that's all.'

I was surprised, but managed not to say so. 'Doesn't it scare you to live in a house where people were murdered?'

'They weren't the first. And I'm not squeamish,' Daffy said. 'Apparently the house used to belong to a family – the Patel house, people still call it. They were murdered in it during the war.'

'The Patel family who owned the oil-palm plantations that were here before the rubber trees were planted?' I asked. I'd heard of how the Japanese had tried to get the Indian Patels to turn on their Chinese neighbours. When they refused, they were all massacred. 'Did any of them survive the war?'

'One son, Jaimin. Captain Henry hired him,' Daffy said. 'Runt of the family, but Captain Henry says he knows the area and the people so he's useful. The Japs should have done us a favour and got rid of him too.'

Daffy left, saying she was going to look for a lighter. I put on my sandals – I was so glad I'd brought them: not as dignified as Western shoes but much more comfortable – and set out to explore the Moonlight Lodge.

We had the largest and most comfortable room with a bathroom attached. The other two rooms shared washing facilities across the corridor, and then there was the locked door. That must be where Mrs Max – Elfrida – was staying. At the back of the building there was a kitchen with basic equipment and no supplies. I guessed that was because we were meant to take our meals at the Emerald Lodge. The kitchen door opened onto a crude network of walkways sheltered by zinc sheets that linked the rear of the three buildings and an outhouse that looked uncomfortably close to the steep drop into the ravine.

I stayed away from it and went to look for the women I'd seen cleaning beans earlier. It's an easy but time-consuming task. You need to snap off the heads of the pods and pull evenly to remove the fibrous strings that run down both sides. Once that's done, the fresh beans can be snapped into inch-long segments for stir-frying. Like picking the tails off bean sprouts, it's a chore that occupies your fingers but not your brain. That was probably why they were working in the open, on the side of the house with a good view of the road, rather than in whichever kitchen they used.

That was where I found the three of them.

'What do you want? We're busy!' one woman said.

She reminded me of Gan Jie, who had been one of the loudest voices against bringing me, a 'bad-luck' child, into Chen Mansion. But it was she who had washed me and my clothes, and kept me safe and well fed. Her kindness had taught me that grumpiness, like beauty, is often only skin deep.

'Can I help?' I asked, in my best Bahasa.

She laughed. I don't know whether it was my accent or my clumsy audacity but I laughed too, which seemed to put them at ease.

'How can you help?' the one who'd challenged me earlier asked. 'Do you know how to roll *nipah*?'

I saw they were smoking low-grade tobacco rolled in dried *nipah* palm-leaf wrappers. They weren't as refined as imported British brands like Player's cigarettes or Wills Gold Flake but likely worked just as well.

I also saw where Daffy's lighter might have gone, if it was the gold-plated Ronson Princess the woman was holding.

'I don't want to smoke. Can I sit with you until my husband comes back?' I said. I smiled. 'Please tell me something about this place. You can call me Su Lin.'

'I am Rakiah,' said the woman who'd spoken first.

'Aunty Rakiah.' I nodded respectfully. 'Aunty' conveyed familiarity and respect for older servants.

'I am Salmah,' the skinny lady said.

'Aunty Salmah.'

The third looked startled and pulled down her headscarf to cover more of her face. I saw she was much younger than the other two, not much more than a girl.

Aunty Rakiah said quietly, '*Dia pekak dan tidak boleh bercakap. Dia tidak dapat memahami apa yang anda katakana.*' She'd said her friend was deaf and couldn't talk, so wouldn't understand me.

I could tell the girl wasn't deaf, but I understood she wasn't comfortable talking to a stranger.

'Deaf Aunty.' When I bowed to her our eyes met and she gave me a very quick, very sweet smile.

Aunty Rakiah looked pleased. 'Tell me what you want to eat, and I will make it for you,' she said. 'I cooked for English, Indian and Japanese people. I can cook anything!'

'I want to help find the missing woman,' I said. 'Do you know where she is?'

Servants can be like ants, spotting crumbs of information others miss.

'Maybe she doesn't want you to find her!' Aunty Rakiah laughed.

I didn't mention the lighter to Le Froy when he got back. I could tell the expedition hadn't been a success. 'No sign of Mrs Max, then?'

'I caught up with the security people and searched with them. The others should be back soon. I'll change out of these wet clothes and then we'll go over to the big house to meet everybody.'

'You saw Prakesh? Did you tell him we're married?'

'He'd already heard. He's looking forward to seeing you.'

'But how?'

Le Froy smiled, 'Never underestimate the bush telegraph,' he said. 'The good thing is, as far as I can tell, no one was trying to come after Max Moreno or his wife.'

'What do you think happened to her?'

'No sign of abduction. No sign she got a ride down out of here. And she's not in any of the other lodges.'

'You can't have searched them all.'

'I talked to the workers,' Le Froy smiled wryly. 'Once they'd finished making fun of my speaking Bahasa with a Singapore accent, they told me they were sure Mrs Max wasn't in the town centre or any of the other lodging houses. Boss Max and his team didn't socialise with the other visitors or residents. He and Terry Cook didn't even sign in at the clubhouse when they used the golf course. They just walked around, played a few holes without paying and ignored complaints. They were ordered off the course, but Boss Max just laughed. I can almost understand his wife walking away from him.'

'She wasn't the first,' I said. I filled him in on what Daffy had told me about Elfrida being Boss Max's fourth wife. 'But I don't understand why she left him up here. Why didn't she leave him when they were at the plantation? She could have gone to stay with friends or got a room at a hotel in Ipoh.'

'Breaking point,' Le Froy said. 'You can't tell when something's going to snap. But the woman may be all right. We'll check the trails again tomorrow. Some locals are meeting me here tomorrow to cover the territory around the trails. They should have done it as soon as she went missing. She could be stuck somewhere with a broken leg. Promise me you won't walk off the side of a mountain if I make you cross, okay? Just push me off if I deserve it.'

The New Planters

———◆———

'How'd you people find out so fast my wife's gone missing? Why are you spying on me?'

Standing in the doorway of the Emerald Lodge, Boss Max Moreno was a bearded *botak*, or bald man, with a brown and white beard. He could have been Portuguese, Spanish or English. And he was already drunk.

'You must be Max Moreno,' Le Froy said. 'The new owner of the Emerald Estate Conglomerate.'

Did the man look disappointed? I thought so.

'So what if I am?' He turned away from the door, waving at us to follow. 'You might as well come in since you're here,' he growled.

Something about the man made me uncomfortable. I know – I shouldn't judge a book by its cover. But haven't you ever looked at one and known at once something's wrong? I'm not talking about the cover design but about dry rot and termites, things that can infect the rest of your shelf.

Boss Max was clearly unwell. His face was too red and he smelt sick. He had a sweet, musty odour that suggested trouble with his bowels and sour breath that pointed to an infection.

I told myself the dislike I felt was an animal reaction against possible infection.

The Emerald Lodge was bigger and grander than the Moonlight, but the furniture was much the same – upholstered armchairs with thick cushions, a couple of wingbacks, oil paintings on the walls and heavy curtains at the windows. There was also a gramophone in the corner and a trolley with bottles and glasses, which Max Moreno was already standing beside when we followed him into the room.

Daffy and two other guests were holding drinks.

'Thomas Le Froy, right? Heard you were coming up. I've not met you before, have I?' A man came up to Le Froy. 'You might not be new to these parts, but I am. I'm Terry Cook.'

He was a redhead with pale skin, the worst complexion for our climate.

Most *ang mohs* (literally 'redheads') either stayed very fair by covering their arms and faces, avoiding the sun (many ladies did), or thought it manly to go out at all hours, including under the midday sun. They ended up with skin so sunburned you could smell it in their sweat.

He wasn't tall for a Caucasian man but round enough to play Santa Claus for the children at the Farquhar Hotel Christmas lunch.

'This is my wife Daffy. And the silent giant is Viktor.'

'Pleased to meet you,' Daffy said.

Daffy acted as though we were meeting for the first time. Le Froy went along with it. 'Thomas Le Froy,' he said. 'And this is my wife, Su Lin Le Froy, or Madam Chen Su Lin.'

He smiled at my surprise at being called 'Madam Chen' for the first time. In Singapore, a woman's family lineage remains part of her identity, unlike Western women who typically take on their husband's family name. 'Madam' is added to indicate her marital status. I smiled back. I liked how it sounded.

'You just got married, you're looking for somewhere to spend your honeymoon and your man decides to head for the middle of the tropical jungle since they're not taking any more reservations in Hell.' Daffy laughed loudly at her own wit. It was a rasping smoker's laugh. 'Girl, take my advice and get away from him.'

Viktor nodded to Le Froy and then to me. He was probably in his mid-forties, a large, deeply tanned man, almost abnormally broad across the chest. He had a shock of heavy dirty blond hair, also a thick beard that he allowed to grow, probably to avoid shaving, and hacked off when it got in his way.

Boss Max was back with his drink. 'So. What are you doing here? People call me Boss Max because I'm in charge in Ipoh town, so out with it or I'll have you kicked out.'

'Arthur Aston didn't mention you,' Le Froy said mildly.

He was the British Resident of Perak, officially an adviser to the sultan, but in reality the Resident's word was law in all state and administration matters. The only place his authority did not reach was inside the mosque. Since the end of the war, there had been talk of abolishing the post and giving more governing power to local people. So far all that had been agreed on was that the term 'British Resident' would be replaced with 'British Adviser'.

'Are you working with or replacing Sands?' Le Froy asked.

'I run things. I don't bow to any of Aston's official rubbish.'

'I'm here because you reported receiving threats to your life,' Le Froy said.

I noticed Viktor looked surprised.

'Meaning you should round up the buggers sending the threats, not hound me!'

'I'm here to find out more about the threats you received.'

'All you need to know is that you're wasting your time. And mine.'

'And now your wife is missing.'

'She'll be back,' Boss Max said. 'Can't imagine her getting far without her shoes.'

'Why would she go out without them?' I said.

'He took her shoes away from her,' Daffy said.

'What?'

Daffy shrugged. 'Shoes. You know. Hard to get anywhere without shoes here. Driveway is gravel and the rest of it is worse.'

'Anyway, where my wife's got to has nothing to do with you,' Boss Max said.

'I need to make sure someone isn't trying to get at you through her,' Le Froy said.

That struck home. Max Moreno stared at Le Froy. 'Impossible!'

'Why?'

'It's just impossible. I don't think you understand the situation, sir!'

'Of course not. I've only just arrived here,' Le Froy said, 'but I'm trying to get up to speed quickly. I've already spoken to your security people.'

'You had no right to go behind my back.' Boss Max was angry again.

'Max, come on. He's got to talk to the security people. If Frida's gone it's because they weren't doing their jobs,' Daffy said. She was one of those women who knew how to talk to men. That was something I needed to learn if I was going to help Le Froy in situations like this.

'Go and get Captain Henry, then. And tell him to bring the other two.'

Daffy wasn't too pleased to be sent off, but she went.

'They don't eat here with us,' Boss Max explained to Le Froy. 'You will, of course. Guest at Aston's lodge and all that. But, hey, it's my woman who's gone missing so . . .' He held up his beefy hands in a 'Don't shoot me' gesture. 'Elfrida looked right for a wife of mine – the kind of woman every man dreams of. She's not like that slab of lard Cook's married to.'

Boss Max was the kind of man every woman dreaded and had nightmares about.

Terry Cook came over to offer us drinks and Boss Max left to refill his glass.

'As I said, I'm here looking into the threats made against Mr Moreno,' Le Froy said. 'Especially given the deaths of the previous plantation owners. Did you know them?'

'Not at all,' Terry Cook said. 'Their processing plant needs updating but that's not going to happen until the money starts coming in.'

'How did you come to be in the rubber business?' Le Froy asked him.

'Moreno. He needs me,' Cook responded. 'I don't know a thing about rubber and I don't give a damn. But he needs me as a partner. Thanks to me, he gets to keep that generous grant, the plantation lands that cost him next to nothing, and enough to pay the staff until our production pays for itself. If I wasn't around there would be no Emerald Estate,' he said, with a triumphant sneer. 'You should ask him why Viktor's working for him. He was with the Walkers.'

'Viktor?' Le Froy looked at the silent giant.

'Viktor Falk.' He could talk when he wanted to. 'I was working for the Walkers, yes, but I was hired originally by Boss Max. I set up the processing facility, the packing area and the transport for Boss Max and Mr Walker. Then Mr Walker and his brother took the plantation and I was working for them. Now I am working for Boss Max again.'

There was a lot to untangle, but it would have to wait. Boss Max was back. 'Did Viktor tell you I hired him straight after he got out of prison?' Boss Max said. 'He killed the man who killed his mother, and they sent him down for five years.'

'It had to be done,' Viktor said.

'And here's Captain Henry,' Boss Max said. 'Captain Henry meet my man Le Froy. Sent up by the governor to find out what you've done with my wife.'

'We've met,' Le Froy and Captain Henry said at the same time.

Captain Henry resembled a Caucasian-Indian, like my friend Parshanti. He nodded in my direction. 'You picked up a translator?'

65

'My husband speaks Bahasa better than I do,' I made myself say. Hadn't I decided to stop playing the stupid smiling Asian girl?

'You wanted to see us? We were having dinner.'

'At this hour?' Boss Max scoffed. 'Just get the others.'

Captain Henry nodded. Prakesh and a young boy in khakis came in through the kitchen. They must have used the rear walkways I'd seen earlier.

'Prakesh!' I said.

He flashed me a smile that showed how glad he was to see me, and mouthed, 'Later.' He was on duty in front of his boss at the moment. I saw bruises on his face. What had he been doing?

'You know Prakesh Pillay?' Captain Henry asked me.

'We worked together in Singapore,' I said.

'Worked? In the police?' He glanced at Prakesh. 'What kind of work?'

'Well, in a case like this, I would talk to a missing woman's friends and ask about her, how she spent her time. Sometimes women find it easier to talk to other women than to a policeman.'

Captain Henry laughed. 'Next you'll be saying the police should hire women.'

But Boss Max said, 'My wife didn't have any friends. Other than us here. Where would she want to go? She joined us for meals. Otherwise she did her arty stuff.'

'She probably wanted to go to the city. You know what girls are like,' Captain Henry said. 'Always looking for something new and exciting. You're all like that, eh?' He squeezed my shoulder, a huge thumb rubbing my back. 'I keep telling Max you have to pay attention to your woman. They'll be offended if you don't. If he'd listened to me, Elfrida would still be here, eh?'

I stepped away from him. It took a bit of effort to yank myself loose because he held on, pretending it was a joke, though I could tell he was annoyed.

'She is smart, this girl. She doesn't like you,' Viktor said.

'The threats probably came from that bunch of people trying to claim the land,' Terry Cook said. 'They'd thought it would be theirs once they'd got rid of the Walkers but then Max and I stepped in and did the deal.'

'Was it really their land before, though?' Le Froy asked.

'Don't be taken in by what they say,' Terry Cook said. 'These locals can claim anything they like, but they can't read or write so how are they going to prove it?' He shook his head. 'They're just lucky we didn't string up the whole lot of them for what they did to the Walkers. It's completely ridiculous.'

'Why?' I asked. None of them seemed to hear me.

'You think the independence movement is what triggered the killings?' Le Froy asked. 'And that the killers are sending you threats now? Do you know why the Walkers picked that particular area to work in?'

'I chose the spot,' Boss Max said. 'I saw its potential at once. I set up the Emerald Estate, before the Walker brothers swindled me out of it. The land was good, but people wrote off the location because it's surrounded by primary jungle and high mountain ranges. I realised that the easiest way to transport our rubber was by river, and everything fell into place. Once I saw that, I had the agreements drawn up and it should have been plain sailing from there.'

'You can sign whatever agreements you like,' Viktor said, 'but the trees will decide. You have to treat them right.'

'There's a British guy in town who's trying to make trouble,' Terry Cook said. 'He was doing it to the Walkers too. Stirring people up, talking rot about their rights, writing letters to authorities and the newspapers about ownership. We had him picked up and worked over a couple of times but he just goes on making trouble.'

'Harry Palin?' Le Froy said. 'The lawyer?'

'That's the one. Claims he's a lawyer. You'd think a lawyer would have better things to do. Keeps whining about treating the locals right and tries to shut down businesses that could be giving them a chance to do an honest day's work.'

'You think Harry Palin could have had something to do with the threats Boss Max has been getting?' Le Froy asked.

'Wouldn't put anything past that one,' Captain Henry said.

But Boss Max seemed to think of something. 'It's that Pillay fellow,' he said, pointing at Prakesh. He and the younger security guard were still standing quietly by the passage to the kitchen. 'I tell you, that Indian was always sneaking around spying on my wife. He must have got her away and hidden her somewhere in the jungle. There's no way she could've got anywhere on her own.'

'We'll talk about it after dinner.' Terry Cook took hold of Boss Max's arm. 'Let's go and have dinner, everyone. Henry, thank you. We'll check in tomorrow.'

For a moment I thought Boss Max was going to hit him. He pointed at Le Froy. 'You're in it with him, I can tell.' His shoulders dropped and he shambled off down the passage.

'Max is very worried about his wife,' Terry Cook said. 'You mustn't mind him. He was always afraid she'd leave him, but I never thought she'd actually do it. I mean, where would she go? The girl's not from around here.'

'Where's she from?' I asked.

'South America,' Daffy said. 'Come on. The food's not bad.'

I really didn't want to eat with those people. I wanted to find Prakesh and . . . I wanted to go home to Chen Mansion and sleep in my own bed.

'Chin up.' Le Froy smiled.

I managed to smile back. This was my duty as Mrs Le Froy. And Chen Mansion was no longer my home.

Prakesh

———◆———

Dinner at the Emerald Lodge was surprisingly (to me) good. We started with prawn cocktail – cold boiled prawns served with ketchup and mayonnaise. The thought of eating cold seafood made me feel sick, but I tried it and really liked it. Then we had chicken à la king served over rice. It was like a Japanese bland sweet curry with chicken. The long beans I'd seen the women preparing were cooked with butter and so were the peas, carrots and cauliflower. They put butter into everything. Even the dessert, which was apple crumble, was rich with it. I enjoyed the meal, but I couldn't have eaten like that every day.

It was a mix of British colonial cuisine and local Malayan ingredients. There were no disagreements over dinner, though Boss Max had his whisky bottle by his side. The others had wine but I drank cooled boiled water.

After dinner, they seemed inclined to sit around smoking and talking. Boss Max was talking earnestly to Le Froy in a corner, now and then throwing baleful looks around the room to see if anyone was eavesdropping on them.

I didn't bother to try. If there was anything I needed to know, Le Froy would fill me in later. Instead I said I was tired, wished a good night to the room in general (since our hostess was missing) and slipped out.

Of course I headed towards the security lodge to look for Prakesh. I was taken aback by how dark it was, once I was a few steps from the lighted windows.

In Singapore at night it's never completely dark because there are so many buildings so close together. Well, maybe if you went out of the city – but where I'd lived, I'd never seen such total darkness.

Because of the heavy cloud cover there was no light from the moon or stars. I could feel the driveway beneath my feet and hear the wind rustling the leaves of the rose apple tree in front of me but that was all.

I jumped when Prakesh spoke to me out of the dark. 'So you two are married,' he said. 'Congratulations!'

'You startled me,' I said. 'It's so good to see you again.'

'Same,' Prakesh said. 'But I wish you hadn't come.'

'Why do you say that?' I asked.

'I can't believe you're here – and that you're married.'

'Le Froy said you already knew before he told you. How?' I stumbled and he caught me.

'Come on, I'll walk you back to your place. We can talk there.'

Prakesh had a torch. Now that we could see the path with the small yellow light, it was a short walk back to the Moonlight Lodge where I managed to unlock the front door without difficulty and find the light switch with just a little fumbling.

We settled down in the living room. I hoped that having the lights on would help Le Froy make his way back more easily.

'What happened to your face?'

'Moving stuff, you know.' Prakesh shook his head. 'I'm not the clumsiest person I know. Second only to you.'

'Huh. So how did you end up working in private security?' I asked. 'I thought you got a captaincy in a police post?'

Prakesh sighed. 'It's a mess, a huge mess.'

'Because of the new regulations?' I knew the recently re-instated force was having problems. Despite all Commissioner Foulger's efforts, the police were in a state of chaos.

For years, we'd all longed for the return of British adminis-tration, the kind of government that didn't cut off your head for not bowing low enough to a passing officer. That was what we all wanted, hoped for, during the war. But now the British were back, people seemed even more discontented than before.

'I don't know what people want from us,' Prakesh said. 'It's easier to do the same job when you're not with the police because you don't have to follow regulations that don't apply out here. And, to make it worse, nobody seems to know what the rules and regulations are supposed to be. They keep changing them.'

Le Froy had chafed at the constant changes too, but he tried to see it as a positive sign that the people in charge were trying to adjust and adapt until they'd established a system that worked. Old regulations no longer held because society had changed.

While I sympathised, I knew that people who had survived the war, thanks to buying and selling on the black-market, were unwilling to return to their old obedient ways. There was talk of secret societies trying to take over businesses, but most of the time it was just people who'd learned to think for themselves not wanting to let go of their new freedom. It wasn't surprising. After years of being put down by the Japanese, many weren't ready to kowtow once more to the British.

You see the same thing when you've pruned your bougain-villaea bushes to bare branches. If they survive, with a little sunshine and a little rain, new shoots sprout from the naked branches in wild profusion, thick with thorns.

That was how we must have seemed to the British law enforcers. It wasn't just gangs or Communists making trouble, but local people wanting equal pay with European men for doing the same work. Also, the Japanese had controlled the police and used them as a means of oppression so it wasn't easy to rebuild trust.

It was difficult within the police force too: now that the Communists were seen no longer as allies but as enemies, the British authorities were cutting down on Chinese officers and putting them on the blacklist.

'I miss the days when the only problem we had was people getting drunk, fighting and gambling,' Prakesh said. 'Those were the days.'

'I know,' I said. 'I can't do any work for the police now, because of my grandmother.'

'I hope she is well?' Prakesh said automatically. It's an Asian thing. You ask after all senior members of people's families whenever you meet up, to show respect.

'She is. Working too hard. She'd like me to help her, but I don't want to.'

Prakesh nodded. 'She should be careful also.'

I wasn't sure where Ah Ma meant to take the Chen family business. I knew that a lot of not-quite-legal stuff happened, although she and Uncle Chen had been moving into property and rentals. 'She's always careful. But she says we have to continue doing business in some areas because so many people depend on her to earn their living.' She'd also said she wasn't harming anything except the British Empire, which took taxes for doing nothing, but I wasn't going to tell Prakesh that.

'How did you hear we were married?' I changed the subject.

'De Souza,' Prakesh said. 'He telephoned me. He heard you were coming up to Ipoh and asked if I knew yet.'

'How would Ferdie know?'

'He telephoned his mother on her birthday and his sister Lizzie told him. I didn't know you knew her.'

'She's teaching my cousin at school,' I said. 'I hope de Souza's mother is well?'

'Alive and kicking. Chasing him and his sister to get married because she wants grandchildren. Poor beggar!' Prakesh laughed. Then he snapped to attention, turning to the door. 'What's that?'

I'd heard something too, 'Maybe it's Le Froy?'

It was the khaki-clad boy I'd seen with Prakesh earlier.

'Jaimin! What are you doing skulking and eavesdropping? Su, this is Jaimin, my colleague at the police post. When Captain Henry quit, he offered us the same pay and less paperwork so we went with him. Jai, this is Su Lin, my friend from Singapore.'

'Hello, Jaimin,' I said.

Jaimin glowered sullenly at me.

'He's shy,' Prakesh said, 'but he's harmless. Come in and sit down, like a civilised human.'

Jaimin wouldn't look at me as he sidled into the room. I could tell he didn't want to be there, but he was going to stay because he didn't trust me and wanted me to know it. I didn't blame him: I was suspicious of strangers, too, especially if I thought they might hurt my friends. I would go on talking to Prakesh and let Jaimin see I was harmless – and might even be helpful. 'Could any of the other people here have taken Mrs Max away?' I asked.

'How?' Jaimin said. 'She couldn't call for a car because she didn't have money to pay for it. And no one here could have driven her away. Boss Max keeps the keys to all the vehicles.'

'Boss Max sounds very controlling,' I said.

'He's careful,' Prakesh said. 'Things have been going missing.'

I thought of Daffy's lighter and the one I'd seen with the cleaning aunties but didn't say anything. I shouldn't assume that just because a woman was working as a servant she couldn't have a fancy lighter.

'Boss Max has a safe in his lodge,' Prakesh said. 'It weighs a ton, and that's when it's empty. We had to lug it all the way up here because he said if he comes across anything valuable he has to have a safe place to keep it.'

'What does he expect to find up here?' I asked. I wanted to say that only his wife was missing and she wouldn't have fitted into a safe. But I'd seen neither the woman nor the safe so I said nothing.

'Daffy Cook wanted him to show her how to use the safe, but Boss Max said no. She said, "You don't trust me," and he said, "Damn right I don't."' Prakesh had mimicked Daffy's girlish whine perfectly.

I laughed, 'Do you think Boss Max has a reason not to trust Daffy Cook?'

'The Cooks are harmless,' Prakesh said. 'They don't know anything about rubber. They're just trying to make some money. If there's anybody he shouldn't trust it's the estate manager.'

'Viktor,' I said, remembering the fair-haired giant. 'Why?'

'Viktor was running the estate for the Walkers, and they all ended up dead. He started working for Boss Max, who received death threats and his wife disappeared. Don't you see a pattern? Plus they've been having big fights ever since the monsoon started.'

'Why?'

'Viktor won't let them tap during the rains. Boss Max says it's just superstition and the tappers are using the monsoon as an excuse to be lazy. He wanted Viktor to order them to carry on as usual. Viktor said the trees needed to rest and refused. The trees are just standing there wasting money, and the boss wants Viktor out, but they don't have anyone to replace him.'

'Mrs Max liked Viktor,' Jaimin said unexpectedly, 'Mrs Max talked to him like she talked to you. More, even.'

'Nah,' Prakesh said.

I recognised the look on his face: Mrs Elfrida Moreno wasn't just his boss's missing wife. Prakesh really liked her. I grimaced inside. Prakesh was always falling in love. And too often with women who didn't appreciate his mix of shyness and bravado. He was so reserved and respectful that most of them never knew how he felt. But now the woman he was currently in love with had vanished. Poor Prakesh.

'It's my fault Elfrida was so unhappy here,' Prakesh said. 'I shouldn't have said anything.'

'You told her you loved her?' I noticed he'd used her given name.

'Of course not! Are you crazy?'

'Then you talk cock for what? Faster state facts can or not!'

Or: *Why are you prattling such nonsense? Pray proceed with the facts expeditiously!* Sometimes Singlish gets the point across faster than the King's English.

'Elfrida told me she couldn't stand being with the two old women who cleaned and cooked in the plantation house. They had worked for the previous owners and she felt nervous with them. She thought they were watching and spying on her. I told Boss Max so.'

'Why?'

'I decided he might not know how uncomfortable they made his wife. And if he could replace them with new staff while they were up here, they wouldn't be around when she went back to the plantation. Instead Boss Max told the locals who usually staff the lodges that they wouldn't be needed because he'd be bringing his own staff – he arranged for the old women to come up here with them so Elfrida didn't even have a few weeks away from them. That was my fault.'

'It wasn't,' I said. 'You couldn't know Boss Max would react in that way.'

'I should have. He is a sadistic bully, but I didn't see that until later. I asked him why he didn't just keep the staff at the lodge, and he said that, because of the threats, he didn't want strangers around. But it was really because it was one more way for him to make Elfrida miserable – and that was thanks to me.'

It sounded as if Prakesh was quoting Elfrida. He might not have known how Boss Max would respond, but she should have. Had she used Prakesh to get her way?

'How well do you know those old women?' I asked.

'Not at all. Down in the plantation, they would bring tea and snacks to the security post for us, but since we came to the Camerons, they've been staying away from me. I think they also imagine it's my fault that they're here.'

'One is deaf. Do you know if she's a bit . . .' I twirled a finger at the side of my head. I'd once been employed to care for someone with the mental age of a child and the strength of a woman. It had been a dangerous combination because she literally didn't know her own strength.

'I don't know her. I think she's a widow that Aunty Rakiah and Aunty Salmah took on. They were working for other expats before the war. I think Aunty Salmah's previous employer was a German with an English wife. But they were interned at the start of the war and left afterwards. I don't think they can have had anything to do with that.'

'No. But that explains why they speak some English,' I said. 'And can cook English food. I wish I could see what Mrs Max left behind in her room. And it's crazy, I know, but could she be hiding in a cupboard?'

'Why would she do that?' Prakesh said. 'Why would you *think* she would?'

'Hey, don't be angry with me – I don't know her, remember? I just think it's strange that she should stay in a room in a different building from her husband. And everybody seems to think she can't have left this place. So what if she's still inside the house somewhere?'

Not to mention it was the house we would be living in for the next seven days.

'I'm not angry,' Prakesh said. 'I just don't like hearing the things they've been saying about her.'

'Daffy said Boss Max took away her shoes because he thought it wasn't safe for her to go walking around on her own,' I remembered. 'I thought that was pretty weird. If someone took away my shoes just to stop me walking outside, I'd go even if I didn't want to. I'd get banana or palm leaves, wrap them around my feet and tie them on with vines. With some grass or moss inside for padding. But I wouldn't let anyone do that to me.'

'I think you and Elfrida would have got along,' Prakesh said. 'Boss Max goes too far sometimes.'

'I hope I get to meet her some day,' I said. 'And I wish I could see her things inside that locked room.'

'Why?' Jaimin asked.

'It might give us some idea of where she's gone.'

'Come on, then.' Prakesh stood up abruptly.

'Come where?'

'To her room. You'll see what I mean and you'll tell us if it gives you any ideas.'

Mrs Max's Room

'Boss Max keeps all the keys, but he gave this one to us to bring Mrs Max to meals and escort her back here,' Prakesh said.

'What? Why?'

'To make sure she doesn't take other people's things and hide them. The Boss says she's a kleptomaniac. She doesn't mean to take stuff but she will if we don't keep a strict eye on her.'

I still didn't get it. 'You mean she's locked up in that room and you're like her jailer walking her to meals?'

'It's to make sure she's all right. But I know what you mean. Just come and look.'

Was Mrs Max a kleptomaniac? I knew there were people who couldn't resist the compulsion to steal. That would explain why Boss Max kept her locked up when there were other people around, though it didn't seem the best way to deal with it.

I followed Prakesh to the door off the right corridor – the room Mrs Max had been staying in.

It was a strange room. It stuck out at the side of the house, but when you looked at the lodge from the front, all you could see was the bamboo fencing around it.

The key Prakesh used to unlock the door was different from the others on my keyring, but it worked. When he opened the door and switched on the light, the room was even stranger inside. It looked like a storeroom, crammed full of bags and cardboard boxes, all sagging and falling apart from the damp. They were stacked in piles, as though they had been dumped there on arrival and left.

I stepped in, careful not to touch and topple anything. It looked like Mrs Max had packed everything she could to bring on this holiday with her ... and not touched any of it. There was a strong, unpleasant smell of damp, dirt and small dead creatures. I saw clusters of rat droppings and the cracked shells of lizard eggs.

There was a single bed against the far wall with a couple of books on it. They looked like children's. I picked one up: the pages inside had been pulled from the spine as though something might have been hidden in the binding. The same with the other. If there had been anything in either, it was gone now. I couldn't read them – they were in German – but I could see from the illustrations that they were fairy tales. One featured a boy with a shock of untidy hair and seemed to be a collection of nursery rhymes. In the other, a child sneaked around a giant with golden hair who got up to all kinds of adventures, before ending up at a palace and marrying a princess. The German fairy tales were not very different from English ones.

A low table beside the bed had been used as a craft area, with buckets of clay, the remnants of clay bowls and clay models of birds. They had all been smashed to bits, as though someone had taken a hammer to them.

Had Mrs Max made these objects and destroyed them? Had she had some kind of nervous breakdown that had led her to smash her models then disappear? There were a few watercolour paintings of birds and fruits, the bright pinks and greens looking incongruously cheerful tacked to the walls. They hadn't been damaged.

Looking at the pathetic attempt to brighten the space I realised something else: there were no windows in the room, just two doors, the one we had come through and one other.

I don't follow all the dictates of *feng shui*. Mostly it seems to be about getting people to buy things they don't need to ward off evil spirits and bad luck. But I believe there's something about energy flow and clearing out stagnant spaces being healthier for the people living in them. This room felt unhealthy. The lack of windows, the disorganised baggage and, most of all, the broken models made me feel there was bad energy in that place, the kind that brings sickness, misery and hopelessness along with everything we lump together as 'bad luck'.

I went to the other door and was surprised to find it wasn't locked.

Prakesh joined me with his torch. We were looking out onto a small, fenced compound. Even in the dark, I could see bamboo fencing with black patches of mildew, and an aggressive roll of barbed wire ran along the top edge, just below sharpened bamboo spikes. It might have looked like a secret garden from outside but it was more like a prison yard, especially as there was no gate and no way out. But a prison yard would have been better tended. This was a wilderness of snakeweed and *duking anak*, which children called 'piggy back' plants because of the tiny round fruits that grew under its leaf stalks. I'd never seen them grow to this size. The weeds were almost a foot high.

'If I were locked in here, I think I would—'

Footsteps crunched on the gravel beyond the bamboo barrier. An angry voice shouted, 'Why's that light on?'

The next moment the door was slammed open against the wall, shaking the whole room. 'What are you people doing in here?'

It was Max Moreno and he was furious.

'Su Lin's good at finding things and figuring things out. I thought she might spot a clue to where your wife went, sir,' Prakesh said.

'You had no business, no right! This is an invasion of privacy. It's trespassing!' Boss Max turned on me. 'What did you take, hah? Let me see your pockets – lift up your skirt. What are you hiding under there?'

He was stopped by Le Froy, who came in behind him. 'What are you doing?'

'What the hell does it look like I'm doing? I'm going to search her. Take back whatever she's stolen. And then you lot of lying, cheating swindlers can get out of here.'

'He locked up his wife in here,' I said. 'There's barbed wire around the top of the fence outside. And the lock and key to this room are different from the keys to the rest of the house. I think he changed the locks. He was keeping her prisoner.'

'That's a lie! And it's none of your business!'

'Barbed wire?' Le Froy asked. I saw him take in the rest of the room and glance out of the open door. Prakesh raised the torch and illuminated the depressing enclosure.

'Barbed wire for the barbed wife,' Boss Max said. 'Exactly! Let the punishment fit the crime.'

'This place looks as if it was set up for Japanese officers to question prisoners at leisure,' Le Froy said. 'Why was your wife locked up in here?' He was no longer the genial retired policeman on holiday. He was investigating what was at best an abduction and possibly something far worse.

'The bitch didn't just leave me,' Boss Max glared at him. 'She robbed me – she pinched my emeralds. The emeralds I needed to keep the Emerald Estate going. Without that money, the estate is dead. We're all dead.'

'Tell me about these emeralds,' Le Froy said.

I expected this to trigger another explosion, but Boss Max seized on the chance to expound on how he'd been wronged,

'They were once part of the Russian Crown Jewels. Sold to rich Germans after the Great War. All the Bolsheviks wanted then was cash so the emeralds were auctioned to wealthy buyers from the West – Elfrida's family. They were supposed to come to me, as her dowry. Enough to buy a tenanted farm in South America, they said.'

'Her family just gave you the emeralds for marrying their daughter?'

'Pretty much.'

Le Froy waited.

'The emeralds were supposed to support her and her family for the rest of their lives – under normal circumstances.'

'What happened?'

'There are no more normal circumstances. Things are unstable everywhere, people demanding their freedom without any idea of how to govern themselves,' Boss Max said. 'You can see for yourself. It's happening here too. No one's satisfied with what they've got any more. Everybody wants a bigger piece of the pie. Anyway, there wouldn't be much left of their lives if those Nazi hunters found out a high-level Nazi was living in luxury in Argentina, hah?'

'Her family bought your silence with their daughter and their emeralds,' Le Froy said.

'We had a deal,' Boss Max said. 'I did them a favour. You might say I saved their lives. I got the emeralds out of South America for them. There's no way anyone could link the emeralds that paid for the Emerald Estate with the ones smuggled out of Berlin by my wife's father!'

I thought of Elfrida, married off to save her father, a stranger in this country, finding herself locked into this room. This was her new home with her new husband. Without ever meeting her I already felt sorry for her and totally on her side – wherever she was and regardless of what she had done. Those two children's books on the bed were something a homesick little girl might carry across the world, dreaming of the adventures she would have, or the prince who would come to her rescue. Or had she dreamed of reading them to her own children?

'Why didn't you take the emeralds yourself?' Le Froy asked.

'Thought I did, didn't I? I had them all safe, under lock and key. Then one day – *poof* – they were gone. There were three emeralds left after the down payment on the estate and they were gone. She said she didn't take them. I said, "Who else would know where they were, hah? Who else would know how to get into my safe? Hah?"'

'You think she took them and hid them somewhere?' Le Froy glanced around the cluttered room.

'Searched it. Searched every bit of luggage before it was packed. Nothing. Checked the linings, everything. Zilch, *nada*. Nothing in there except her rubbish,' Boss Max said. 'I've gone through everything. No secret compartments, no hidden drawers. But I had it all carted up here in case she managed to pull a fast one. You know what I told her? I could burn all this,' he waved at the bags and boxes surrounding us, 'burn all her books and dried flowers and whatnot and I would find the emeralds in the ashes along with her bones.'

His words hung in the air. For a moment Boss Max looked as though he meant to set the room on fire there and then, but he walked out of the room and we filed after him.

'I'm locking up,' Boss Max said. 'Everybody out of here.'

'This is our lodge so we're staying,' Le Froy said. 'These are our rooms, including this one.' He indicated the one we had just left.

'You have no right to—'

'You can leave your wife's things in here till she comes back to get them,' Le Froy said.

Boss Max departed, taking the key to his wife's room with him.

'I'll see you tomorrow,' Prakesh said. 'Good night, sir. Good night, Su. And congratulations again.'

Le Froy locked the door after them.

'If he wanted to lock his wife into the Japanese interrogation room, why didn't he take this lodge for himself?' I said. 'Then he could have done what he wanted with nobody knowing anything.'

Much as the Japanese officials had.

'You've met Boss Max,' Le Froy said. 'Can you see him staying in anything but the grandest lodge?'

He had a point.

'Happy honeymoon,' he said. 'No regrets about coming here, I hope?'

'You can't trust the cleaners,' I said. 'I've got to tell you about a cigarette lighter I saw one with.'

'Prakesh knows something about the missing woman,' Le Froy said.

'Yes. Otherwise he would have been full of ideas. Either that or . . .'

I didn't have to finish. We both knew Prakesh Pillay's propensity to fall in love. And once in love he seemed to lose all common sense.

'Why is Jaimin here?' I said.

Le Froy nodded, 'He can read and write. He could have stayed as a constable in town. Even if he has family here, he could earn more there to support them better.'

'It's the way he watches everything? It makes me uncomfortable. And yet at the same time there are things he doesn't know that he should, if he's been working with the police for any length of time.'

Even if things were run differently here than they were in Singapore, surely the basic training would be the same,

'Jaimin must have done his basic training before the occupation. Otherwise he would be an intern now. But the boy's very young and we don't know what he went through during the war.'

Le Froy's use of 'we' instead of 'you' was enough to tell me that he had noticed too.

'Captain Henry might have told him to keep an eye on Prakesh. Report back anything we might tell or pass him.'

'Captain Henry?'

'As Indian was treated better by the Japanese during the war. Now the British are back he feels they despise him for the colour of his skin. And he's always felt the Chinese looked down on him. He got some of his own back during the war, but now he's being accused of collaborating, which isn't easy for him.'

In other words, I should watch what I said to Prakesh when Jaimin was around. But there was more than that in the way the young former constable lurked and watched. I could tell he wasn't just following orders.

'Part of me wants to believe it's possible to fight for independence and redistribute the wealth Western colonisers have stolen . . . but the upheaval that would cause makes it seem impossible.'

'There's always going to be chaos when things change,' Le Froy said.

'I love you,' I said. 'And I love the Mission Centre teachers, all their English books, the ideas and ideals in them. I don't want to throw all that out.'

'Why not keep the books?' Le Froy said. 'And me? Just throw out the bathwater.'

First Night and Morning After

◆

'I don't see it,' I said.

'You don't see Max as a suspect?'

'I don't see him as a boss. If you're a big-time boss, you don't have to act like that all the time. People know. You don't have to call yourself "Boss". And you don't go around getting drunk and locking up your wife.'

'Maybe Western bosses are different from Chinese bosses,' Le Froy suggested. 'I've come across quite a few loud, bossy police chiefs.'

But I knew he was thinking about what I'd said. Le Froy was good at processing information he didn't agree with. That was what made him successful as an investigator. I just tossed in all the facts I had and made a *rojak* of it.

Rojak describes something that's jumbled. It can be delicious, like the *rojak* salad of fruits, vegetables and fried dough sticks tossed in spicy sweet shrimp paste. Singapore's mix of ethnicities, languages and cultures can also be described as a *rojak* – as could the melee of thoughts in my brain.

'Max feels more like my uncle Chen than my grandmother.'

'Agreed.'

I enjoyed the coolness and the sound of rain outside while I was dry, snug and warm under the bedcovers with the man I loved, discussing stolen emeralds, wrongful imprisonment and possibly murder, with digressions into Nazi war criminals and looted Russian treasures.

I was so tired I fell asleep without even thinking about lovemaking. I know Westerners consider it a very big deal. That's why they've invented so many social, legal and religious laws controlling how, when and with whom people are allowed to do it. I'd believed the most compelling reason white people get married is so they can go to bed together legally.

But, anyway, the shameful truth is that on the first night of our honeymoon, instead of slipping into sexy underwear and seducing each other, Le Froy and I snuggled together in our pyjamas and discussed what we'd learned about Missing Mrs Max since we'd got there and how it connected with the threats made to Boss Max and the Walker family.

I didn't know I'd fallen asleep till I woke, vaguely aware that Le Froy was awake beside me, reading papers by lamplight. And though the heavy curtains were drawn, I could see it was already morning.

'Didn't you sleep at all?' I asked. 'You should have woken me.'

'I like watching you sleep,' Le Froy said. 'It makes everything worthwhile.'

'But I want to help you.' I stretched luxuriously. It felt good being on a huge bed with clean sheets.

'You're on holiday,' Le Froy said. 'You don't have to do anything except have a good time.'

'But as your wife—'

Le Froy laughed. 'As my wife, I order you to do whatever makes you happy. Then the worst anyone can say is, "That poor woman having to put up with him. But at least she looks happy!"' He leaned over and kissed me. 'That's what makes an ideal couple.'

'If we were an ideal couple I would be a white woman without a crooked hip,' I said.

'Or I would be a Chinese tycoon with two good feet,' Le Froy said. 'Otherwise I'd say this is pretty good.'

The way he said it made me laugh. All my life I'd been told to mind my behaviour, because it would reflect badly on my family, but since I was the bad-luck girl, with dead parents and a polio limp, there was no way I could reflect well on the Chens. I was only now grasping that my family and race would reflect badly on my husband. And that didn't even come close to my greatest fear: my parents had died soon after I was born – what if I really was some kind of walking disaster zone, spreading bad luck like Typhoid Mary spread germs?

'What are you thinking?'

I couldn't explain, even to him.

'But you know that being married to me will change how people see you. Not just because of me but because of my family.' I knew that not everyone – least of all the British governing class – shared Le Froy's attitude towards locals. 'I don't want to be bad for your career.'

Le Froy took off his reading glasses. 'What's brought this on? You're supposed to get cold feet before the marriage, not after.'

'I was thinking about that poor woman. Getting locked up by her husband and running away from him. What kind of man marries four wives?' I'd told him what Daffy had confided to me.

'I'll have someone look into what happened to the previous Mrs Morenos,' Le Froy said. 'But there's no law against having four consecutive wives.'

'And what if she did take the emeralds? They were hers, weren't they? She had every right to take them back if she wanted to leave him.' I thought of Ah Ma instructing me not to tell Le Froy about the gold bars she'd given me. Did all families do that? Make sure their girls had the means to get out of the marriage they were sending them into?

'Ready for some breakfast?'

We'd been told breakfast would be served in the Emerald Lodge dining room from seven a.m. until everyone had eaten. The food would be on warmers on the sideboard, and if we wanted eggs, we should tell the aunties how we'd like them to be cooked.

'I wish I'd known there was a kitchen here,' I said. 'I would've brought stuff to make our own meals.'

'You're on holiday,' Le Froy said again. 'Relax and let someone cook for you!'

* * *

At my suggestion, we walked to the Emerald Lodge via the sheltered walkways at the back of the buildings. The view across the valley was breathtaking after the night rain. Below us, the forest canopy stretched out, wisps of mist curling from the treetops. We could hear the birds' morning calls. They always seem to me to be saying, 'I survived the night! Anyone else still alive?'

Despite everything that was going on, I was glad to be there and alive. The smell of damp earth and fresh greenery, the glimpses of pale blue sky between the clouds, the crisp morning air made everything seem more hopeful.

For all I knew, we might find Mrs Max returned from her adventure and sitting down to breakfast.

We entered the Emerald Lodge through the kitchen. Aunty Rakiah, Aunty Salmah and Deaf Aunty were there, and I introduced them to Le Froy as my husband.

The aunties giggled when he greeted them in Bahasa, adding that he would take local coffee if they had it and scrambled eggs.

No, we were told, Mrs Max hadn't come back in the night.

Once Le Froy had passed into the passage to the dining room, Aunty Rakiah whispered, 'Very handsome man! Kind also!'

Aunty Rakiah was a smart woman with good taste.

We found Daffy and Terry Cook had already arrived. 'We have to serve ourselves. Viktor's already had his,' Daffy said. 'He's up so early he usually collects his breakfast from the kitchen and eats outside. Boss Max . . .' she jerked her head towards the door where the dining room joined the living room '. . . I can't hear him snoring so he should be here soon.'

On the sideboard warmers we found sausages, baked beans and fried potato cubes. On the table I saw a toast rack, with butter and marmalade beside it, and a fruit salad made with chunks of papaya, pineapple and rose apple. It was all good. It was strange eating raw fruit in the morning but when Aunty Salmah brought out my eggs, the whites soft and cloudy, the yolks liquid gold, my breakfast was perfect.

'I don't suppose there's any news of Elfrida?' Terry Cook said. 'She's been out all night. You'd think she'd have made it back by now if she could.' His face was grim.

We could no longer believe the missing woman had gone off by herself to worry her husband. She might yet be alive, might yet be found, but where was she and what hell was she going through?

'Thoughts and prayers,' Daffy said, helping herself to more orange juice. 'That's all any of us can do right now.'

I'd already sent prayers to the Christian God (who protects lost sheep) and all the others I could think of, especially Bixia, who's said to protect women and children. I would light an offering to her when I got back to Singapore, I promised, if Mrs Max was found safely.

'I'm going to walk around the golf course,' Le Froy said. 'A lady's not likely to have gone into the jungle when there's all that flat grass to walk on. No one's playing in this season so she might just have fallen into a ditch.'

Even if she had withstood nothing more serious than a sprained ankle, Elfrida had already spent most of a day and a night out there.

'I'll get the aunties to pack you a lunch to take with you,' I said. I didn't offer to go with him because I knew I would slow him down. Le Froy would want to cover as much ground as he could as quickly as possible.

'That's being a good wife,' Terry Cook said. 'Making sure he's got his lunch. When's the last time you made sure I had a good lunch?'

'Why would I? You've never missed a meal in your life!' Daffy said. 'You two make a sweet couple, like Laurel and Hardy.' She laughed.

Daffy and her husband reminded me of Mr and Mrs Bumble from *Oliver Twist*, but unlike her I was too polite to say so.

'Where are they from, those servants you brought up with you?' Le Froy asked.

Neither of the Cooks knew or seemed interested. 'They work in the plantation house,' Terry said. 'We took them on along with the house. Probably from some nearby village.'

'Any idea who they worked for before?'

'You can try asking Max, though I doubt he knows.'

As though summoned by mention of his name, Boss Max appeared. 'Bloody lot of noise you all make.'

I noticed his knuckles were bruised – something had happened since he'd left us last night. Maybe he'd been punching the walls.

'According to some reports there might be Nazi hunters in the region,' Le Froy said. 'Could they have kidnapped your wife to use her against her father?'

'I don't know anything about that. Why would anyone bother?'

The Cooks seemed surprised by the mention of Nazi hunters. I suspected that was the response Le Froy was looking for. They didn't know the story of how Boss Max had got his wife and the emeralds.

'And the missing emeralds, did you or Elfrida mention them to anyone else?'

'What's he talking about?' Terry said. 'You sold those emeralds for the down payment.'

'Nothing,' Boss Max said. 'I had one too many last night. Don't know what I was talking about.'

'God, Max! What happened to your hands?' Daffy said. 'Who'd you punch this time?'

Boss Max looked at me and said, 'I had that fake cop Prakesh Pillay arrested for abducting my wife. Last night I saw him using my key – the key I entrusted to him so that he could protect my wife – and letting a stranger into my wife's room. It's obvious, isn't it? I saw him betray my trust with my own eyes. He's clearly done it before.'

'No!' I said. 'I asked Prakesh to show me your wife's room. I wanted to see if there was anything in there that might show where she went.'

'Ssh,' Daffy said, as Aunty Rakiah and Aunty Salmah came in with more food. They must have been listening for Boss Max.

'Doesn't matter. They don't understand English,' Boss Max said, as Aunty Salmah put his coffee and three fried eggs in front of him.

Didn't he wonder how his cooks got his orders right if they didn't speak English? But that was a question for another time. 'Sir, Prakesh wouldn't do anything to your wife. He showed me the room because we're staying in the same house and I wanted to make sure no one was there.'

'You know what? I think that Indian abducted my wife and that you lot are in cahoots with him. Otherwise how did you happen to turn up just after she disappeared? Hah? Answer me that!'

'Max, honey, you're just upset,' Daffy said. 'That's understandable. But you can't go around accusing your security men and the guests.'

'I caught him hanging around my wife,' Boss Max said. 'I knew he was up to something. I tried to make him 'fess up,' he clenched his fist, 'but he wouldn't say a word.'

I felt as though I was going to throw up the eggs I'd just eaten.

'Where is he?' Le Froy asked.

'Locked up in the security post. And he's going to stay there until I get my wife back.'

'What would he want with Frida?' Daffy asked.

'What do you think?' Max's laugh was ugly. 'Come on. You know as well as I do that these foreign devils would do anything to get their hands on a white woman. You'd better watch yourself.

'That man Pillay, he's been carrying on with my wife. I catch him hanging around her all the time. Fine, I think. Can get lonely for a woman out here. More fool me, right? Next thing I know she's gone. I tell you, he's got my wife hidden somewhere out there and I'm going to get it out of him!'

The security officers had set up a temporary post in the annexe adjacent to the third lodge where the staff were staying. Le Froy and I headed over there, barely pausing to assure Aunty

Rakiah everything was fine when she hurried after us, worried breakfast hadn't been to our liking.

'You cook English food very well,' I said.

'Salmah cooks,' Aunty Rakiah said. 'Last time she had a ma'am who taught her to make English and German dishes.'

'What do you think?' Le Froy asked, as we walked on, braving the drizzle for a short distance rather than going the long way around under shelter.

'I think Boss Max believes what he's saying. I don't think Prakesh would do anything to hurt his wife but . . .' But we knew Prakesh's penchant for falling in love. 'You think we fit together like Laurel and Hardy?' I asked.

'More like prunes and custard,' Le Froy said. 'I'm good for the system and you make me more palatable.'

'I'm badly brought up,' I said.

'Thank God, yes,' Le Froy said, 'because you have more colour and life in you than any well-brought-up young lady. And you're decent. Plain decency is an increasingly rare quality.'

'Decency? Me?'

I'd been called indecent for everything from wearing Western-style dresses to marrying an *ang moh*.

'Decency is the ability to tell right from wrong. And to act on that,' Le Froy said.

'You're decent too,' I said.

And in that moment it really felt as though that might be enough. And once we talked to Prakesh, surely we would get everything there sorted out too.

Prakesh Imprisoned

———◆———

But, as it turned out, talking to Prakesh wasn't such a simple matter.

'He's under detention. I locked him up for his own safety,' Captain Henry said. 'Give the man time to get over it.'

'On what charges?' Le Froy asked.

'Assault, rape, abduction,' Captain Henry said, 'and kidnapping.' He yawned hugely.

'What?'

'The man was drunk. There was no reasoning with him.'

'Prakesh wasn't drunk when we saw him last night.'

'Not your Prakesh, Boss Max.'

Apparently Boss Max had attacked Prakesh after leaving us last night.

The security post was little more than a concrete floor with a slanting corrugated-metal roof and three wood-plank walls. The fourth side was open, apart from the woven rattan chik blind that could be lowered to shut out the elements. It was lowered halfway now and, given the weather, the whole floor was wet.

There was also a rail set in the concrete for the sliding panel of metal bars that could be pulled across the front to turn the whole place into a prison. Positioned where the ascending road split to form the roundabout, it was the ideal spot from which sentries could check vehicles entering or leaving.

I was shocked when I saw Prakesh curled up in a cage, horribly beaten up. 'This is inhuman!'

'It's not as bad as it looks,' Prakesh managed a grin.

Captain Henry came over to join us by the cage. He didn't look in great shape either, but at least he wasn't bruised and bleeding. 'Tiger cage,' he explained. 'We use it as the drunk tank. Boss Max wanted him chained to the fence outside. Believe me, this is better.'

'Yeah,' Prakesh agreed. He seemed strangely passive. I wondered if he was feverish.

'It's not locked.' Le Froy swung open the cage door.

'Pillay's not dangerous,' Captain Henry said, 'and he's not going anywhere. But he's safer in there than out. I'll lock it if the boss man comes around.'

'Why is Boss Max so sure Captain Prakesh had something to do with his wife's disappearance?' Le Froy asked.

'Your man Prakesh had a big motive. Boss Max gave him a good beating for assaulting his wife.'

'Prakesh assaulted Boss Max's wife?' I said. 'I can't believe that!'

'You think you know a person,' Captain Henry said, as though I'd just agreed with him, 'plus there's the uniform and the position. That's going to be big trouble for him once the roads are clear, believe me.'

'How long have you been here?' Le Froy asked him.

Captain Henry rubbed bloodshot eyes, 'Since I got woken by Boss Max trying to pound this man into the wall. Arrested him so I could stop the boss killing him.'

'Why don't you go and get some coffee?' Le Froy said. 'Take a break. We'll keep an eye on your prisoner.'

'If Boss Max shows up when I'm not here . . .'

'He's not in any condition to do that. Not for a while,' Le Froy said.

'Thanks,' Captain Henry said. 'I owe you.'

As soon as Captain Henry walked out of the security post and into the lodge I started trying to drag Prakesh out of the cage.

'Help me!' I told Le Froy, who stood there doing nothing.

Prakesh wasn't helping either. In fact he was pushing me away. 'Stop! Su, what are you trying to do?'

'I'm getting you away from here, of course,' I told him. 'Le Froy, help me lift him.'

'Where are you going to take him?' Le Froy asked, still not helping.

'Away from here!' That was all that mattered. 'Anywhere away from here and away from those crazy people.'

'Stop, Su.' Prakesh clamped a hand over mine. 'We're not going anywhere, not in this weather.'

'We just have to wait it out,' Le Froy said. 'Right now he's in there and the best way to get him out for good is to find someone to take his place.'

'We can make it back to the town with him – get him to a doctor.'

'They'll all have moved out of town by now. Or be more than fully occupied,' Le Froy said. He turned to Prakesh. 'What do you say? You want us to get you out of here?'

'I have to stay, sir,' Prakesh said.

Le Froy didn't look surprised. I realised I wasn't either.

Le Froy extended an arm to help me out of the cage. I crawled out without taking it. Prakesh stayed where he was.

'Better I stay inside here. It was Captain Henry's idea,' Prakesh said. 'He's old school, but not a bad sort. Boss Max got it into his head that I know where his wife is.'

'Do you?' I asked.

'No,' Prakesh said. 'And if I did I wouldn't tell him. Captain Henry told him it's no use trying to beat information out of a Singapore-trained officer, but a few days in the cage would change my mind. You shouldn't be here.' His eyes were bloodshot and his skin was damp and too hot.

'Why did you quit your post in Ipoh?' Le Froy asked. 'How did you come to take this job? What's going on?'

'There's nothing going on. I was offered a job in private security, that's all.'

'What happened to the captaincy you got?'

'This pays a lot more money,' Prakesh said. 'Or it's supposed to. If we ever get paid!'

We just looked at him.

'All right, I might have got into a fight and quit.'

Some things never changed.

'They were picking on Jaimin, giving him all the night shifts and pissing all over the floor, making him clean up. Then Boss Max commissioned Captain Henry to set up a private security unit and the pay was good so I thought, Why not? Jaimin and I both signed on.'

'And now Boss Max thinks you had something to do with his missing wife. Why does he think that?'

I reached inside the cage and took Prakesh's hand in mine. When he squeezed it I knew he wasn't upset that we were there, just eager to show he'd not sent for us. The metal rods of the cage felt almost like protection.

'What are these people doing here?' Jaimin's sudden appearance made Prakesh uncomfortable enough to shake off my hand. Jaimin, the third member of the security team, whom Prakesh had got into trouble for defending in his previous post. It was natural that he'd be defensive of Prakesh who'd stood up for him. I'd just have to give him time to get used to me.

'They're my friends. From Singapore,' Prakesh said. Then to Le Froy, 'Jaimin's a good corporal.'

'How old are you?' Le Froy asked Jaimin.

'Old enough to qualify as corporal before the Japanese came,' Jaimin said. He sounded sensitive about his age – not surprising, perhaps, given how difficult it must have been to do his job while looking like a child. Likely much of that was due to malnutrition during the war years. Hopefully things would get better now.

'You're Bengali?' Le Froy asked. He sounded like a job interviewer, but I knew he was watching how the boy answered as well as what he said. He was deciding whether or not he could be trusted.

Jaimin hesitated, then nodded.

'You're not sure?' Le Froy prompted. 'Or something else?'

I saw Jaimin smile slightly, acknowledging that Le Froy had picked up on his moment of indecision. He struck me as smart – a smart man. I was sure he would use that knowledge in future to mute his own unconscious signals and watch for any that other people might give off. But he was so young. It would be more difficult for him to maintain authority. Especially in a village setting where the white men ruled.

'I'm only half Bengali. My mother's family is *sakai*.'

That was what the British colonials called indigenous people. I was so used to hearing people use terms like '*sakai*' or '*jakun*' as insults that even though I knew better, it sounded as though he'd just called his mother a dog or something worse . . . a female dog.

'That's why you're so sure-footed on the forest trails. I was watching you when we were searching for Mrs Moreno yesterday. *Sakai* can navigate forests and rivers better than any other people,' Le Froy said. 'We could learn so much from them. Are your mother's people from around the Emerald Estate? Petani Village? Ampai?'

'They are in the forest around Kesumbo Ampai,' Jaimin said, his eyes lighting up with pleasure.

'Did you ever see Mrs Max on any of the mountain trails?' Le Froy asked. 'Did she like to go for walks?'

'When they first came, yes, she wanted to,' Jaimin said, 'but Boss Max said no. He said it's not safe. Later she stopped asking.'

'There are some good things up here,' Prakesh said later. 'Whatever happens to me, get the chief to keep an eye on Jaimin, will you? I don't want that lout Henry taking it out on him. He's a good boy.'

I nodded. I agreed, although 'He's very quiet, isn't he? I can't see him dealing with most of the stuff that must come up here. Drunken workers and so on.'

'He manages. You told me everybody works in a different way. As long as the job gets done, who cares how?'

I wasn't sure I believed that now. Captain Henry was determined to keep the peace here in the only way he knew how – by pinning an abduction and murder on Prakesh and closing down all alternatives.

Caught in my old thoughts I thought I misheard what Prakesh was saying. 'What's that again?'

'I said I shouldn't have talked about Harry Palin as I did. Even though it's nothing I would ever get involved in, I can see how deep friendship could maybe – you know – come to mean something more between a couple of men.'

'Jaimin?' I asked.

'I don't want him to get into trouble for trying to help me,' Prakesh said. 'But don't say anything to him. I don't want to mess up anything further here.'

'Don't worry,' I said. 'You're brothers in arms. Of course you're concerned about what will happen to him. There would be something wrong with you if you weren't. And he's going to be working under Captain Henry. That's not something I'd wish on my worst enemy.'

Prakesh nodded. But I knew he was still troubled.

Even before he brought it up, I'd sensed the bond between him and the young corporal. It wasn't surprising. Stuck in this desolate outpost, you either hated your colleagues or you became family. Or both.

In this case, I thought it was hero worship on Jaimin's part. He had risked getting into trouble with his boss when he allowed us to help Prakesh.

'Maybe Le Froy can see about getting him a post in the city, in Kuala Lumpur, perhaps. There would be more people around. It would be harder for one bully to get away with it.'

'I suggested it,' Prakesh said. 'Can you believe he's never been further than Batu Gajah? Not even to Ipoh!'

Ipoh was the capital of Perak, the state we were in. I could well believe what Prakesh had said, though. There are people who live their whole lives without moving more than ten miles from where they were born. If you have your farmland and your local shop to buy the things you can't grow yourself, it makes sense to marry and, later, marry your children to people from the next village so that there is always someone to continue farming and caring for the land and livestock. Until they built the railways and motor-cars became popular, that was the usual way to live.

Jaimin brought a bowl of water and a cloth and I cleaned Prakesh's injuries. I was glad to see the damage wasn't as bad as I'd first thought. Prakesh grinned. 'Just giving Boss Max a chance to blow off steam.'

I smiled back, relieved. Most of the blood had come from his nose, which wasn't broken.

Jaimin got up abruptly and walked away with the soiled cloth, emptying the bowl into the rain.

'He's not going to say anything about us being here, is he?' I worried.

'Nah. Jaimin's okay,' Prakesh said. 'He's very young.'

'Where was he trained?' Le Froy asked. 'Which division?' For some reason he seemed very interested in the boy.

'Before the occupation,' Prakesh said. 'I don't know under whom. He had papers and everything, but he didn't know anything when we started. He tried really hard. He's not involved in any of this.'

'But you are,' Le Froy said. 'Why does Boss Max think you had something to do with his wife's disappearance?'

'Because he's crazy.'

'But why you?' I asked. 'If he's crazy, why doesn't he accuse Captain Henry or Jaimin? Or Terry Cook?'

Prakesh snorted at the suggestion, then shrugged. 'We used to talk. We got along quite well. She could speak some English and she was trying to learn more. When they first arrived I used to drive her and Mrs Terry to Ipoh town to go shopping. But Mrs Terry always took such a long time so Elfrida and I would sit in the car and talk.'

I wondered if Prakesh realised he'd called his employer's wife by her name.

'It sounds like you got along very well,' Le Froy said. 'Why would he think you would attack her?'

'There was a misunderstanding.'

'Go on.'

'One day when I came to take her to the main house for dinner, I saw some rotten *jambu* in her room. They were on a paper on her bed. I was going to take them and throw them away. Everybody knows that when they look like that they're rotten inside and you can't eat them. I just wanted to throw them away, but she didn't understand and she started scream-ing at me to leave them alone. I thought, Is she worried I'm going to eat them? I was just going to grab them and throw them over the fence to show her I wouldn't eat them. But she screamed and went crazy and started hitting me and tried to push me out of the room. Boss Max turned up and I tried to explain but he punched me for attacking his wife.'

'Oh, Prakesh,' I said. Prakesh might have been falling for women as long as I'd known him, but he'd not upset any *ang moh* women until now.

'I didn't,' Prakesh said. 'I know what you're thinking. Even she tried to tell Boss Max I didn't do anything, but I think he enjoyed making her watch him hit me.'

I believed that.

'That room she was sleeping in,' I said. 'Why are there broken pots and red clay everywhere?'

'Making pottery was Elfrida's hobby. When she was growing up her family had a country estate in Bavaria and she used to play with the local artisans, who taught her to make clay vases and bowls. Her mother liked art-nouveau and

Bauhaus designs and let her take lessons from a master potter. She left all that behind after the war, but when she saw the Ipoh red clay pots she got some clay and started making pots and models of coconuts and rubber seeds . . . She's very gifted, a real artist.'

Le Froy and I looked at each other. I could tell we were thinking the same thing.

So could Prakesh.

'Come on, you two,' Prakesh said. 'It's nothing like that. There's nothing between us. People talk about her as if she just ran off and left her husband. What if he did something to her? That's a lot more likely, if you ask me. She loved those clay pots and models. She would never have broken them.'

'I'm going down to town to see if I can get any information on anyone else here,' Le Froy said. 'I can take you with me, try to get you to a doctor. But with the floods, it's chaos down there.'

'I know. Thanks, but I want to stay here until we find her – or find out what happened to her.' Prakesh grinned painfully at Le Froy. 'Some honeymoon, sir. You really know how to show a woman a good time.'

'Careful,' Le Froy said. 'You've already antagonised one husband here!'

People and Paths

———◆———

Le Froy and Boss Max headed down to the town. Boss Max needed 'supplies', grumbling about people pinching his bottles, and Le Froy suggested they drive together to the resort centre because he wanted to find a working phone.

'Do you want to come for a ride?' Le Froy seemed torn between whether I would be more uncomfortable stuck in a motor-car with Max Moreno or left alone among strangers, but I made it easy for him.

'I'm not driving anywhere again so soon.'

After waving them off in Boss Max's vehicle, I wandered under the rose apple tree to see if there was any ripe fruit within reach. I was standing on tiptoe reaching for a branch, using the bamboo fencing of the secret garden as a support, when I was startled by a voice.

'There are many evil things here,' Aunty Rakiah said.

'Ssh!' Aunty Salmah said fiercely, and muttered something in Bahasa about not talking nonsense. She was as skinny as Aunty

Rakiah was plump and looked younger than Aunty Rakiah, despite daring to tell her off. They were probably in their forties or fifties. The third aunty looked unwell given the way she hunched over. Though they all wore headscarves only Deaf Aunty covered her lower face, which made me think she wasn't comfortable with being looked at. I made a point of not looking directly at her. Maybe she would get used to me when she realised I didn't mean her or her companions any harm.

'What's wrong with that?' Aunty Rakiah waved a hand up, making the birds in the foliage above us flutter and cackle. 'So much evil up there. They're waiting for you to stand here so that they can poo-poo on your head.'

I laughed, and Aunty Rakiah looked pleased.

'Better not stand here.' She urged me away from the fencing. 'The problem with evil is that it comes in so many varieties. Some do evil on purpose. Some do evil believing they are doing good. And some just need to shit and don't care who they are shitting on.'

The last was directed at Daffy as she came towards us from the Moonlight Lodge.

Aunty Rakiah and the others stood meekly aside as Daffy took my arm and hurried me away from them.

'I was looking for you, but you weren't inside.' She was wearing a sun hat with a long brim round the back that made her look somewhat like a dung beetle. 'Let's get out of here. I can't stand those old crones,' she said. 'Now it's stopped raining for a bit, I'll show you the walk Frida always wanted to explore.'

I was tempted, but I couldn't just walk away. Some people are uncomfortable around the elderly, but I'd grown up with my very powerful grandmother: she'd enjoyed scaring people but had a good heart.

'Just a moment, Mrs Cook,' I said politely. Resisting Duffy's tug on my arm, I turned and bowed respectfully to the aunties. 'We are going now.'

People have all kinds of reasons for looking down on other people, but old age is one of the most ridiculous. It's something that comes to us all – if we're lucky.

They were already melting away, heads bowed.

'Come on now,' Daffy said. 'Everybody calls me Daffy.'

'Short for Daphne?' I asked.

'No,' she said. She didn't sound like the Mission Centre British ladies who had come out to teach us. But she did sound British. More like the girlfriends of servicemen who had come out before the war.

'It doesn't have to be short for anything, does it?'

'No, it doesn't,' I said. 'I just wanted to be respectful.'

Daffy shrieked with laughter. 'Respectful? Of me? That's a good one. I thought I'd love that, being waited on hand and foot, having everyone bowing and scraping to me. But you get tired of it, you know. At least you speak pretty decent English. You're someone to talk to. Now that Frida's gone there's no one else for me to talk to here. Not that Frida ever had the time of day for me. God knows what she found to keep herself so busy. She just didn't want to be with me. Well, no loss.'

It was too easy to forget that white people have their own caste systems. If anything, they're more rigorously defined and observed than anything you find here or in India. Though for Indians, as Dr Shankar had pointed out, the main problem with a girl marrying out of her caste was that that would make it much harder for her relatives to set up her husband in a family business: he probably wouldn't have any experience in it. He'd brought that up after his daughter Parshanti had told him she was marrying an *ang moh*, who was a doctor, like Dr Shankar himself. Thinking of that made me smile. Oh, I missed Parshanti so much. We were both happily married, but there are things you can say to your girlfriend that you can't to a husband . . . mostly things about that husband.

And talking to Daffy wouldn't be the same at all.

'I want to live closer to the coast. We'll be moving, once this stupid rubber plantation is all set up and running on its own. This is just the start-up phase.' Daffy sighed heavily. 'I want to be on the beach in a coconut grove with cool breezes all day long. Not the awful damp heat of the plantation. I hate it there!'

'At least it's cool up here,' I said.

'I'll tell you something, can I? Since you asked? It's a secret, okay.' Daffy linked her arm in mine, and leaned in close to whisper. I smelt alcohol on her breath and steeled myself not to pull away. 'You want know what my name really is?' She looked around, even though we were alone on the plateau. 'Daffodil! Can you believe it? My mum thought it was such a pretty name. And she's always loved flowers. My older sister is called Lily. That's not so bad. There are lots of Lilys around, Lilys and Roses. You'd have thought she'd pick something like that if she wanted a flower name, but no, it had to be Daffodil for me and the one who died was Carnation. When my dad was drunk, he'd say that was what killed her, being saddled with a name like that. It wasn't much fun growing up with a name like Daffodil, but now . . . I don't know. I like to think of my mum and her love of flowers. And I like to think, too, that maybe if I have a daughter I'll name her Orchid. The school kids would give her hell but it's exotic, isn't it? I wouldn't mind being called Orchid. Better than Daffodil. But such a common flower, don't you think? Not so common where we lived, of course. But that was my mum. She was into her poetry and everything. And wanted to travel. If she could see me now, eh? She'd be blooming jealous.'

'Where did you grow up?' I asked.

Daffy seemed to tense. Then she shrugged. 'Hackney,' she said. 'Council estate. I know it's not something to be talked about but, hey, it wasn't too bad when it's all you knew.'

'When it's all you knew . . .' I said.

'Exactly,' Daffy said. 'You said it exactly.'

Even though I had only repeated her words, I kind of knew what she meant.

'Not that I'm saying I would ever go back there,' Daffy added, 'after all I did to get out. But with half the people saying you can't ever go home, and the other half saying you can get the girl out of Hackney but you can't get Hackney out of the girl, what are you supposed to think, eh?'

She looked at me. 'How are you finding married life? That Le Froy's not a bad catch, I must say.'

'I don't know what to think yet,' I said honestly. 'It hasn't been a week. How about you?'

'If I had to do it again, I'd get married but I might hold out for someone a bit further up the ladder. Terry's always talking about how much he's going to earn, the profits he's going to make, how it all takes time. How much time? That's what I'd like to know. And Boss Max isn't God's gift either. What do you know about him? Did your Le Froy tell you anything?'

'I know his wife is missing,' I said.

'She'll be back.' Daffy seemed unconcerned. 'By the way, word to the wise – be careful of Viktor. He hates women. He only spends time with them for their . . . shall we say attractions?' It was clear what she thought those attractions were. 'Otherwise he doesn't even talk to them.'

'What – really?'

'Absolutely. Why do you think he's sleeping in the staff lodge with the servants even though Boss Max said he could have a room in the big house with us?'

I could think of a couple of reasons to sleep anywhere other than in the Emerald Lodge, but I guessed Daffy was hoping for genteel horror rather than an honest answer. 'You mean the cooking and cleaning staff?'

'Whatever. They're all his mistresses. You know what loose local women are like. They'll do anything to hook a white man.'

'All three of them?' The aunties didn't meet my idea of loose women. 'He got his mistresses to clean and cook for Boss Max?'

'Of course not. They're locals. They work at the Boss House on the rubber plantation. They've always worked on the plantation. Max brought them up with him so they couldn't steal or sabotage anything, left alone down there.'

'Why do you think they're Viktor's mistresses?'

'Isn't it obvious? Why else would he camp out in the staff lodge unless he wanted to get access to those sluts?' Daffy glanced about to make sure no one could overhear, and hissed, 'My guess is those old servants ganged up together to get rid of Elfrida. I've noticed them following her and spying on her. They hate us, you know.'

'Why?'

'Isn't it obvious? They're jealous. We've got money and nice clothes, and we're living this life of luxury while they're wearing rags and eating our leftovers. You see them with their head coverings and you know what kind of life they would have if we weren't around. They'd be in harems, being powdered and pampered, no better than prostitutes, really, for all the men who come in to use them. I read books, you know. I know what it's like in places like that.'

I could just imagine what kind of racy romantic novels the woman had been reading.

'You don't have to worry, though. I don't think they'll be jealous of you. You don't look white and even they wouldn't want your clothes.'

Well, thank you very much, Daffy. Maybe she wasn't that far wrong. I could well imagine someone wanting to do away with a woman like her.

'But Boss Max arranged for them to live with Viktor?'

'Boss Max said they could set up quarters in the garage,' Daffy said. 'But my Terry didn't want the cars standing out in the rain. Viktor said there was plenty of room in the staff lodge for them and for the security people too. Can you imagine? Just as though they were regular guests here.'

Maybe Viktor wasn't so bad after all.

The path Daffy had spoken of was really more of a narrow dirt track that led down from the edge of the plateau with the jungle pressing in close on both sides.

'That's the path Frida used to want to go walking on. But she wasn't supposed to go anywhere alone, and I didn't want to, so we'd just look at it from here.'

'We should explore it,' I said. 'She might have gone alone and fallen. Did they search down here?'

'I'm sure they did. But why would anyone want to walk down there when it's so much nicer up here?'

The gardens surrounding the lodges were charming, if more than a bit soggy at the moment. There were carefully laid-out pebbled paths between cultivated rose and jasmine bushes surrounded by green lawns, with a riot of wild orchids flowering in the trees beyond and below. But there was nothing to see – and if Elfrida had indeed wandered down the path and fallen, something as minor as a broken ankle would have rendered her unable to return.

'I want to go down the path,' I said.

'I said no. Stop being so stupid and stubborn,' Daffy turned and set off in the direction of the lodges, taking for granted I would follow her.

I stepped out carefully – the ground was soggy there too – onto the path and pretended not to hear the exasperated sighs coming from behind me.

I would go just a little way. If Elfrida had followed her fancy, I could too. And if I found her, well, that would be the first problem of our stay solved. Though I wished I had a map. It would be too easy to get lost – and it would be pointless to find Elfrida only to disappear alongside her.

'Hey! China girl!' Viktor Falk came from further along the trail, rather than behind me. 'What are you after?'

'I'm not after anything,' I said, 'just walking.'

'Everybody is after something.' Viktor stared at me. 'Your man. He is an investigator. He looks for money and murderers, am I right?'

I stared back at him. He hadn't said or done anything threatening but he was a large man saying strange things in an unfamiliar place. My fingers found Ah Ma's *kris*. It was tucked inside its sheath tied around my waist under my frock, but I could have it out in a second. It probably wouldn't do him much damage, but it would buy me enough time to shout for help and scramble away – though how far would I get?

'Are you holding a weapon?' Viktor asked. 'Is it a knife? What kind of knife is it?'

I couldn't tell his background from looking at him or his country of origin by listening to him. And even though he'd somehow seen through the material of my dress that I was holding my knife, I didn't feel afraid of him.

'It's a *kris*,' I said. I pulled it out to show him.

'Keris dagger. Very old,' Viktor said.

'My grandmother's.'

'Yours now?'

He was asking if my grandmother had died and left it to me. 'No. She just lent it to me because I was going somewhere dangerous.'

'Here it is dangerous,' Viktor agreed. 'I show you what my *abuela* left me.'

With a quick, smooth move, he slid a knife from the leather sheath attached to his belt. 'This was her gaucho knife. She used it every day on the farm. And you want to see another secret?'

Of course I nodded.

He pulled open his shirt and showed me the knife he was wearing on a rope – sheathed in a leather case. 'Neck knife. Not as useful as the *facón* but it is always good to have a little secret.'

We were behaving like children on the first day of school, showing each other our pencils and erasers for the new year, a tentative overture of friendship. But his *abuela*? That sounded Spanish.

'Did Boss Max bring Le Froy here to get rid of me?'

'Why would Boss Max want to get rid of you?'

'Because we fight.'

'About what?'

'Everything,' Viktor said. 'All the time.'

Rubber Trees

———◆———

Viktor Falk reminded me of a big jungle cat – or a fighting dog eyeing its competition.

Last night I'd had the impression he'd been deliberately staying in the background, as a tiger or a panther might, circling and watching the clearing where Boss Max was tying up a goat as bait.

Then his eyes switched to me before I had time to look away. I was surprised by his eyes. I'd seen *ang moh*s with blue eyes before, of course, but Viktor Falk's eyes were the very pale blue of *pulot tai tai* – the glutinous rice cakes delicately coloured with butterfly pea flowers.

'What did you and Boss Max fight about?' I forced down my sudden craving for rice cakes. After exchanging information about grandmothers and concealed weapons, I felt I knew him well enough to ask.

'Why do you want to know?'

'Le Froy is trying to find out who sent threats to Boss Max. Did you?'

Viktor shook his head. 'You think I am stupid,' he said.

'I don't. But you're not saying you didn't.'

'Max thinks I am stupid. But I know things he doesn't know. None of them know. They don't understand rubber trees. Rubber trees suffer torture daily. Death by a thousand cuts. That's how ancient Chinese tortured people to death.'

I was surprised. He was talking about *lingchi*, one of the cruellest tortures ever devised. When people talk about the good old days, they're forgetting how bad they were for some. 'You like trees,' I said.

'I have always liked trees,' Viktor said. 'The trees on the plantation, they are still young. Ready for years of tapping if they are treated well. You should see them. They are so beautiful, so tall – sixteen feet at least – with trunks as wide as the waist of a perfect young woman, just enough to hold with your two hands.'

He held them apart to show a twenty-inch circumference. Mine wouldn't have gone around a trunk that size. And I didn't think much of him equating that to perfection in a woman's waistline. Western men wanting women corseted into hourglass shapes were as bad as the Chinese who wanted wives with agonisingly tiny bound feet.

We were walking slowly as we talked. The path descended very gently but even without bound feet I found it difficult not to lose my footing.

The jungle in the Highlands differed from the lowland rainforest with which I was more familiar. I saw more pitcher plants, wild orchids and ferns there. Even the insect sounds and bird calls were different. I was the alien in that space, even though it looked like home.

I was a little surprised by what Daffy had said, that Viktor was a woman-hater who never talked to us. Maybe he just didn't talk to Daffy.

'Max does not understand rubber trees, that you should not tap when it is raining. He should not be in charge of them. You cannot cut trees when the trunk is damp, or the latex will not follow the narrow channel but will flow like floodwater all over. It's like when you kill a pig. You want to cut dry, healthy skin to save the blood. If you cut wildly, the blood goes everywhere. All wasted. And bad for the animal.'

It sounds brutal, but if you eat meat you must know that animals are killed to provide it. And it makes sense to want the knife in the hand of an expert slaughterer who will get it over quickly. 'Did you grow up working with rubber trees?' I asked.

'No, but I studied them. I like studying,' Viktor said. 'I spent the war years working with rubber trees in Sumatra. The Japanese needed rubber, so they allowed the plantations to operate.

'The tree is divided into four layers: bark, pink flesh, paper-thin pale-green water tissue and its core. You must make sure your tappers know to stop before the third layer, because you only get latex in the second, the meat of the tree. If you cut too deep, you destroy the tree.'

It's the same with any kind of exploitation. You need to ensure survival to extract all you can.

'One experienced tapper can cut five to six hundred trees a day. Boss Max wants to pay less to fewer people. If he won't pay for experienced tappers, how can he expect me to train inexperienced workers to work faster than they can? It's not just a matter of walking around slashing trees. You must first pick off the encrusted latex from the previous day. If your tappers are careful – if they are experienced – the scraps can be sold, also the crust from the bottom of the tapping cup. But it takes skill. How do you expect workers to learn if you are always shouting at them to go faster, faster?'

I could imagine Boss Max yelling at his workers. 'If he hired you to manage the plantation he must trust you,' I said.

'Boss Max walks through a rubber plantation once and thinks he knows everything about rubber trees. In South America the rains don't last as long as they do here. And you know how they tapped trees in Brazil? They would cut through the bark to get the sap and the trees would die. Here they use a scientific method from the Botanic Gardens in Singapore. Did you know that, Singapore girl? They use the fish-bone method – two incisions in the shape of a V, like bones sticking out of the spine of a fish. The sap flows through a metal funnel to a ceramic cup. You can slash a tree only once a day, the incision to be neither too deep nor too shallow.

'You cannot tell people to go faster or produce more. And the trees cannot be tapped during the monsoon season because if the bark around a cut gets wet, it will scar and become vulnerable to infection. Boss Max refuses to understand that. He wants to work my trees and my workers to death.'

I wondered if Viktor realised he was talking about 'his' trees and workers. Maybe that was just how a good plantation manager saw his responsibilities. But I wondered how far he would go to defend 'his' trees?

'You know much more about running a rubber estate than Boss Max does,' I said. 'He's lucky to have you.'

'I know more than all the rest of them,' Viktor said. 'That is why they have me in the group. They want me to run the rubber plantation while they play golf and spend all the money I make for them. And all that while they call me stupid!'

'Then why do you work with them?' I asked.

'Because I am very good at it,' Viktor said. 'And I like rubber trees.'

'There are other plantations,' I said, 'or you could start your own.'

'I have no money,' Viktor said. 'That is because I am not as big a crook as Boss Max. But I have the knowledge,' he tapped the side of his head, 'and I have the skills.' He held out his hands. They were strong-looking, misshapen from hard labour but still agile. They reminded me of lion dancers' feet: muscular from use yet finely tuned for precisely accurate movement.

'Most plantation owners don't care about their workers,' I said. It was one of my grandmother's tenets that if you wanted a profitable business, you had to pay good people and treat them well. It was more expensive and a waste of time always to be training new workers. 'They should. If they treat their workers badly, they'll leave.'

'Or die,' Viktor said.

'Or die,' I acknowledged.

'You think workers are treated badly here?' Viktor said. 'You should see what it's like in the Amazon. They set crazy impossible targets for latex collection. If the workers don't make the target, they make a big show of cutting off their fingers. Anybody who resists or cannot go on working is killed, slaughtered. I hate the Amazon rubber business. And that's where Boss Max comes from. He thinks that that's how he can run things here. But the workers will not stand for it. I will not stand for it!'

'But you're still working with him,' I said. 'Why do you stay?'

Viktor reached out and patted the trunk of a nearby tree as we walked past it. It was a gentle, affectionate gesture that reminded me of Uncle Chen reaching down to rub the ears of the old family dogs when he thought no one was watching and he didn't have to act tough. I don't think anyone – especially not the dogs – was really taken in by Uncle Chen's tough-boss act. But maybe outsiders were, given the dogs put on their savage-brutes act to back up their master.

'I love the trees,' Viktor said. 'A beautiful tree is like a beautiful woman. They don't have to do anything. Just being near them makes me happy. It is not an easy life for the tappers. They start before six in the morning, with paraffin lamps fixed to their foreheads because they have to finish by noon when the overhead sun thickens the sap and stops it flowing freely. Once a tree has been tapped from top to bottom, you can tap into the new layer that grows over the scars. But the latex will not be as good as from a virgin tree. The trees in the Emerald Estate are all virgin trees.'

What is it about the English language? The word 'virgin' was correct in context but made me uneasy. It wasn't Viktor's fault but my Mission Centre school education. Words like 'virgin' and 'nylon stockings' were taboo because the sweet Mission ladies who taught us believed they were the first rungs up the ladder of sin that led straight to damnation.

'You know a lot,' I said.

'I know a lot about a lot of things,' Viktor said. 'When I am interested in something, I learn about it. I find you very interesting.'

I'd found him interesting too, up to a point. 'I'm sure you must find everything here very interesting. Is this your first trip east?' I said, in my most formal, social and distant voice. We had stopped walking to lean comfortably against trees and look down over the rainforest canopy that stretched beside our path, but I straightened now. 'I should get back to the house,' I said. 'Le Froy might be back by now.'

'No,' Viktor said.

'No?'

'He is not back yet. We would have heard the car.' He pointed. 'The road is down there, under the trees. Because of the steepness, it goes back and forth on the side of the drop. This path here goes down more steeply so you have to cross the road three times.'

'Oh, I see,' I said. 'That's interesting. So if we could climb down the slope we could reach the resort centre?'

'It is not safe to climb down. You should not try. Most women would not think of such a thing. But you are different, yes? You think and smell different from the other women here.'

I should probably have been morally offended by that. But, then, most morally righteous women probably found me morally offensive. I was finding Viktor interesting again. Strange, but interesting.

When he said, 'We walk down a bit further?' I agreed. If we got as far as where the trail met the road, I could meet Le Froy in the car there and surprise him.

'I like strawberries immensely,' Viktor said. 'Do you like strawberries?'

It wasn't that the man spoke bad English. In fact, I realised his spoken English sounded strange to me because it was too good – too proper, almost as though he was reading from an English textbook. But where did strawberries come in? I couldn't help wondering if it was English slang I was unfamiliar with, like 'cheaters' are sunglasses and when they say 'muddy water' they want coffee.

'Strawberries?' I said carefully.

'Like so many others you think strawberries are English. Strawberries and cream, you think, like Henry the Eighth. You have heard of Henry the Eighth? Even earlier, the strawberry appears in German art and illuminated manuscripts.'

It was a bizarre conversation to be having along a sodden goat trail – but it was interesting.

'So strawberries as in the fruit,' I confirmed.

'Strawberries were cultivated in South America for centuries before the Spanish arrived,' Viktor said. 'Same with rubber. So why not here?'

The goat trail was terrible in the best way: the weather, the fire ants crawling out of buried nests, the ankle-deep puddles disguised with dead leaves and the dead animals. Just pushing on I felt I was achieving something, as though being uncomfortable was a virtue. And when Viktor came to a stop: 'The view!' I exclaimed. The mist all around us was water vapour, evaporating out of the damp rainforest below us, but it looked like clouds. I felt as though we were in the heavenly cloud palace of the old stories. 'I've got to bring Le Froy here to see this.'

'Your husband, you call him by his family name?'

'It's the name you know him by,' I said, 'and what I called him when we first met. I got used to it.'

'Why is he really here? What is he after?'

'It was supposed to be a holiday, a chance for us to spend some time together,' I said. 'but now, of course, he wants to help find Mrs Max and clear Prakesh.'

'But why did he come here with you?' Viktor asked. 'Why here? When you started out you did not know anyone was missing because at that time no one was missing.'

'Because we have just been married. This was supposed to be our honeymoon,' I said again. I tried to look sad, as a newlywed abandoned for work on her honeymoon should. I didn't think I was doing very well so I countered with my own question: 'What do you think happened to Boss Max's wife?' I'd much rather talk about a missing woman than worry about familial responsibilities.

'Her name is Elfrida,' Viktor said. 'I call her Elfrida.'

'What does she call you?' I asked, wondering if there was any truth in the rumours I'd heard.

'She calls me "the fiery giant who knows all the answers".' Viktor laughed.

I laughed too. I had no idea what he was talking about, but that man's laughter was infectious. 'What?'

'*Der Riese mit den drei goldenen Haaren,*' Viktor said, 'the giant with three golden hairs. He is a big, fierce giant, but he is good to his grandmother, and he helps the child in the story get everything he needs to survive.'

I remembered the book of fairy tales on Elfrida's bed.

'So why is Le Froy after Boss Max?' Viktor asked. He was like a dog with a bone.

'He's trying to find out who killed the Walker brothers and their families,' I said.

'Exactly,' Viktor said. 'So Le Froy suspects Max?'

Walking with Viktor

◆

'No!' I said, startled. 'I didn't say that at all!'

But my brain was already spinning. Le Froy hadn't said he suspected Boss Max in particular. That suggested Viktor was trying to use me to turn Le Froy towards Max. And why, honestly, would he bother to do that unless he was trying to deflect suspicion from himself?

I'd not considered Viktor Falk a prime suspect until now. After all, he'd worked as plantation manager for the Walkers, too. But was it just conceivable that if the Walkers had damaged one of Viktor's precious trees he might have snapped and massacred them?

I didn't think so. But even I could see that walking alone on a trail running alongside a steep drop wasn't the best place to ask a semi-stranger if he was a murderer.

'I don't think Le Froy suspects Boss Max,' I said instead.

'Boss Max hated the Walkers,' Viktor said.

'I didn't know he knew them.'

'Of course they knew each other. The elder Walker and Boss Max were partners,' Viktor said. 'Jonathan Walker and Max Moreno put up the down payment on the rubber estates. Only the down payment. The rest would be paid out of the profits once they started exporting rubber. Max hired me to run the estate. When Jonathan Walker brought his brother in to buy out Max's share he asked me to stay on as estate manager, so I did. After the Walkers died, Max asked me to continue, so I did. So many changes, but for Viktor and the rubber trees, nothing changes except the weather.'

'Right now the weather is changing a lot.'

'It is normal,' Viktor said.

He was right, though during the monsoon season, it was usually either raining or about to rain. At that moment, though, we were between rains and the air was beautifully fresh.

'You know your way around these trails. Which direction might Elfrida have gone in if she was on her own?'

Viktor shrugged. 'The things I know about women, they don't like me to tell other people,' he said. 'Especially not husbands. Husbands don't have to know everything. If you would like, I will show you a place with a view all the way down to the bridge that you have to cross when you turn off the main road to come up here. I told Elfrida about it, and she wanted to see it, but . . .' he shook his head '. . . she didn't go.'

I hesitated but only for a moment. Wasn't this the classic case of following (or, rather, not following) a stranger into the woods? Especially after one woman had already disappeared?

But I wanted to see where he might have taken Elfrida. And, besides, I had Ah Ma's *kris*.

'Let's go on,' I said.

I followed in Viktor's footsteps, managing better than I'd expected to, especially after Viktor cut and trimmed a stout branch for me to use as a walking-stick. Which showed me how strong and sharp his knife was . . .

'Elfrida and her husband, did they get on?'

Sometimes it's easier to put invasive questions to someone's back than to their face. If Viktor took offence, I would say something like 'What's wrong with asking whether they were married for long?' while looking indignant.

I didn't have to.

'They are married,' Viktor said. 'They don't have to get on.'

'That's not very nice,' I said.

'It is true. Once you get the bacon, you don't have to go on feeding the pig.'

'Which of them is the pig?'

Of all the stupid things to say, I thought, as soon as the words came out of my mouth. Comparing husbands and wives to pigs and bacon? Any respectable married woman should have been offended by that. But it's easier to be morally offended when you can make a dramatic exit without tumbling into a ravine.

'Where?' Viktor stopped abruptly and scanned the area around us. 'Where is the pig?'

'What pig?' I wasn't sorry to take a break from walking.

'There are wild pigs in the jungle. That is why we talk and make noise as we walk here, so they hear us and stay away. The same with panthers. Unless, of course, they want to eat you. Where did you see the pig?'

'I didn't,' I said. 'Sorry.'

It was too complicated to explain. But since Viktor didn't mind my asking questions, I pressed on: 'Do you think Elfrida was uncomfortable with her husband bringing his partners and the security people up here with them?' I asked. 'She might have wanted to spend some time alone with him.'

In a way I was in Elfrida's position – a newly married woman, surrounded by strangers. The main difference between us was that I had a much better husband – the difference between Heaven and Hell.

'She seemed not to like them,' Viktor agreed. 'But Captain Henry, he has the smell of her perfume. It is different on him, of course, but you can tell it is Wishing.'

'Wishing for what?'

'The Wishing scent that Elfrida uses is aldehydic, made of synthetic ingredients. It doesn't smell as good as the natural aldehydes in roses and orange peel. On her it smelt good. On Captain Henry, it did not. When people spend time close together, their smells mix.'

'Really?' It was an effort not to giggle. Was he saying that people who got on well started to smell the same?

'The same perfume smells different on different people because their bodies react differently,' Viktor continued. 'A perfume is just a combination of chemicals. When somebody smells good naturally, it is a biological and chemical reaction telling you they are healthy. I smell very good. You smell good too.'

Should I be offended by that? But I didn't find Viktor offensive. He was like a big, earnest dog fascinated by different scents.

'Did you tell Elfrida she smelt good too?'

'No. I told her she didn't smell good. And I told her that covering up her smell with synthetic aldehydes wouldn't help her become healthier.' Viktor sounded sad.

'What did she say?'

'She said to me, "Thank you for telling me honestly how I smell. I believe we can be friends now." And we became friends. So now, when I meet a woman I want to be friends with, I tell them how they smell.'

Elfrida sounded like a clever, tactful lady, not the spoiled rich woman I'd imagined, who would deliberately wander off to worry her husband.

And maybe it says something about my morals (or lack thereof) but I felt comfortable with Viktor now we'd discussed how we smelt.

'Why aren't you staying in the big house with the other Europeans?' I asked, remembering what Daffy had said.

Viktor shook his head. 'They see me as a servant. Those in the big house, they need me for my knowledge and skill. I like to work in the East, and I like to work with the trees, but I don't like those people.'

I nodded sympathetically. 'Your family doesn't mind?'

'Luckily I have a younger brother, who is very good at producing sons to run the family business. So I am free to fulfil my destiny.'

'Which is?'

'To work outdoors, not in an office.'

'Some of my family started in the rubber plantations, too, when they first arrived in Malaya after leaving China. But that was long ago,' I said. 'A lot of Chinese immigrants worked on rubber plantations in Malaya.'

'Same with Brazil,' Viktor said. 'There are Chinese in Brazil also, transplanted like rubber trees and growing like them. We were the biggest producers of rubber in the world. We had the whole rubber industry, until you people in Asia started doing the same thing but more cheaply. So I decided this was where I would come, to see how you do it.'

'Will you take what you've learned back to Brazil?'

'I like it here,' Viktor said. 'But strawberries I think are the next thing. Up here it is too cool for rubber, but the British like to eat strawberries. The climate here would be very good for growing strawberries. I would like to stay in Malaya. I would grow rubber in plantations down there and strawberries in plantations up here. And I would be happy. Not unhappy like those people.'

I risked asking, 'Was Elfrida very unhappy?'

'Of all of them, Elfrida was the unhappiest. I told her she must be quiet and rest, like trees after pruning.'

I remembered what Daffy had said. 'Was it because she hated living on a rubber plantation in the middle of the jungle?'

'Not at all. When Elfrida first came to the plantation, she was happy. She wanted to learn about the rubber trees and she wanted to learn about the trees in the jungle. She told me, "City people think it's all wild beasts and poisonous snakes and insects in the rainforests but it's not. And when at the end of the season the rubber-tree leaves change from green to yellow, then red, before they are shed in the rain, even though it's still hot, it's like autumn. Only time you could see the sun from within the plantation."'

'She doesn't sound as if she was unhappy.'

'At first she was very happy. She wanted to learn about life on the plantation so that she could find something to love here.'

'Didn't she love her husband?' I asked. 'What made her unhappy after that?'

Viktor shrugged. 'She learned what had happened to the family who lived on the plantation before them. I thought she already knew about it. I thought everybody did. It was – how do you say it? A boiling hot topic. But one day she asked me, "What are they doing there? The offerings of joss sticks and fruit outside the porch of the Boss House?" I told her it was for the Walkers, who had been killed there.'

I knew the offerings he meant. After a death, especially a sudden or tragic one, people often leave such offerings to comfort any spirits that linger around the site.

'I didn't expect her to mind so much,' Viktor said. 'She said she had to talk to her husband right away.'

'You mean she wanted to leave the place because she was scared of staying in the house where people had died?' I could understand her shock, but she had been living there for a while and it wasn't as though there were bodies and bloodstains all over the place – at least, not by the time she arrived.

'No. It was as though she thought he'd had something to do with it,' Viktor said. 'But I don't know. After that she wouldn't talk to me at all.'

· Much as I liked Viktor, I knew Le Froy would suspect he had been involved in the Walkers' murders when I told him all this. Otherwise why was he trying so hard to implicate Boss Max?

'Elfrida is a good woman,' Viktor said. 'It is not easy to be a woman in the world today. I hope that she will be all right.'

It was as though he was offering a blessing to her, wherever she was. His affection for her seemed genuine. I nodded. 'It's not easy for anyone at the moment,' I said.

'Do you think there are different degrees of criminal?' Viktor asked.

'Of course,' I said. 'Otherwise you would be sentenced to death regardless of whether you'd stolen somebody's sweet potatoes or murdered their sons.'

'True,' Viktor said.

We had reached a part of the path that looked over a steep drop. I could see the foot trail winding on to our right, along with glimpses of the road.

In front of us the ravine plunged down to waters we could hear far below but not see. I had to stifle an absurd, dangerous urge to launch myself down. I quashed it, of course, but even if I'd tried I probably wouldn't have reached the rushing waters. I would likely have been stopped by the cluster of rocks below us – like that glimpse of something blue . . .

'Viktor! Look! Over there! Do you see that? That blue thing?'

'What are you talking about?' Viktor frowned. 'I see . . . Is it a bird? No. Too big.'

'Somebody's down there! Did Elfrida have a blue dress?'

'Yes.' Viktor was staring now. 'She had a blue dress with white spots and a white collar. She was wearing it the night before she disappeared.'

He was just staring with a puzzled expression. Why were men so useless in a crisis? I started to try to scramble down the slope, but Viktor grabbed me and wouldn't let go. 'Wait! Stop! We must go and get help!'

'She might still be alive! We have to get to her as soon as we can! We don't know how badly she's hurt!'

'We need ropes. We need people and equipment to lift her. If you try to go down now we will have to lift you both – and you might kill yourself!'

He was right. But I couldn't understand why he wasn't more frantic. After all, he knew the woman lying down there.

Or maybe he knew her better than he'd let on. And had he meant to send my body after hers?

I was extra careful making my way back up the slope. It didn't help that Viktor stayed behind me all the way. How much strength would it take to throw another body down that slope? Especially if you weren't concerned about getting either of them back up?

'This way.' We'd reached the ledge of the ravine behind the lodge buildings.

The sky looked as if rain was about to pour at any moment. Shaken by the wind, tree branches scattered droplets over us as I climbed back onto the safety of the Moonlight plateau.

Elfrida's Body?

———◆———

'Elfrida's body is down the slope!'

I made it safely back up to the lodge plateau and charged into the security post, the nearest building to the trail.

'What are you talking about?' Captain Henry gaped.

'Down the slope where?' Prakesh jerked up and banged his head against the roof of the cage. 'Is she all right?'

'We need ropes.' Viktor came in behind me. 'Good, strong ropes. And pulleys.'

'No pulleys here, no ropes that I know of.' Captain Henry looked around the bare wooden walls of the security post.

'Where is she?' Prakesh crawled out and got to his feet stiffly. 'Which slope?'

'The south-west side of the ravine,' Viktor said.

'No way to get down there till we have the equipment. Rappelling ropes and men who know how to use them,' Captain Henry said. 'No point risking more lives.'

In other words he wasn't going to risk his own neck. Why were these men so useless?

'We have to go to her! Now!' I believe I stamped my foot. I couldn't believe everyone was standing there so uselessly. It was just possible Elfrida was still alive and every minute wasted made it less likely we would reach her in time to save her. Why couldn't these men see that?

I turned and went out, almost colliding with Jaimin, who'd been standing silently against the sliding barrier.

'Wait! Where are you going, Su?' Prakesh called. 'Show me where you saw her!'

'I'm going to see if anyone in the big lodge has rope,' I said. 'It's no use us going down to her if we can't get her up.'

Terry and Daffy Cook weren't much help, though Daffy at least understood the urgency of the situation. She wanted to dash out in the rain to see the body straight away. In fact I was the one saying, 'Wait! We need a way to get her up. It might be hard to move her. I'm trying to find ropes, pulleys and a first-aid kit.'

I had brought iodine, cotton swabs and bandages in my own first-aid kit, but nothing that would help broken bones or a broken neck.

'There should be a rope in the van,' Terry Cook said. 'We made sure to bring rope and chains, in case one of the motors went over the side. Viktor? You said you'd take care of all that.'

Only then Viktor remembered there was a tow rope in the old van. Why couldn't he have thought of it sooner?

We also got hold of an old wooden cart that looked as if it had been designed for a small bullock to pull. If two men each pulled one of the cart's shafts they should be able to get Elfrida – or her body – up the steep incline.

It would have been much easier in dry weather, but now the detritus swept down from the slopes made everything slippery with decomposed leaves, mud, rocks and branches, ready to send you down into the rushing water at the bottom.

Viktor proved to be best at deciding how to anchor the ropes to the sturdy trunk of a large tree and he improvised a pulley system by running the rope through knot loops.

Then came the question of who was going down to get Elfrida.

'I think a woman should go,' I said. But between my dodgy hip and Daffy's bulk . . . Practicality swept aside female niceties.

'The captain and I can pull those two and Elfrida back up easier than they can pull us.' Viktor nodded to Prakesh and Jaimin, who immediately agreed and moved to the edge. Viktor fashioned rope harnesses and attached one to each man, in addition to what he had already tied around the cart.

It was frustrating how long all this took, but I could see the sense of not adding more bodies to the one already there.

In fact, Boss Max and Le Froy returned just as Prakesh and Jaimin had made it within three body lengths of the blue figure . . . which hadn't moved since I'd been watching it. That was not a good sign.

'What are you all doing out here?' Boss Max and Le Froy were carrying canvas satchels with bottles of liquor – which explained the reason for Boss Max's excursion – when they joined us by the tree Viktor had designated as the anchor. 'What the hell are you up to, hah?'

'There's what looks like a body in a blue dress down there, sir,' Captain Henry said. 'Not saying it's your wife, but...' He shrugged.

Boss Max peered down. 'Well, go and find out, you fools!'

Prakesh gestured to indicate he'd heard. The rain was lighter now, but the thick layer of leaves on the ground covered a multitude of pitfalls and they moved slowly.

I worried that Boss Max would object to Prakesh being the one to go to his wife, but he seemed to have forgotten their previous altercation.

'You okay?' Le Froy came to my side and put an arm around my shoulders.

'Could she still be alive?' I whispered.

'Not likely after that drop,' Le Froy said. 'Not the way she's lying.' Sometimes I hated his honesty as much as I counted on it.

Standing pressed together, we watched as Prakesh and Jaimin made their way down the last few feet with their cart to reach the blue material. I saw but didn't understand their surprise, relief and frustration.

Boss Max burst out, 'What are you doing? Is there anything on her? Look around! Make sure you pick up anything she has with her!'

Prakesh shouted something.

'What? We can't hear!'

Jaimin seemed to be laughing as Prakesh tried again: 'It's not her!'

'Who is it, then?' Le Froy shouted down.

They were loading something blue into the cart, but from the way they were handling it, it didn't seem to be a body.

Viktor and Le Froy started hauling up the cart while Captain Henry and Terry Cook kept the ropes taut on Prakesh and Jaimin as they climbed up.

It wasn't a body. But it was a blue dress. Someone had deliberately made it look as though Elfrida had fallen.

Boss Max had to be held back from kicking the cart and its contents back down the slope. He stormed away, ranting.

Of course we were relieved it wasn't Elfrida's body. But . . .

'Why would someone try to make it look as if there was a body down there?' I wondered.

'I think the dress was just wrapped around some rubbish and thrown over, not to look like body, just to get rid of it,' Le Froy suggested thoughtfully.

'Well, where is she, then? And without her clothes?' Daffy asked.

No one could answer. Things were looking worse and worse for the missing Mrs Moreno.

Back in the Emerald Lodge, Boss Max was drinking again. I couldn't blame him for that but then he turned on Le Froy. 'What use are you? You can't find my wife, and if your job is to discover who murdered the Walkers, why aren't you down in the city questioning suspects? I could have your job for harassment! You don't seem to get it. We're the victims here! You're supposed to string up the locals!'

'I'm here to follow up on the death threats you reported,' Le Froy said.

'No one had death threats,' Captain Henry said. 'They would have come to me. That's what I'm here for.'

'The governor said . . .' Le Froy took his time, leafing through his notebook. I knew very well that he didn't need it, but it gave him time to study their responses. I saw the look Captain Henry directed at the plantation owners. Terry Cook shook his head, but without conviction.

'Maximilian Moreno. You said you and your wife were threatened and felt unsafe at the Emerald Estate –'

'After what happened to the Walkers there that's hardly surprising,' Captain Henry said. 'That doesn't mean—'

'– because of the threats you received, directed at you and your wife,' Le Froy said. 'You wanted the down payment on the estate returned to you until you could be sure that you and your family could live there without fearing for your lives.'

'There were threats,' Boss Max said. 'I couldn't risk my wife's life, could I? I had to protect her. The threats were driving her crazy! She was getting depressed, refused to leave her room—'

'That's true!' Daffy said. 'Frida didn't want to eat, didn't want to go to town, didn't want to play rummy. I thought it was just being in this country, but if she knew people were threatening her, that would explain it.'

Boss Max nodded. 'Exactly.'

'Tell me about these threats,' Le Froy said. He was still studying his notebook. Anyone would have thought he wanted to match their accounts to what he had written there.

'How would I know?' Boss Max asked. 'It's not the kind of thing you remember. You get the damn notes, you tear them up and – and burn them. And then you put them out of your mind. You don't memorise them, for God's sake! Or maybe you would. I wouldn't know what tickles your fancy.'

'So they were notes,' Le Froy said. 'Written? Typed?'

Boss Max didn't answer.

'On what kind of paper?' Le Froy said. 'How easily were you able to tear them up and burn them?'

'I was speaking generally,' Boss Max said. 'That's the kind of thing normal people do with nasty, anonymous threats.'

'Some people save them as evidence,' Le Froy said agreeably. 'You received them in the mail? Or were they delivered by hand?'

'Might have been delivered by hand,' Boss Max said, 'and then mixed in with the mail to look innocent. Who pays attention, these days?'

That didn't make sense. If I'd wanted to deliver an anonymous threat, wouldn't it be more intimidating to give the impression you could deliver it by hand, unseen? Unless you didn't want to let on that you were already on the premises. I managed to keep my mouth shut. I would bring it up with Le Froy later.

'They were expressed in English, if you and your wife could understand them,' Le Froy observed. 'What makes you think they were written by a local?'

Boss Max sighed heavily. 'Le Froy,' he said, 'you've spent too many years in the force. You're seeing suspicious things everywhere. We all need to calm down. I think we could use a drink.'

I recognised the move. Boss Max was behaving just like my grandmother when she felt manoeuvred into a corner and needed a distraction to give her time to re-plan her strategy. Ah Ma would have called for sweet tea and *kueh*, or complained that she was too hot and called for the new electric standing fan to be brought in . . .

'Scotch and soda?' Boss Max said, when he came back. 'That's what Churchill was putting down, right? Three Scotch and sodas before lunch is the way to win the war.'

Daffy and Terry Cooke followed him in with glasses and bottles.

'This is supposed to be good stuff,' Boss Max said. 'It'd better be! We used to set the gin alight, back in the day. If the alcohol content isn't high enough, it won't burn. That's how you tell.'

Le Froy accepted a glass but didn't drink. I took a sip of mine. Ordinarily I would have been fascinated by the British ritual, but I didn't want to be distracted.

'The thing is,' Boss Max lowered his voice, 'I didn't want to bring it up but it was my Frida who got the notes. You know what women are like. Emotional. She was upset, wanted to leave the country straight away. Get as far away as possible. I had to tell her to be reasonable. "This isn't just some holiday trip we can cut short. It's a business we have to keep up or we lose everything we've already put into it." She destroyed the notes. They frightened her, so she tore them up and burned them. I never saw them so that's why I can't tell you what kind of ink was used or whether they were written by a left-handed man or an elephant with his trunk. You know, all those things you detectives ask. But you can't blame her. Women get upset easily.'

'Was that what prompted her to make off with your emeralds?'

'She did?' Daffy's eyes were wide. 'I didn't get that. There were more of those emeralds? Those emeralds that are more valuable than diamonds?'

For a while after that no one said anything.

'The roads will be closed soon,' Le Froy finally said. 'The rains aren't stopping for a while and the tides will keep rising till this moon cycle is over. We've cleaned out the liquor supply at the resort centre so we may as well resign ourselves to the fact we'll all be up here for a while.'

'You've already had quite a day,' Le Froy said, when we were safely back in our lodge. 'Do you want to stay here? I'll bring you something for dinner.'

Because of all the excitement – even the aunties had come to watch the rescue operation – we'd missed lunch and I was hungry.

'I'll come with you,' I said. 'At least it wasn't her body so she may still be alive.'

I didn't tell Le Froy about Viktor's opinion on how I smelt. Men can be funny about these things. Le Froy had been born an Englishman, after all, however far he'd come since, and he might feel obliged to be offended. I didn't fear Viktor, though, and Le Froy didn't need anything else on his mind.

The *Keropok* of Courage

———◆———

Idetected a familiar spicy smell as we approached the Emerald Lodge. Aunty Salmah was sitting behind the kitchen, frying *keropok* over the charcoal. When she saw us approaching, she stirred the charcoal and tossed another handful of the small dried prawn crackers into the pan. The oil must already have been hot because the crackers were swelling immediately.

'Frightening day.' Aunty Rakiah came out of the kitchen with a rattan tray lined with banana leaf. 'People climbing up and down mountains in the rain looking for dead bodies.' She gave an exaggerated shiver.

I understood. Prawn crackers were a comfort food. 'Luckily there was no dead body,' I said.

Aunty Salmah stirred the crackers with a pair of tongs. When they floated, she fished them out and deposited them on the tray.

'Try first?' Aunty Rakiah offered.

I took a couple, of course. I could get *keropok* in Singapore but would it have come so light, crisp and crunchy on a banana leaf with *cili kucai* on the side? We had banana leaves in Singapore, of course, just as we had *kucai*, Chinese chives. At least the plastic plates and bottled chilli sauce that had come with modernisation had left behind something familiar.

'Tried it before.' Le Froy shook his head as he walked along the passage to the dining room.

He was open to new experiences, but now he was focused on the job in hand, and when he was thinking about work, things like eating and sleeping were pushed aside. Maybe that was part of being British. It wasn't my problem. In fact, it's probably easier to feed a husband who doesn't much care what he eats. But very often it's when you're eating or sleeping that you discover the answers to your problems.

Often you find they aren't problems at all.

'These are very good,' I told the aunties.

'We are happy that you like them. You must teach your man to like them, too. Take some more. By the time Boss Max comes out to eat, all soft. Not nice,' Aunty Salmah said. 'My *keropok* should be eaten when it is almost too hot. My old boss called it "the *keropok* of courage". The first time my old mother tried *keropok* she thought it was going to be hard and that her teeth wouldn't take it. My father laughed at her and shouted, '*Mut! Mut!*' pretending his mouth got burned and his teeth broke! Take more, I give you the basket.'

'*Wah*, today you talk so much,' Aunty Rakiah said.

'It's the relief,' I said. I accepted the banana-leaf basket. 'We're all so glad it wasn't Mrs Moreno's body.'

But where was Elfrida?

Daffy came into the kitchen and grabbed me. 'You're here! I've been waiting for you! Come with me, quick. I've got to show you something.' She grabbed me and dragged me away, never mind that her husband and mine were already sitting at the dining table with Viktor.

'Call me when Boss Max comes out,' Daffy called to her husband, without looking at him, as she pulled me past the men in the dining room.

I saw Le Froy raise his eyebrows but he seemed happy to let things play out since there was no way in or out of the bedroom suites without passing the dining room.

The Cooks' room was about the size of ours. 'What do you think of these?' Daffy held up some bracelets. 'Made by Frida.'

They were three red clay bangles, the same colour as Ah Ma's *labu sayong* pots, delicately patterned and studded with red *saga* seeds.

'She made these? They're beautiful.'

'No, they're not. They're hideous. Could she have hidden the emeralds she pinched inside them? That was why Max smashed up all her clay stuff in that room, isn't it? I get it now. He thought she put the emeralds into her clay to hide them. But he didn't know about these. Can you smash them?'

'I don't think there's anything in them.' I hefted the bangles. 'How big were the emeralds?'

'I don't know. Bigger than would fit inside here, I suppose.' Daffy slumped. 'I just thought since there were three of them and she gave them to me just after she took those emeralds . . . Those stones are worth more than the whole estate right now.'

'Max is probably exaggerating,' I said. 'The plantation is worth a lot. Everybody wants rubber now. How soon after they went missing did Mrs Moreno give you these? It would have taken days to air dry them without cracks, and then she probably slow-baked them in the oven if she didn't have a kiln. Anyway, she'd hardly give them to you if she'd hidden something so valuable inside.'

'She didn't exactly give them to me,' Daffy said. 'Hey, don't judge me. People are always nicking things off me. I don't see why I shouldn't nick stuff back!' Her eyes narrowed when she spotted the basket of *keropok* I was still carrying. 'What's that?'

'Spicy shrimp crackers.' I offered her the basket, but she refused.

'I can't stand what those old idiots churn out.'

I liked the aunties' food, but I wasn't entering that battle now.

'Max made the down payment on the estate with two of the emeralds. But he didn't think about what we were going to live on until the estate started paying, did he?'

'I don't understand,' I said. 'If Max had already cashed in his wife's jewels, why does he think she ran off with them?'

'There were three left,' Daffy said. 'He had them in his safe. He was so pigheaded about keeping them safe. I thought, Why not let us girls wear them for a night out? I could get a simple setting made but, oh, no, they had to be locked away. And then, just when they were telling us we had to evacuate, he found they were gone.

'He already had those security goons of his keeping all the locals away, so he knew it had to have been her. No one else could have got into his room and his safe. It was such a joke. Max thought he'd got himself a good little wifey who'd do whatever he wanted and she went and pinched his emeralds!'

'Well, they were hers to start with,' I said.

'I begged her to tell me where she'd put them, but she wouldn't. You think you'd like to find a woman who can keep a secret, but I tell you it's a damned nuisance. I had a good look around her room at the plantation while Boss Max was grilling her, but found bugger-all.'

Daffy tossed the bangles back into the drawer. 'You know what I think? I think she got that Indian guard to smuggle her out of here.'

'But Prakesh is still here.'

'Meaning he's got her hidden somewhere and he's got your Le Froy to help him smuggle her down.'

'Smuggle her down where?'

She ignored my question, 'That's what Max suspects, you know. I heard him telling Captain Henry. Elfrida's emeralds are worth more than the estate so you're all in cahoots to steal them from her.'

This was so crazy I just ate another *keropok*. Would it spoil my dinner? Not likely: I was starving.

'Or Max wants to cheat Terry and he's got Elfrida hidden somewhere and the two of them are in it together,' Daffy said. 'She was a Nazi, you know.'

'Really?'

'Max thought he had it made. Instead he gets the ice queen all the way here then – poof!' Daffy blew a (not very good) smoke-ring, distracting me momentarily. I'd seen *ang moh* men blowing smoke-rings before, but it was the first time I'd seen a woman do so. Smoking was one of those things that the Mission Centre teachers warned would lead straight to Hell. And you can't blow smoke-rings without smoking, so . . .

I saw a jewellery box. 'She gave it to me,' Daffy said. 'Are you listening or not?' She sounded peeved. 'Why the hell are you looking at my mouth like that?'

Alamak. I pulled myself back from wondering if smoke-rings worked like clouds, and 'Your lipstick,' I said. 'It's nice.'

'It's Red Velvet.' Daffy looked pleased. 'Very exclusive. It's very popular. Jealous? Can't take your eyes off it, eh?' Daffy cackled.

'Did Mrs Max wear lipstick?' I asked. I'd not seen any makeup or toiletries in her room. If she'd taken them with her that would indicate she'd planned her disappearance.

'What a daft question—' Daffy coughed. Something had gone down her windpipe the wrong way. 'Who cares what lipstick that woman used?' She looked at me more closely. 'You're thinking I pinched this from her too, aren't you? Oh, I can't stand all you judgemental people! Get out of here! I'm not having you in here accusing me of things!'

I'd not meant to accuse her of anything, but I was happy to leave. All the *keropok* was gone and maybe the others were already eating dinner.

'Sorry.' I got up and started for the door.

'Hey, where are you going? Can't you take a joke?' Daffy's mood changed again. 'You locals have no sense of humour. Frida didn't get it either. She got upset when I scolded the servants for not understanding and, frankly, they understood

English better than she did. She was the boss's wife, but she was so totally hopeless I had to take them in hand and make them do their job properly. I wouldn't let them get away with anything. My family wasn't rich but we always had a servant and I learned from my mum to keep an eye on them. That skinny one was so lazy – mopping with half a bucket of water. I scolded her until she cried and Elfrida got so upset she cried too. She really doesn't know how to handle servants.'

'Dinner might be ready,' I said.

'Nah, they won't serve it till Boss Max makes his appearance and when he does we'll hear him.'

'Poor Mr Moreno,' I said. 'At least his wife's not dead.'

'Max blows up on a regular schedule. He'll be all right once he's had a couple of drinks,' Daffy said. 'He used to blow up at Viktor. Frida spoke German to him. Her German was better than her English, and Max would threaten to beat him up for flirting with her. It was hilarious!'

It didn't seem funny to me, but I smiled. Maybe she was right about my lack of humour.

'One more thing, girl. Be careful of that Indian you're so friendly with,' Daffy said. 'I don't know what promises he's made you, but let me tell you this, he and Frida were close, very chummy, if you know what I mean. You don't want your Tommy Le Froy to think you two being together gives him the right to wander off.'

'Oh, no,' I said. 'There's nothing like that between us. Prakesh is like a brother to me. We used to work together before the war.'

'Mind you, I'm not saying he's bad-looking,' Daffy said.

'Right now he's rather bashed up,' I said.

'Max does get a bit carried away,' Daffy said. 'If you ask me, he's getting desperate. He must have got into something he's not told Terry about. But if he thinks he's going to dump the bloody estate on us, and run off with those emeralds, he'd better think again.'

I wanted to ask her what she meant, but then we heard a roar that indicated Boss Max had put in an appearance. We jumped to our feet and headed for the passageway.

Sometimes opportunities are like *keropok*. If you bite down on them at the right time they are the most crispy, tasty and delicious treat in the world. But if you wait too long they become soggy and there's no way to reverse the process. Always seize your opportunities and *keropok* when you get the chance.

Max's Proposal

———◆———

'That damned Indian guard's behind it, I tell you!' Boss Max was in the middle of throwing a huge tantrum, like a big and not very bright child.

Something about the brightness of his eyes and the redness of his face made me think he was either crazy with fever or drunk. But he had a lot more energy than most men suffering from a fever. And he had purpose.

The last time I'd seen an *ang moh* with that kind of almost manic purpose was when an American Baptist preacher interrupted a Thaipusam procession to expel demons from the *kavadi* carriers and fire-walkers. The man had been screaming at the demons in them to fear God and be gone while the procession organisers were shouting at him to move out of the way, trying to show him their written and signed procession permits. The watching crowds cheered both sides on. He was thanked by many, after the event, for his contribution to the devotees' practice of penance and devotion. Although invited, he did not return the following year.

But though the feverish gleam in Boss Max's eyes and the redness in his face might have come from a mix of whisky and passion, there was something more than that. This was a desperate man, already driven to his limits and in fear of worse to come. I could understand him being in a panic over his missing wife. I could even sympathise with him. But was there even more to it than that?

When Daffy and I took our seats at the dining table, Aunty Rakiah and Aunty Salmah were already serving dishes of mushroom soup, dodging Boss Max, who was walking around the table in full tirade. He seemed not to see them, but I winced when one of his wild gestures narrowly missed hitting Aunty Rakiah in the face and left a splash of whisky on her shoulder.

'But that doesn't make sense because the Indian guard is still here,' Terry Cook said. 'He risked his neck this afternoon, climbing down to get that dress.'

The plump man was in a good mood after the day's exertions.

'Only because I was on to him and had him locked up before he had a chance to get away with her,' Boss Max said. 'I would have got the truth out of him by now if all you people hadn't come in interfering.'

He'd gone back to ranting about Prakesh.

'You can't get him out of this, my man.' Boss Max jabbed a finger at Le Froy. 'I warn you, if you don't do something about it soon, you'll force me to take things into my own hands. I'm just giving you people a chance not to look stupid.'

'What exactly do you mean?' Le Froy said. His tone was pleasant. His eyes were not.

'The issue is, what's that man done with my wife? And what do you mean to do to compensate me for that, hah?'

'Your wife?'

'Look, get that fellow to tell you what he did with my wife. Make him bring her back. If he does, we can forget this whole business. That's all I want. Get him to see that, can't you?'

It made sense that a man whose wife had run away wanted her back. He was upset because he didn't believe his wife had a chance of surviving in the rainforest in the monsoon season. He knew she had run away because of how he had treated her and was looking for someone else to blame.

'Or you know what? You tell that man, if he returns what she took from me, he can have her.'

Then again, maybe he didn't really want her back.

'We should search through the things in her room again first, just in case,' Daffy said. 'Let me have a go this time. You don't have any idea where women hide things.'

Boss Max turned and glared at her.

Daffy put on a baffled expression and gave an exaggerated shrug. 'What? I'm only offering to help.'

'As though you aren't helping yourself to everything you can get your greedy hands on.'

'Hey, no need for that,' Terry Cook said mildly. 'Sit down and pass the mustard, would you?'

Boss Max took his seat, but ignored the mustard.

'Le Froy, I have something very confidential to discuss with you. It's what you might call an exchange of information. You get me the information I want, and I'll give you something very important to your investigation. Everybody knows the force is looking for an excuse to push you out. That's why they're handing you dead cases. But what if you manage to turn that around, hah? What if I give you a case so big they'll have no choice but to give you a bunch of medals and send you and your wife back to London, hah? What would you say to that?'

Despite his misreading of Le Froy's position and what would appeal to him, he had Le Froy's – and my – full attention.

'I'd say I have no idea what you're talking about but I would like to hear more.' Le Froy's duck was untouched on his plate as he nodded to Aunty Salmah to clear it.

And I was so caught up in what Boss Max was going to say that I didn't even think about what a waste it was. Well, maybe a little.

'I heard the people around here set up systems to hide women from the Japanese during the war. That means there must be hiding places. The locals would know where they are. That Indian guard probably found one and sent her there to hide from me.'

To hide from him?

'Look, old man, I know you don't want to face it but it's most likely that she went for a walk and got lost,' Terry Cook said.

'Not your business. Nothing to do with you,' Boss Max said, without looking at his partner in the plantation business. 'You know how much it cost me? To bring her here, halfway around the world? All that just to have her sabotage me and wreck everything I've worked so hard to put together. You know what? I'm not going to let that happen.'

Boss Max was focused on Le Froy now.

'What are you going to do?' Le Froy asked.

No one was eating. No one was talking. I saw Aunty Salmah and Aunty Rakiah standing in the kitchen passage, hesitant to clear the half-empty plates and serve dessert. (I was the only one who'd finished everything. Stress might stop others eating but it makes me eat faster.) I saw the shadow of Deaf Aunty in the corridor behind them, probably with the coffee things.

'It's what you are going to do for me,' Boss Max said. 'You are the great detective, right? You are going to detect my wife and bring her and my emeralds back. And I will give you some very interesting information on the Walker case.'

'We got the killers in the Walker case,' Terry Cook said.

'The alleged killers,' Le Froy said, 'who aren't alive to testify.'

'Alleged killers. Alleged. That's exactly what I mean,' Boss Max said. 'Do we have a deal, then? You hand over the emeralds and I hand over the man who had the Walkers wiped out.'

'As I've said, I have no idea what's happened to your wife,' Le Froy said, 'but if you know anything about who organised the attack on the Walkers and their families you should—'

'Hah! No, no, no, no, no,' Boss Max said. 'I'm holding the cards now. First, you produce my wife and the emeralds she stole. Then we talk. I'm not an unreasonable man. I don't even need to know where she got to. Just get me my emeralds back and I'll give you what you need and walk away from this damned place. The rubber man,' he nodded to Viktor, 'he can do what he likes with those bloody trees, but I've had enough. "Make a fortune on a sure thing," they said. "America's gone crazy for the motor-car. They'll buy all the rubber you can produce for tyres," they said. They didn't warn me it'd take six bloody years to break even. Hah!'

'Hey, I'm involved in this too,' Terry Cook said. 'You can't just walk away from a partnership.'

'What partnership?' Boss Max said. 'You didn't put in one red cent of your own money. You and your wife just came along for the ride, two fat deadbeats. You've been living off me ever since.'

'Well I never!' Daffy said. 'What kind of man are you, Terry, letting him talk to your wife like that?'

'He's drunk,' Terry said. 'I may not have put money into the project, but he knows that without my name on the contracts, his estate wouldn't have any of its grants and licences. And given it's my name on the contracts and grants, he can't just kick me out.'

'I'm sick of this bloody plantation business and people who promise to handle things and don't keep their word,' Boss Max said. 'I'm not kicking you out. You can keep the place and your precious name. Good luck to you and that pig of a wife.'

'Maybe you could ask to see the records of those deaths,' I said quietly to Le Froy.

'I have all the records of the Walkers' deaths,' Le Froy said.

'I mean, check on the deaths of the five killers in police custody,' I said. 'Those five men who were arrested and shot trying to escape.'

Daffy made an impatient sound and I turned, startled. But she was looking at Boss Max. 'You won't be wanting your nightcap.' She pointed to a glass on the sideboard beside her I'd not noticed till now. Boss Max held out his hand but she stayed where she was so he had to walk over to get it. For a moment I thought he would hit her but, after snatching the glass, he picked up the whisky bottle from the sideboard and headed down the passage to his room.

Viktor got up and followed him. I heard the door close. Then we heard Viktor shouting at Boss Max and Max laughing, then shouting back.

'If he tries to walk out, we'll show him,' Terry said. 'Viktor and I will be making pots of money and laughing all the way to the bank.'

'Ssh!' Daffy said. 'What's Viktor yelling at him about?'

I couldn't make out what they were saying. That the loudest shouts were in German didn't help. But they were definitely not happy with each other. I started helping Aunty Rakiah clear the table. When I carried a stack of plates to the back I saw why she was working alone.

Aunty Salmah was standing by the back door holding Deaf Aunty. They seemed traumatised by what was going on. The shouting was much louder in the back because the windows of Max's room were open.

Viktor stormed through the dining room and out into the rain, leaving the front door to slam shut. Max yelled at everyone to leave him alone.

'I hope Boss Max isn't accusing Viktor of hiding his wife,' I joked, as I scraped food off the plates into the pig bucket.

'Viktor is angry because, as estate manager, he needs money to pay all the men they hired who will be coming to work once the monsoon rains are over. Also, there's processing and packaging equipment and other materials he needs to order. Boss Max hasn't given Viktor the money yet, even though he already collected the government grant money,' Aunty Rakiah said, in a low voice, glancing at Aunty Salmah and Deaf Aunty, who had moved to the very edge of the shelter, still huddled together.

'Viktor is worried that if the equipment isn't paid for, they will not be able to process the first few months of latex and it will be wasted.'

So Viktor was also pushing Max for money . . . I wondered how much rubber-processing equipment one of Elfrida's emeralds could buy.

Dead Max

I had a surprisingly good appetite the next morning. Almost as though yesterday's yelling match had cleared the air.

Neither Viktor nor Boss Max was at the table when Le Froy and I went into the dining room but the Cooks were already halfway through breakfast.

Before taking his seat, Le Froy looked enquiringly at Boss Max's door, just visible down the corridor.

'He's already up,' Terry said. 'Says he's working on new plans for the plantation. He's got toast and scrambled eggs in there and Daffy insisted on bringing him coffee. I don't know what that double-crosser is up to now. I'm going round to the main resort to make a couple of calls. He's not the only one who can make plans.' He looked grumpy.

'Where do you telephone from?' Le Froy asked.

'The bungalows on the other side of the golf course,' Terry said. 'The main resort is over there. The Princess Elizabeth

Lodge is unoccupied but the caretakers are there – ours too – and we should be able to use the phone.'

Le Froy nodded. 'Can I have a lift? When are you leaving?'

'As soon as we've finished here,' Terry told him.

Le Froy nodded yes to coffee as Aunty Rakiah appeared with the pot.

'I'll come with you,' I said. I hadn't seen anything of the rest of the resort and didn't mind making myself scarce before Boss Max appeared. And it would give me a chance to ask if anyone had seen Mrs Max. I had no intention of returning her (or anything she might have taken) unless she wished to come back, but I would like to know she was safe.

'No, don't go. Stay with me,' Daffy said. 'I don't want to be alone here.'

'Come along too, then,' her husband said.

'No,' Daffy said. 'I need to stay here.' She looked aggressively uncomfortable in a way that made both men uncomfortable too. 'With her.'

'Woman stuff,' Terry said lightly. 'Come on, Le Froy. Best thing we can do is leave them to it.'

Le Froy didn't laugh, but acquiesced. It was almost funny how fast the two of them scuttled out of there.

It was unfair that, just because I was female, I was stuck with Daffy. But we women have to stick together, right?

'I have some pads,' I said, once they were gone. It was not my time of the month, but it's always safer to be prepared. 'And safety pins. I can let you have two pads and two pins.'

'What the blazes are you talking about?'

'For your woman stuff. They're not new but they're clean.' I'd made them out of old towels and though they were scratchy they were absorbent enough.

'Gawd, no!' Daffy looked offended. 'I use Kotex. I would never touch your . . .' She shook her head.

'Then what is it?'

'I want to check Max's room to see if Elfrida's hiding in there.'

I had misjudged the woman. Okay, I was on board. 'How? If he's in there and he locks the room when he comes out?'

'He has to come out sooner or later. There's no connecting WC.' Same as in our lodge. 'As soon as he does, one of us gets him talking and the other checks to see if she's in there.'

'If she is, we'd have heard her. And she could walk out when he's not there.'

'She might have a memory-loss thing,' Daffy said, 'like that woman mystery writer who disappeared in England before the war. Things like that happen all the time. Some people said she ran away to scare her husband who was playing around – sound familiar?'

'If Elfrida ran away to scare her husband, she wouldn't be hiding in his room, would she?'

Daffy shrugged with bad grace. 'Anyway, I want to check the room.'

She had filled a plate with bacon, beans stewed with tomato, and fried eggs from the chafing dishes on the sideboard and she was taking her time over it. I ate more toast and Marmite. Marmite is like a thick, salty soy sauce and one of the few things (other than *kaya*) that tastes better on bread than on rice. *Kaya* is a thick, creamy coconut jam flavoured with pandan leaves, and one of the first things I intended to cook in my own kitchen – but until I had one I might as well have a look around this room, too.

Well, why not? Even if I only had the briefest glance into it, I could tell Le Froy I'd not seen (or smelt) Elfrida or her decaying body in there.

'What if we knock and ask if he wants more coffee?' I suggested.

'Good idea.'

To my surprise Daffy marched straight over and banged on the door to his room. 'Max! They want to clear the breakfast things. Do you want more coffee before they clear it?' She tried the door handle as she spoke, but it was locked from the inside. Then she sprang back. 'Oh, sorry!'

'Did you hear him growl at me?' Daffy hurried back to her chair, giggling in excitement. She had provoked the wild boar. I braced myself, but Boss Max didn't appear.

'What did he say?' I asked.

'Busy and wants to be left alone,' Daffy said. 'You heard him.'

All I'd heard was a growling mutter, but I couldn't make out what was said.

'He'll have to come out sooner or later to use the lavatory,' Daffy said.

We continued sitting there while the aunties cleared the remnants of breakfast. It wasn't as though there was anywhere else I had to be. We were still there an hour and a half later when Captain Henry turned up.

By then we'd discussed the weather, whether Boss Max could be working for the British government undercover, whether Elfrida could be a Russian spy . . . In other words, we'd exhausted all relevant and irrelevant topics.

'He doesn't want to be disturbed,' Daffy said, before Captain Henry could ask for Max. 'He's completely dead to the world!'

'Too bad. I need to talk to him.' Captain Henry had a strange look on his face. I remember wondering if it had something to do with Boss Max's outburst last night. He knocked on the door.

'Told you,' Daffy said. 'You'll have to break it down if you want to get in.'

'Maybe he didn't hear you,' I said. It was possible, given the way the rain was pounding down.

Captain Henry banged on the door again. 'Max! I'm not joking. Wake up and open the door.'

Still no response.

'How long's he been in there?'

'Since breakfast,' Daffy said.

'Boss Max!' Captain Henry shouted. I could see that beneath his bravado he was worried. That made me worried too. Captain Henry was the security chief: if he thought there was something to worry about . . .

'I'm going to break the door down,' Captain Henry warned. 'Stand back.' He put his shoulder to the door and the flimsy hinges gave way almost immediately. 'Max?' He strode into the room.

I started to follow him, but Daffy grabbed me. 'Something terrible's happened. I know it! I can feel it! Why ever did we come to this terrible place? Oh! I think I'm going to faint.' She leaned heavily on me.

She was a large woman and her weight almost brought us both down. 'Come and sit,' I tried to disengage myself. I wanted to see what had shocked Captain Henry into silence.

But Captain Henry was back, and ushering us both into the dining room. 'Don't go in,' he said. 'The poor bugger's dead.'

This brought on a fresh round of wails, shrieks and moans from Daffy, but I left her to Captain Henry and darted past him into the room. It wasn't morbid curiosity. Sometimes people look dead even when they're not, and if you act fast enough you still have a chance to save them.

But even as I stepped through the remains of the door I could smell the sweet metallic odour of fresh blood and the stink of faeces and knew it was too late. Captain Henry was right. Boss Max, in his pyjamas, was sitting in his armchair with a bottle and a glass beside him on the low table to his left. His rifle lay on the window ledge to his right and the handle of a knife stuck out of his chest with a dark red stain radiating from it.

I know many people can't imagine being in a room with a dead body, let alone touching it. But unless you are vegetarian, you've been in contact with dead meat all your life. Touching the skin over one of his arms, I found he was still warm, and rigor mortis had not fully set in. His eyes were not cloudy, suggesting he'd been dead for less than two hours.

I prodded him. I remembered Ah Ma teaching me to poke at fish, lifting their gills, using the same finger to poke prime ribs of pork and hairy melons, insisting I learn to tell freshness and quality in this way. The man had indeed not been dead for long. But it was cooler and wetter here than it was in Singapore, so I couldn't trust my timing.

'I'm taking the knife,' Captain Henry said, behind me.

I didn't watch him extract it. But Le Froy would ask what kind of knife it was, so . . .

'Can I see it?' I asked.

My voice sounded shaky and I expected him to brush me off. But, to my surprise, Captain Henry said, 'Go ahead,' and handed me the towel on which he'd laid the knife.

So wrong, I thought, for fingerprints and bloodstains. But I was glad of the towel and knew better than to tell a security chief how to manage a crime scene. I was shocked to see it was a *kris*.

'Recognise it?' Captain Henry said.

'What?' For one crazy, wild instant, I thought it was the *kris* Ah Ma had given me . . . but, of course, it wasn't.

'No,' I said.

This *kris* blade had an asymmetrical base, like mine, but was slightly longer. It had a wooden handle; the one tucked into the pouch on my hip was carved ivory. But aside from that, they were very similar. They had clearly originated in our region.

But thinking of Ah Ma's *kris* flipped some kind of switch in my brain. I wasn't just a silly local girl helplessly over-whelmed by circumstances, I was the holder of a *kris*: weapon, heirloom and supposed conduit of magical powers . . .

'It's a *kris*,' I said. 'The killer wouldn't have left it behind unless something really terrible happened.'

'Same as the ones they used on the Walkers,' Captain Henry said. 'I'd call murdering a man pretty damn terrible. Shows it's the same people behind this, doesn't it?' He held out his hand for the *kris* and I passed it to him on the towel. 'You're a witness to this being the murder weapon. It's evidence.'

'What are you going to do about . . . him?' I asked.

'Too late to do anything.'

'We should cover the body. Or wrap him in something,' I said. 'Just to keep the bugs off. Otherwise there'll be nothing left for the medical examiner to look at by the time the roads are clear.'

'Cold-blooded little witch, aren't you?' Captain Henry was incredulous. 'This kind of thing seems normal to you, then? I'm getting the feeling you know more about this than you're letting on.'

'No! No, I don't.'

I was upset, though it was right and necessary to suspect everyone in the vicinity, of course. What struck me was how relieved Captain Henry looked when I cried out. I understood. I hadn't been responding as a woman was expected to. I could still hear Daffy wailing and moaning in the dining room.

'What should we do, then?' I raised my voice to a girlish squeak.

It worked.

'Don't worry your little head about it,' Captain Henry said. 'Leave it to us. Why don't you two ladies go to the kitchen and find something to calm your nerves?'

I nodded. But I stayed in that terrible room, sinking onto the floor in the doorway and curling up, as though my legs could take me no further. I could do nothing for Boss Max, but for Le Froy I could preserve the crime scene.

I stayed there until Le Froy returned. 'What happened?'

Viktor was with him. I gathered they had already heard a version from Captain Henry, and Terry Cook was with his wife.

I told them what I'd witnessed, then left the room when they went in to examine it.

'Su Lin,' Le Froy said, when he finally came out of the room, 'you were here when Max was found? And you've been here ever since?'

I nodded.

'Good,' he said. I knew that meant we would rehash the details later. 'What's wrong with your stomach?'

'Nothing,' I said. 'At least they'll let Prakesh out of that cage now.'

The only reason Captain Henry had kept his own man locked up was to placate the crazy (now dead) Boss Max.

I could understand someone wanting to murder Boss Max. What I didn't understand was how he could have been murdered inside a locked room.

Locked Room

◆

Captain Henry was convinced that Boss Max had been killed by a local, and not only that, it must have been one of the same gang who had killed the Walkers: a *kris* of the kind that had done for them had been found in his chest. But all the men guilty of murdering the Walker brothers were already dead. And even if not, how would they have found their way up, in the rain and flooding, to the most isolated part of the Cameron Highlands Resort? And if that were possible, how had they got past me and Daffy without us seeing them?

'It's impossible that anyone could have got in to kill him without him knowing them and letting them in,' Terry Cook said. 'He was paranoid about strangers. Always had that rifle with him. It had to have been someone he knew.' He glared at Viktor. 'Someone who had just had a big fight with him.'

'I did not see him again after last night,' Viktor said. 'I had no desire to see him.'

'What were you two fighting about?' Captain Henry asked.

'It is not relevant now,' Viktor said. 'And it is none of your business.'

It's funny that a man trying to prove his innocence would make himself sound guiltier than anyone else could.

'Where was everyone last night?' Le Froy asked casually. 'We should go through that while it's still fresh in our minds. Captain, would you mind starting? Just to show them how it's done? Su, if you would take notes . . .'

'Of course,' Captain Henry said. 'I was with Mrs Cook for much of last night.'

'What?' Terry said. 'No, you weren't. I was with her. Tell him, Daffy! This is ridiculous.'

'Why?' Le Froy asked Captain Henry.

'She found some of her things were missing. She thought they might have been stolen. She was giving me a list, telling me who might have taken what and where she had last seen them.'

I saw the look he gave Daffy. I saw Le Froy notice it too. But it was the look she gave him that struck me. It lasted only an instant but was the kind of look you give a child who's made a mess yet again of the instructions you gave him and has embarrassed you in public.

'I don't know what he's—' Daffy caught herself quickly. She turned to Terry. 'You were fast asleep. I couldn't sleep and I didn't want to wake you. So I thought I'd go through my jewellery box and organise my things. You know, all the pretty things you've given me. But I got a shock because several were missing. And some of my blouses and handkerchiefs had gone too. I didn't know whether it was the monkeys or the workers who were stealing them. And I was still so upset over Max carrying on that I knew I'd never drop off. I looked out of the window and saw the light in the security post was still on, so I went over and made a report to Captain Henry. I wanted to tell someone about it.'

'You went out alone? In the dark?' Terry Cook couldn't seem to process that. 'You never go out in the dark. Why didn't you wake me?'

'You needed your sleep,' Daffy said. She turned to the rest of us. 'He's been having so much trouble sleeping, what with worrying about Frida and Max acting crazy.'

'That's true,' Terry said. 'But last night I was out like a light. All those sleepless nights caught up with me and knocked me out.'

'So when the poor man managed to get to sleep, I wasn't going to wake him, was I?' Daffy said. 'But I was worried about my things and the light was on so I went over to make a report. You always say to let you know everything that's happened, don't you?'

'That's the way things should be done,' Captain Henry said. 'I took down what she said was missing and told her I would look into it.'

'Can I see the list?' Le Froy asked.

'There's a murderer on the loose, man!' Terry Cook said impatiently. 'Why are you wasting time over some missing hairpins? Could those renegade Nazi hunters be behind this?'

'Max had German ancestors but his people have been in South America for years. He wasn't even in Germany during the war.'

'What about his father-in-law?' I asked. 'Elfrida's father.'

'What the hell are you talking about?' Captain Henry said.

'Could Elfrida have told her father she didn't want to stay with Max? She might have taken the remaining emeralds and arranged for her father to send someone to fetch her. They might even have put her dress down there to make it look as though she fell. They probably thought by the time someone saw it they would have had time to get away. But somehow Boss Max found out and was going to stop them so they killed him.'

'Frida's family did come from Germany,' Daffy said. 'She said she and her father escaped. They went from Germany to Spain and ended up in Argentina. Max was their contact in South America who helped them get settled.'

'Why didn't they return to Germany after the war?' Le Froy asked.

'They didn't leave till the war was almost over. Elfrida's father was a high-level Nazi who escaped from Germany after the war. I don't think they had anything to go back to.'

'This is murder,' Le Froy said. 'Never mind whether it's Communist vigilantes, Nazis or Nazi hunters. We're going by the book from here.'

'We've *been* going by the book.' Captain Henry was clearly distressed. There was more to this security job than he'd bargained for, I thought.

'Tomorrow we'll telephone down to Ipoh and tell them what's happened. They should send a team up to get the body.'

'If they can,' Captain Henry said. 'The roads are bad.'

'They were fine this morning,' Le Froy said shortly. I could tell he was annoyed with himself for not having got us out sooner.

I might have dreamed of visiting the England I'd read about in books, but I wasn't enjoying the *Northanger Abbey* atmosphere here. Did that come naturally with the cold and dark, or was someone creating it?

'Look at these.' I'd waited till we were alone together, in our own lodge, to pass Le Froy the papers I'd discovered during a quick search of Boss Max's room. I'd slipped them under my skirt and held them in my knickers. That's one advantage of wearing Western-style frocks.

Le Froy looked at me.

'Prakesh said Boss Max always had a notebook with him,' I said. 'I didn't see it there, but I found this. I didn't want the others to see it before you did. It looks like Boss Max was trying to frame Harry Palin for the Walker murders. I didn't want them to assume Harry had somehow found out and was motivated to have him killed. Boss Max has all these notes on who Harry was seen with. And it looks like he was trying to write out the confessions Captain Henry took from the dead assassins implicating Harry. That he met them and promised to pay them a fee and so on. I think he meant to give them to you as "proof".'

Le Froy studied the papers. I wondered if he'd believed Boss Max could come up with any real evidence.

'Captain Henry wasn't there when Boss Max talked about giving you information on the Walker murders,' I said, 'but

Daffy, Terry and Viktor were,' I remembered. 'Could one of them have thought he was threatening them?'

Le Froy and Captain Henry went back to the resort centre to telephone through the news of Boss Max's murder. I know Le Froy had intended to make arrangements for transporting the body down, or do so himself, but he was told not to.

'With all the flooding casualties being brought in, they don't have enough manpower, resources or space,' Le Froy said. 'We're in the middle of a national natural disaster. They want us to stay put till they can send someone.'

'They can't expect us to stay up here with the body,' Daffy said.

'Where do you want to go? We're all stuck here, dead or alive,' Terry said. He looked unwell, which wasn't surprising, of course. His partner had been murdered, right after announcing plans to jettison him. He had to be wondering if he could get away with it or whether he would be next.

'Tell me again,' Le Froy said, when we were in bed that night. 'Tell me, exactly, everything you saw today.'

I suspected Le Froy wanted me to disgorge the images from my mind so I would be able to sleep. It probably wasn't the kind of love talk most married couples indulged in, but I could handle it.

'I saw Boss Max sitting in his chair with that knife in his chest.'

'What else? It was dark?'

'Yes. Not too dark to see, but the curtains were drawn and the windows were closed and latched.'

'You sure? All the windows?'

'I checked. And I tapped the windows with a broomstick. Every bar was secure, not a single one out of place. And the curtains . . . nothing behind them.'

'Nothing under the bed?'

'Not within reach of the broomstick.'

'And the last time you saw him this morning?'

'I didn't see him at all. Daffy tried to get him to open the door but he wouldn't.'

'She did? Why?'

'It was silly. We thought maybe he was hiding his wife in that room. That that was why he always kept the door locked and wouldn't let anyone in to clean. Daffy said the servants wanted to clear the breakfast things, and if he wanted more coffee he should come and fetch it now.'

'Surely the servants would have made him more coffee at any time.'

I shrugged. 'It was just an excuse to see inside his room. But he told us not to bother him.'

'What did he say, exactly?'

'I'm not sure. But it certainly wasn't "Please come in."'

It was a locked-room murder. They're fun to read about, but when you're living in the presence of something inexplicable, everything around you starts to feel creepy.

'Do you think Boss Max killed his wife?' I asked Le Froy.

I was holding on to him as a source of warmth and comfort. But I needed mental comfort too.

'It's not impossible,' Le Froy said.

'Even if he did, she couldn't have come back to murder him.'

'Arguably . . . but depending on what you believe, she may have to wait till she's reincarnated.'

The problem with a man who doesn't lie to you is that sometimes you just want to be petted and told that everything's going to be all right, even though you know it isn't.

'That is, if she's really dead.'

I forgot my need for comfort. 'I searched the room for any other exits,' I said. 'Not even a monkey could have got out. The bars on the windows were fixed solid. I promise you, no one went past us into the room, and no human being could have got in there.'

'But someone did,' Le Froy said.

Calling Harry

———◆———

Early the next morning, Viktor drove Le Froy and me to use the phone in the Cameron Highlands Resort. It wasn't much of a town. There were several restaurants and a bicycle rental office, but they were all closed for the off season.

We headed for the shop that apparently served as a post office as well and collected payment for petrol from the pump outside. There was a sign that said 'Emergency Meeting Point', and a phone kiosk inside.

At least we could make a call from the shop instead of having to ask for help at one of the other holiday lodges we could see on the slopes around the central plateau.

'They're mostly unoccupied right now,' the shopkeeper explained, then apologised that he had only dried and canned goods. 'No golfing because of the weather. And,' this to Viktor, 'I'm afraid you'll have to tell the lady the cigarettes still aren't in. They won't arrive till the lodges open.'

Viktor didn't seem surprised, or inclined to be conversational. As he went to hunt down supplies, Le Froy rang Harry Palin. I leaned in to listen when he was finally connected. 'Tried to reach you yesterday,' he said. 'You've been busy.'

'Yeah. What can I do for you?'

I could tell Harry was busy. At least I hoped he was, and not angry with Le Froy or about to slam down the receiver and dash off.

'I wanted to ask about your encounters with Max Moreno. You're not very popular with him or his partner, Terry Cook, are you?' Le Froy said.

'Hah!' Harry laughed. 'Did they get you to warn me off? I didn't think you caved to people like that.'

'Part of a case,' Le Froy said. 'What did you do to the man?'

'I've got clients with a pretty good case against Max Moreno.' Suddenly Harry was no longer in such a hurry. 'I suspect he was paying off the local police. What are you after him for?'

'Some notes Su Lin found suggest the man was trying to set you up for the Walker murders. Any reason why he'd pick on you?'

'To get rid of me. I've got some good proof that he paid – or threatened – land rights officials to ignore evidence that he'd seized properties belonging to local families. Any chance I can see those notes? Say hello to Su Lin for me.'

'I was hoping you could find out something for me – about the *kris* daggers found at the site of the Walker murders,' Le Froy said.

'What? You're joking!'

'What's so funny? How many of them, descriptions, identifying features, where they might have come from.'

'I'm also looking into who hired the killers. Again, why are you asking?'

'I'll call again tomorrow to hear what you've found out. Got a dead body here to see to.'

'What? Not Max Moreno's?'

'It'll be a few days before we can transport the body down and make it official, but yes.'

'Strewth! That's too bad after all our work on this, but there'll be no tears from me. One other thing, though. There's been talk here that Nazi hunters were after one Martin Rauff, who changed the name on his passport to Max Moreno. Could they have got him?'

'No,' Le Froy said. 'I've seen a photo of the real Wilhelm Maximilian Rauff, Mrs Elfrida Moreno's father. It's a grainy print but it's not Rauff. He and his daughter were smuggled into South America courtesy of clerics in the Vatican, passports from the International Red Cross, the Argentinian Consulate and his friend President Juan Perón. They didn't even bother to get someone who looked like him when they persuaded a factory foreman to set up a passport trail leading away from there.'

'Wait–' I said. 'Elfrida is Max Moreno's daughter and not his wife? I'm confused.'

'Elfrida is the daughter of Max Rauff, who escaped with her to South America under the name of Max Moreno.' Le Froy said. 'Where he seems to have handed both his identity and daughter over to a factory employee to create a false trail for the Nazi hunters.'

'That's so horrible!' I said. 'Poor Elfrida!'

'Is that who I think it is?' Harry said.

'I think Su Lin wants to say hello.' Le Froy offered me the receiver and I grabbed for it, but there was barely time for me to me to cry out, 'Harry! Harry!' and hear his laughing 'Suzie Poozie! How's my girl?' before Le Froy reclaimed the receiver.

'So,' Le Froy said, 'what else have you got on Boss Max? Who are you acting for?'

It's funny how such a brief exchange made me feel immediately better. But it also filled me with longing for my friends. I'd not talked to Harry or Parshanti since I'd got married, and the side of myself that came out when we shared our nonsense had been stuffed under the shell of the good Asian girl, Le Froy's helpmate, for far too long.

But I could think about that later. For now I focused on what I could hear from Harry's side of the conversation.

'You know Moreno picked up the estate during the restitution of properties seized by the Japanese. The Japanese formed the estate by combining the rubber holdings of several Chinese and Malay families, putting many of the former residents to work on the lands that had been theirs. They're the ones I'm helping. They have documentation and property records to prove this, but they can't get anyone to pay attention.'

'I know there was a falling out between Moreno and Walker, his partner. The government-aid grant was in Walker's name and he cut Moreno out. Can't say I blame him. Moreno is no joke to work with or for. With all the people needing work here, he wanted to import labourers from India because they're cheaper and had been talking about how he wanted to bring back indentured labour. If you ask me, Moreno had the biggest motive to kill the Walkers. My guess would be that he hired some goons to get rid of them and, being Moreno, refused to pay them so they killed him because they got fed up with him.'

Le Froy hadn't mentioned the locked-room aspect of Boss Max's murder, and I knew better than to mention it. Harry was a dear, but the reason he was such a good source of information was because he loved sharing what he knew.

'A couple of weeks back, Moreno set up a deal to sell some gemstones at a lower price than they were worth if the buyer could come up with cash immediately. He must have needed money urgently, because he had a reputation for bargaining. But he backed out of the deal at the last minute.'

'How much?'

'Enough for him to pay off whoever he'd commissioned to handle the Walker family hit. But, like I said, he backed out of the deal, so there was nothing to tie him to the killings. Don't think I didn't try. As I said, he's the one with the greatest motive, and he swooped in to claim the estate right off. How can I reach you? Give me a number – wait, I'll get a pencil.'

'No working phones where we're staying. Find out what you can about the *kris* daggers,' Le Froy said. 'I'll phone you again tomorrow.'

'I may not have anything by tomorrow.'

'Just to check in.'

'Say goodbye to Su Lin for me.'

'Goodbye, Harry!' I shouted into the receiver.

So the threats Boss Max reported might have been warnings from someone he'd hired to murder the Walkers? If so, I was surprised they'd let him leave the plantation. But clearly he hadn't managed to get away.

Still, I was feeling good after hearing Harry's voice. I didn't regret marrying Le Froy. I would never regret it. But even if you love chilli crab more than anything else, you can't eat it for three meals a day every day. After a while you find yourself longing for some plain rice congee with a touch of fermented bean curd. Harry Palin, like fermented bean curd, was an acquired taste that grew on you.

Driving us back to the Moonlight Plateau after he had loaded the sacks of charcoal, cans of paraffin and other purchases into the back of the van, Viktor asked, 'What were you saying about Nazi hunters?'

'Rumours,' Le Froy said. 'People getting worked up over the war trials.'

The Tokyo war-crimes trials were still ongoing, but we hadn't heard much about what was happening. Nobody expected too much after hearing that Emperor Hirohito and all members of the Imperial Family had been exempted from trial. The Emperor hadn't even been asked to apologise or step down, after all the atrocities committed in his name.

'The Nuremberg trials were over last year,' Viktor said. 'Not satisfactory. But these trials are useless. They would do it all over again, given the chance. People will never learn.'

* * *

We got back to find Boss Max's body had been moved out of his room and Captain Henry, Daffy and Terry were searching it.

No one had cleaned the area where he'd died and the stench was terrible.

'We have to find what evidence he had on the Walker killings,' Terry said. 'That's clearly what his killer was after.'

'And?' Le Froy asked.

'Nothing,' Captain Henry said. 'There's nothing here.'

'He made the whole thing up, that stupid, stupid man.' Daffy's hair was straggling over her face and she was sweating, despite the chilly drizzle outside. She was clearly unused to physical exertion.

'Or someone else took the evidence.'

Was Captain Henry looking at me? I was about to say that the killer had probably taken whatever it was he'd killed Boss Max for but Viktor interrupted before I could.

'Where is the body?' he demanded.

'Out behind the kitchen,' Terry said. He seemed to think he should take charge after Boss Max's death. 'Thought it best to move him to the coolest area. There's no ice but I got the servants to cover him with cloths soaked in cold water.'

Viktor nodded, appeased. Had he thought they'd sent Boss Max into the ravine where we'd found Elfrida's dress?

'I have tarpaulin sheets,' Viktor said. 'Better to wrap the body in.' He headed out to deal with it.

'So, are they sending help?' Daffy sidled up to Le Froy and clasped his hand in both of hers.

I winced for him: those hands were probably dirty as well as sweaty and they had been all over this room, which stank of blood and bowel movements,

'When are they getting here? Do we have to wait for them? I'm not the kind who would ever say I'm glad a man's dead, but now that he is, can we leave this place?' Daffy asked.

'The roads aren't very safe just now,' Le Froy detached his hand, peeling her fingers off his, 'and the floods below haven't improved. Even if you make the drive down from the Highlands you won't get much further and there's nowhere to stay.'

'Wait,' Daffy said. 'So no one's coming? They can't expect us to stay here with a dead body.'

'A murdered body and a murderer on the loose.' I didn't mean to add to her anxiety, but I thought having an unknown murderer in our midst was even more unsettling than a dead body behind the kitchen.

'Several of the other lodges in the resort are unoccupied at the moment,' Le Froy said. 'We could ask if they could take you in.' He turned to me. 'Do you want to move?'

I didn't. It wouldn't necessarily be safer. Whatever had followed us up to the Moonlight Plateau and walked through walls to kill Boss Max could follow us down to the resort centre and whatever defences the other lodges provided.

Besides, I wanted to take a more thorough look through the things in Elfrida's room, now Boss Max couldn't stop me.

'I want to stay,' I said. 'Elfrida might still be out there. I keep thinking she's still alive. What if Boss Max hid her somewhere? Now he's dead she'll die too if she's not found soon.'

Le Froy shook his head. 'I saw the man when we were searching for her. He was desperate. He wasn't pretending.'

'Someone else took her, then?'

'Why? To pressure Max? If that's the case, they've no more reason to keep her alive. But they had no reason to kill her either. The estate won't be paid off if they don't find the emeralds he promised.'

'What happens if they can't pay for the estate?'

'The government will take it back, most likely to auction it again.'

'What about my share?' Terry demanded.

Le Froy shrugged. 'You may have to return the grant if you don't get the estate going.'

'I'll search Elfrida's room now,' I said. 'She might have left something there that points to someone she met or talked to.'

'There's nothing,' Captain Henry grumbled.

None of the others took up Le Froy's offer to speak to the owners of the other lodges on their behalf.

Suspects and Nazi Hunters?

———◆———

'Pontianak,' Aunty Rakiah said. 'Around here there are many pontianaks.' The other two aunties nodded. Pontianaks, the ghosts of pregnant women, are believed to attack only men, which makes them popular with women.

'From the plantation. Rows and rows of rubber trees for them to hide in. Easy for them to follow him up here.'

'Pontianaks?' Terry said. 'What are—'

'Ghosts of women who died during childbirth or after being betrayed by men.'

'I thought that was banana trees,' Le Froy said mildly.

'Or hantu tinggi, a type of ghost that disguises itself as a tree in the forest. You look up and see the body above the trunk. But once you see the body it's too late because its roots will have grabbed you.'

'Why would the pontianaks go after Boss Max?'

'The area has always been big in rubber and tin so the people here should be wealthy. But the outsiders came. And the ones who grabbed the most control were also the worst offenders when it came to local women. So of course the *pontianak*s seek revenge on them. They have the huge radios, and they think they know everything. But they don't know anything that is happening around them. Remember when they got the man to carry the giant radios through the compound and set up? And then they found that the wire was not long enough to reach the generator?'

They cracked up laughing.

There were women like them everywhere. Grumpy or generous, the old aunties might curse you for stealing fruit from their trees but they knew what leaves and roots were needed to cure you of the worms causing your stomach-ache. They were the ones who kept watch and knew what was happening. Their warnings were ignored because no one listened. Then, after time had passed and their predictions came true, they buried the dead and fed the survivors. And they would go on believing what they believed, as they had done all their lives.

Dinner hadn't been up to the usual standard – just some chicken and potatoes – but no one was very hungry. It's hard to have much of an appetite when you know there's a corpse behind your kitchen.

Growing up, I'd discovered that keeping quiet was the best way to learn anything. Whether at home, in school or at the market, a pretty, smart-talking child might get pats and praise, but the child who kept quiet and blended into the furniture heard the gossip and information. I'd mastered the skill of being overlooked, and it worked here too.

The trick is to appear occupied with something stupid, so that they can see, dismiss and forget you. I positioned myself on a footstool by the open fireplace and watched miserable flames trying to make inroads on damp logs. After a few comments like 'You'd think she'd never seen a fireplace before!' they forgot me.

But sometimes, if people aren't talking, you need to seed the conversation.

'I keep wondering who would want Boss Max dead,' I mused. 'If it's the same people who wanted the Walkers dead that would be a clue. Or maybe they're after all the plantation owners. Maybe they're just getting started. Maybe they mean to kill all the white plantation owners so that the land goes back to the locals.'

Viktor gave a bark of laughter.

'Hey, that's not funny,' Terry Cook said uneasily.

'And, second, who's been around to kill the Walkers and Boss Max? That's where it gets narrowed down. Even if we can't figure out how they did it, the killer or killers have to be close by, right?'

They looked at me. All except my husband. Le Froy appeared amused, but he was watching everyone else's reactions, not mine. Lucky for him I wasn't one of those wives who complains, 'My husband never pays any attention to me ...'

'The servants!' Daffy said. 'You're suspecting the servants, aren't you? They could have had family working for the Walkers. This could be their revenge. Or the guards! Captain

Henry, do you know anything about where your men came from?'

Prakesh and Jaimin weren't around. When Captain Henry ate with Boss Max and his guests, they were off duty. I wasn't sure what they were guarding now that the man they'd been protecting was dead.

'My men have nothing to do with anything,' Captain Henry said. 'I don't know about your servants. Question them yourself.'

So I did. 'Do any of you know anything about what happened to Boss Max?' I asked the aunties, as they carried our half-consumed chicken dishes out to the sink. Washing dishes is seldom a pleasure, but be grateful that most of the time you're not scraping chicken bones off plates beside the fresh corpse of your former boss.

'I know!' Aunty Rakiah said, as the other two shrank away. '*Pontianak!*'

At least it made us laugh, if a bit nervously. 'So many superstitions out here,' Terry Cook said.

'But that Indian guard of yours.' Daffy was as tenacious as an *ular sawa* with a rat in its jaws. Once that python got hold of something there was no shaking it off. 'Prakesh should be your number-one suspect because of all his run-ins with Boss Max.'

'Max was no angel there,' her husband said, 'but even if he tried to frame Prakesh for his wife's disappearance, he can hardly be framing him for his own murder.'

'You think he was framing Prakesh?' I said, though I'd intended only to listen. Why hadn't he said something earlier?

Luckily my non-white female camouflage held and he didn't hear me.

'I warned Max,' Captain Henry said. 'The workers were getting superstitious, saying there were ghosts in the plantation. He tried to get the old workers, the ones the Walkers sacked, to come back and start tapping during the rains. He said working through the monsoon was the only thing that would put the estate ahead, that he couldn't have the processing plant standing empty for three months just because some witch doctor says it's bad luck to collect latex in the rain. He said he would hire them back if they started straight away. Otherwise he would use the labourers the Walkers were having shipped in from India.'

'I don't know anything about that,' Terry said. 'I don't know anything about the rubber business, but even I could see the rain's going to dilute anything you collect during the monsoon.'

'How did you get into partnership with Max Moreno?' Le Froy asked him.

'One day I woke up and thought, Why am I taking orders from some idiot when I could be making my fortune? So I quit and came out east. Moreno needed me: couldn't have got the land contracts without my British citizenship. I told him this is going to be semi-retirement for me. I'll just sign papers and receive cheques!'

He laughed, but no one else did.

I wasn't very impressed by Terry Cook. Men who gave up their jobs ended like Britain's traitor king, living lives of pointless privilege.

'There might be Nazi hunters involved,' Terry said. 'I heard that some time ago but didn't pay any attention. Apparently diamonds and emeralds from some old German family tiara purloined by the Nazis have been showing up all over the place and those Jewish underground tribunals sent someone to investigate.'

'Rubbish,' Viktor said. 'No such thing as Jewish underground tribunals. You are being paranoid.'

'Oh, am I?' Terry backed off with bravado. 'Anyway, that's what I heard.'

I suspected Viktor at once. He seemed the sort to have been either a Nazi war criminal or a Nazi hunter, I wasn't sure which. I looked at Le Froy. Whoever had information wasn't showing it, and there were things I wanted to discuss with him.

'I'm tired,' I said.

'Wait. I asked the servants to make us some herbal tea,' Daffy said. She looked into the pot. 'What is it?'

'Chrysanthemum,' Aunty Rakiah said. 'To help calm down and sleep.'

It was one of my grandmother's favourite 'cooling' concoctions, known for alleviating tension and inflammation. This tea wasn't as good as hers, I thought, but warm, sweet and soothing nonetheless.

'Why didn't the killer take Max's notes if that's what he was killed for?' Le Froy asked, as we walked back to Moonlight Lodge.

'You're not wondering if I killed him but if they were left there for us to find?' I said. 'I thought of that. They were stuffed into the side of the chair as if Boss Max had been reading them and fell asleep. Maybe they didn't see them there and didn't have time to look. I didn't until I checked to make sure he wasn't breathing.' But I had my own questions for my husband. 'Why didn't you tell me you knew Boss Max was a fake? What else haven't you told me about this case?'

'Only what I read in the file on the way up,' Le Froy said. 'You looked at the file too, didn't you?'

I hadn't seen anything interesting in it. All it had done was threaten to make me car-sick. 'Sum it up for me.'

'The Emerald Estate rubber plantation covers fifteen thousand acres and a hundred and eighty thousand trees. Under the Japanese, estate workers cultivated coconuts and tapioca for their own meals and to sell. The Walkers claimed all the produce as theirs and wanted to charge the workers rent. The Walkers dismissed all their existing workers after rent negotiations broke down and arranged for labourers to be shipped in from India after the monsoon season.'

'Was it the workers they fired who killed them?' It didn't justify the act, but I could almost understand their desperation. 'Did they find them?'

'They were mostly still squatting on uncultivated estate land. The Walkers hadn't got the production side running so they probably weren't aware. They needed a processing shed, a drying shed, a copra shed and dormitories for some two hundred labourers with a room and an office for the estate manager.

'That was where they'd always stayed during the rainy season. It suited the Japanese because they cleared the jungle and kept it free for new rubber trees, thus saving money for the estate. The tapioca and the other vegetables they planted meant their chickens didn't interfere with the rubber trees. Many of them were locals, who had lived on the land before the Japanese time. They had nowhere to go when the Walkers fired them.'

'I can see why any of them would want revenge on the Walkers,' I said. 'The problem is, they weren't up here in the Camerons. And even if they had been . . .' They couldn't have got past Daffy and me to kill Max Moreno. 'Could it have been something entirely separate?' I asked. 'Someone else wanting to kill the Walkers? Did they run plantations elsewhere before the war?'

'The Walker brothers were businessmen, not planters. They were good at spotting deals and buying low, selling high. The two wives were sisters as well as their husbands being brothers. They had not been living together for long. In fact this was reconciliation. In favour of his brother, Walker Senior had dropped the partner with whom he'd originally arranged to buy the plantation. No doubt prompted by their women.

'Max assumed control of the majority of the business he shared with Jonathan Walker on Walker's death. Which would have given him a strong motive to get rid of the Walkers. If he wasn't dead himself.'

'What are we doing here?' I said.

'What?'

I yawned. Suddenly I didn't care any more. I was so tired of complicated problems and rainy weather and being shut up with strangers who might be murderers. If this was our honeymoon, could I expect any better from the rest of our married life?

I lay back on the bed. It was so comfortable and I was very sleepy. I felt Le Froy pulling off my shoes. He looked groggy, and as I watched he slapped himself in the face. I giggled. He was struggling to loop the heavy curtain cord around the window handles, then moved the dresser in front of the door so the door handle couldn't depress.

'Come to bed and sleep,' I managed to say.

'Coming, darling,' he said. The last thing I remember before I fell asleep is watching him get his gun out of its case and check it.

Elfrida's Room

———◆———

I woke with a throbbing ache in my head. Le Froy wasn't in
bed beside me. I sat up and saw he was in the chair by the
window, twisted to one side but still facing the door. His
pistol was on the table beside him. In other words, he was
sitting much as Boss Max had been when I found him. For
one horrible, shocking moment I thought—

I leaped – or, rather, stumbled, tumbled and rolled – off
the bed towards him, thanking God, Buddha, Kuan Yin and,
yes, even the Kitchen God and the Jade Emperor that there
was no *kris* dagger sticking out of his chest. He woke as I
shook him.

'Oh, my head,' Le Froy said. 'Oh, my neck. What happened?
Why are you . . . why am I . . . why's the dresser . . .'

'I think you did that last night,' I said.

Le Froy rubbed his temples. 'It made sense at the time.'

I looked around the dim room. The cords holding the
window handles together, the dresser preventing the door

handle from being turned, both of us in the clothes we'd been wearing at dinner last night . . .

'We're alive, so it made very good sense,' I said. 'We'd better go and see if the others are all right.'

'I need to wash first,' Le Froy said. 'Oh, my head . . .'

'We were drugged!' Daffy shrilled, as soon as she saw us in the Emerald Lodge dining room.

I winced. I found her voice unpleasant at any time, but that morning it was physically painful.

There was no sign of Viktor or Captain Henry, but Terry sat at the table looking miserable. The dining room wasn't in very good shape either. Not only was there no sign of breakfast, last night's coffee cups and the chrysanthemum tea glasses were still there.

'We woke up here this morning, me at the table, Terry and Captain Henry in the lounge. And no sign of Viktor or the servants.'

I went to the kitchen to check. The dishes from last night's dinner were still soaking in the prewash sink but there were no bodies, other than the one wrapped in tarpaulin out at the back. I guessed the aunties had gone to the staff lodge. I would check on them later, but first I needed to make us some coffee.

'It was the tea. Those damned servants poisoned us,' Daffy was saying, when I returned with the coffee pot and clean cups. 'What else could it have been? They must have mixed in some of their local leaves or whatever they're always messing with.'

'At least we're still alive,' Terry said.

'Does anyone want something to eat?' I asked.

No one did, which was just as well. I sat down with my coffee and thought about what had happened the night before.

Had I heard someone in our lodge during the night? Thanks to Le Froy, no one had come into our bedroom. Had anyone tried to?

In the Emerald Lodge, Daffy and Terry had fallen asleep in the lounge and dining room and woken unscathed. So had it been an accident? Something noxious left from the Japanese time released into air? Or something in the chrysanthemum tea? I knew there were things like snakeroot that induced sleep, but none would have acted so strongly.

Where were the aunties? And where were Viktor and Captain Henry?

Another thought struck me. 'I'm going to check Elfrida's room,' I said. 'Where's the key?'

The room in which Elfrida had been imprisoned had clearly been turned over again since I'd last been in there. They must have got in with Boss Max's keys but not bothered to relock it. Now the previously stacked boxes had been opened and their contents scattered. Folders had been emptied and papers (in German) scattered.

If there had been anything to find, it had gone.

'If someone wanted to search in here, why didn't they just say so?' I said to Le Froy, when he came to stand beside me.

The drawers by the bed had been upended and shaken out onto the floor, and all of this had been done while we slept just along the corridor.

Le Froy asked, 'I don't suppose you can tell if anything's been taken?'

I shook my head. 'They've smashed her clay models even more thoroughly. I'll do some clearing up and see if anything comes to light.' Even if I didn't find anything, I would feel better after putting things in order in here. 'Did you find the aunties? Is Prakesh all right?'

'They were passed out in the kitchen and are back in the servants' lodge with Prakesh and Jaimin now. Captain Henry spent the night in the security post. They're dehydrated but they'll be fine,' Le Froy said. 'I'm going to get a motor and drive down to phone Palin.' He gave me a quick hug, 'Sorry,' and was gone before I could ask what the apology applied to.

'What are you doing?' Daffy appeared in the doorway.

'Just tidying up a bit in here.'

I had swept up the mess of pottery shards and accumulated dust and was trying to repack the boxes in some kind of order.

'Why?' Daffy came in and hovered, unable to find anything to sit on. I was squatting in front of the piles I was sorting things into – broken beyond repair, recoverable after cleaning or fixing, and safe to put away – but *ang moh*s are so used to sitting on chairs that they can't squat.

'I think we were all drugged. I don't know what those servants are trying to do to us. I have such a fearful headache. Can't you come over and sit with me? I'm tired of being alone – no, I'm scared of being alone!'

Her disgust at the mess in the room was evident. 'It's not your job to clear up in here. It makes your husband look bad if you're doing the servants' work for them. Take some advice from me. If you don't want to be treated like a servant, you shouldn't behave like one.'

If this was Daffy trying to be nice to me, I preferred her when she was being herself.

'Where's Le Froy?' Then again, maybe it wasn't me she was trying to make friends with.

'I like to clean,' I said. When I was too exhausted to focus and too wound up to rest, cleaning was an easy, mindless occupation that left things a little better than before. And no one asks you what you're doing – most of the time, anyway. 'Besides, I don't like sleeping next to the mess in here. Bad energy. You know, *feng shui*.'

'I know what you mean,' Daffy said. 'Not the superstitious foo-foo stuff, but you know that room Max died in? Even with the door closed just walking past it gives me the creeps. Where did you say Le Froy is?'

'He went to the resort centre to use the phone.'

Daffy pouted. 'Why didn't he say anything? I could have gone along to keep him company. God, how I hate it here. What's Le Froy really after, then?'

'Like he said, the threats Boss Max received—'

'Come on! You don't really expect anyone to believe that?'

Why not? Especially now the man was dead. I didn't say so, though. 'I believe it,' I said.

'Huh,' Daffy said. 'Don't waste your time. You won't find anything here worth taking. That woman had a couple of nice brooches and necklaces but she took the real stuff with her.'

'The real stuff?'

'The emeralds she pinched from Max's safe, you dummy. Don't pretend that's not what you're looking for.'

'I'm not looking for anything.'

I glanced around the sad little room. The few dresses were of good-quality linen and silk, not really suitable for the climate in Malaya, and had been washed till they were worn and fading. There were some European ladies' undergarments of similarly good quality and similarly threadbare.

Many of the scattered papers seemed to be letters, some with pressed flowers, strands of lace, drawings of hearts and little dogs. They were loose, the glue that once held them in place having peeled away long ago. Had Boss Max sent her these? I couldn't imagine him doing so. Had they come from another man? But the drawings were childish rather than romantic.

'Do you read German?' I asked Daffy.

'Of course not!' Daffy looked offended. 'Are you calling me a Nazi?'

'No, I just wondered about these . . .'

Though I didn't understand German, I guessed Elfrida was the 'Fridachen' they were addressed to, and that these letters must have been from someone very important to her, for her to have carried them with her into exile. I would keep them safe and hope I'd have the chance to return them to her.

'Get out!' Daffy shouted suddenly. 'How dare you come sneaking in here?'

It was Aunty Salmah and Deaf Aunty, with buckets and cleaning rags. Aunty Salmah mimicked a wiping gesture.

'We should let them clean in here,' I said. I pulled together as many of the letters as I could, putting them into a bag that had been tossed aside.

'What are you going to do with those?' Daffy asked.

'She'll want these back if she's alive,' I said. 'I think they're from her grandmother.'

The birds on the branches of the rose apple tree overhanging the bamboo fence set up a racket as Aunty Salmah opened the door to the outdoor enclosure and stepped outside. They were mostly mynahs, barbets and parrots, feasting on the rose apples. Naturally there were bird droppings on the ground beneath the tree.

'So disgusting,' Daffy said. 'Someone should shoot those nasty dirty creatures. If I had a gun, I'd do it myself.'

'Look,' Aunty Salmah said. She was pointing to a pair of *jambu* doves. She put her palms together and bowed slightly.

I did too. '*Jambu* doves,' I told Daffy. 'They're supposed to bring good luck and happy relationships.'

'No such thing.' Daffy stalked out of the room without making clear whether she was referring to the luck or the relationships.

The cleaning aunties seemed to make her uncomfortable so I took my time with the letters, being in no hurry to catch up with Daffy outside.

At least Elfrida had had the tree and the birds for company. The rose apple isn't often cultivated, so old trees like this one were treasured as bringing good luck, like the *jambu* doves they attracted.

Eventually I stepped out into the compound, which looked even worse by daylight. It was overgrown with wild plants, which grow rapidly during the rainy season, almost as though they're trying to gain all the territory they can before the rains stop and people grab back their land.

I wanted to see if I could spot the *jambu* doves again and I did. The young birds can be mistaken for any other species of dove, but the rose-apple-pink patch on the white chest of the male, along with the white-rimmed eyes and bright orange bills of the adult birds are unmistakable.

I sent up a silent prayer for happiness for Le Froy and myself. We could use some good luck in our life together. For Elfrida too, wherever she was, that things would get better for her.

I followed the path through the weeds to the corner where the *jamban*, or traditional WC, stood. The smell told me what and where it was, but I went closer to look. It was an old structure, likely also built during the war years. There were ventilation gaps between its weathered wooden planks, and it stood on a concrete base with a squat-style hole in it. A small water tank, set up to collect rainwater from the slanting corrugated metal roof, was overflowing.

In other words, it was a traditional pit latrine outhouse. I wondered what Elfrida had made of it. At least it was clean and well maintained.

Three rose apples sat in a row on the cement slab just inside. They looked as though they'd been there for a while, with brown and black splotches on the pink skin. They were probably already rotten inside.

I wondered if a bird or squirrel had been intelligent enough to stash them there to eat later and forgotten them – or had Elfrida collected them but been afraid to eat them?

I decided the least I could do was get rid of them.

I reached out, and was stopped by a cry of alarm. It was Deaf Aunty. I'd not heard her coming after me. She gestured urgently for me not to touch the fruit. I tried to convey that I wasn't going to poison myself by eating them, only wanted to throw them away, but she grew so frantic in her insistence that I mustn't touch them that I left them where they were.

The rotting fruit were part of some ritual, I guessed. As a child might put out a missing dog's favourite snack, Deaf Aunty might have placed Elfrida's favourite fruit there in the hope of luring her back.

And just as a parent might shy away from saying, 'It's no use because the dog is dead,' I nodded and let her pull me back inside the lodge. There's too little hope in the world to take away the sliver someone is clinging to.

The Messy Afterlife

———◆———

Whatever might await us after death, there's always cleaning up to do for those still alive.

Le Froy wouldn't be back from the town centre for some time. I was dying to hear what Harry Palin had had to say, reminding myself it might have been nothing, but I couldn't just sit around waiting. Anything helpful in Elfrida's room would already have been taken: why else would you waste whatever you had used to drug a group of people? The aunties were cleaning in there now and had made clear they could do a better job without me around. They'd agreed to call me if they found anything that hinted as to who Elfrida might have been in touch with, but my hopes weren't high.

I wasn't keen on being stuck with Daffy either. So, remembering what she had said about being uncomfortable around Boss Max's room (and the stink I'd experienced for myself in there), I decided to start cleaning. Someone had to do it, and it wasn't fair to leave all the dirty work to the aunties.

I was doing this out of respect for Dead Boss Max too. Whatever the man had done, and however he'd died, no one deserved to be remembered for the stench they'd left behind.

I knew Le Froy would already have recorded how the body had been found; probably Captain Henry had too. And Terry Cooke had gone over the place and collected anything that might be useful as evidence. I saw no point in taking samples of the dead man's blood or what had come out of his bowels because I had no way to preserve it for testing.

First I put some joss sticks and rose apples (oranges would have been better, but I had to use what was available) just outside the door to the room. If his spirit – or any other – returned to its point of departure, that should placate it. I hadn't done the same for Elfrida's spirit because I had no idea where it might be roaming, and there was a chance she was still alive.

Then I reached for the little jar of tiger balm lotion in the cloth bag around my waist, safely under my dress with my dagger, and rubbed some under my nose. It stung, but it was better than the smell.

Then I opened the door, shut down my thoughts and got busy with the cleaning.

'We help you.' Aunty Rakiah and Aunty Salmah had followed me back to the room after I had emptied the first bucket of water and returned to the kitchen for a refill. They brought their own buckets and a tin of lye powder, which I accepted with relief.

'That's all right,' I said. 'It's very good of you, but I know you don't want to be here because of the spirits.'

'What spirits?' Aunty Rakiah asked.

'You were talking about the *pontianak*s,' I reminded her. 'You said maybe it was Boss Max's wife coming back to punish him by killing him.'

'Ha! Why would she punish him by killing him? Why wouldn't she leave him here to make the other people suffer?' Aunty Rakiah shouted. Both women laughed uproariously. I laughed too, because their childlike glee was infectious. 'True or not, if somebody finishes you off and sends you to the other side, you don't want him to come and join you too fast. That is the last thing you want. You want to get away from him.'

'Do you think Mrs Max wanted to get away from her husband?' I asked Aunty Rakiah. I hadn't thought to ask till now. After all, they'd lived in two separate spheres even though they'd shared the same space.

'Oh, yes,' Aunty Salmah said. 'Missy Elfrida is a good girl. She is a very good girl. Very poor thing.'

At least she was all right with me seeing she spoke English.

'You knew her from the plantation?'

Both aunties had wound scarves around their faces to filter out the stench as we scrubbed. I think they felt as if we were speaking incognito, which made it easier for us to talk.

'When they first arrived, in her early days at the plantation, Missy Elfrida would come to the kitchen and ask us to teach her to cook our food. She was very playful, like a little girl, very fun. She would pretend to be a servant girl, even,' Aunty Rakiah said. 'One time she pretended to be a *pontianak*!'

'How did she know about *pontianaks*?'

'We told her stories,' Aunty Salmah said. 'She wanted to hear all the ghost stories about the plantation.'

'So she wasn't unhappy that she had to come to stay in Malaya?'

'She was only sad when her husband got angry with her. He always got angry when she had her period because she was not pregnant and wasting his time.'

Oh dear. That was awful. Poor Elfrida.

'Men are like that,' Aunty Salmah said. She patted my arm. 'Men are stupid. Don't worry. You will have healthy sons when the time comes.'

'What?' I wanted to ask her what she meant, but—

'I told Missy Elfrida about the *tompu* my mother saw at the plantation,' Aunty Rakiah cut in. 'You know the *tompu* are shape-shifters. You must be very careful of them. This was long before the Japanese time. She was at the family plantation. It was raining even though the sun was shining and she was tapping. She had bent down for a long time and her back was aching so she stood up to rest. And when she did, she saw a handsome young man leaning on the tree next to hers. He was watching her and chewing a blade of *rumput* grass and he had such beautiful eyes that she felt shy and quickly bent down again to continue cutting her tree. But she couldn't help herself so she looked at the man again but this time there was no man. What she saw standing there and chewing was a cow. And she knew it was him because it had the same beautiful eyes. Oh, my mother was so scared she ran home crying and after that for one week she couldn't work on the plantation or go to school. That's why they always warned us that when it's raining you shouldn't tap the trees.'

Aunty Salmah laughed. 'You're just too lazy to tap on rainy days, that's all.'

'Aunty Salmah,' I said. 'What do you mean about . . . sons?'

'And then there's the *orang bunian*,' Aunty Rakiah said. 'Only some people can see them. They live deep in the forest or high in the mountains. If you see them, you should not follow them. They can look like people you know or people you find attractive. There are stories of men who see a beautiful woman in the forest and follow her. And they think they were only talking to the *orang bunian* woman for ten minutes. But when they go home, they find that many years have passed and that their families and everybody they once knew is dead.'

'Good excuse for philandering husbands!' Aunty Salmah said.

'Maybe Elfrida met an *orang bunian* and she'll come back safe, thinking she was only gone for a few minutes,' I said. 'When I was young, my friend and I used to wish we could see a *pontianak*. Some of our friends said they had seen a very beautiful woman dressed in a shining black *kebaya* with very red lipstick behind the church cemetery at night . . . One evening when I was staying at her house, they told us to meet them there and we would see for ourselves, but her mother said, "No such nonsense," and made us go to bed. Even though I pretended to be disappointed, I was really glad and I suspect she was too.' I shook my head, thinking of those days. Parshanti and I had been so eager to explore the rest of the world.

The aunties laughed, and Viktor laughed too, coming in with Deaf Aunty behind him.

'You and your girlfriend wouldn't have seen anything,' Viktor said. 'The beautiful demons appear only to men they want to lure to their doom.'

'What do you want?' Aunty Rakiah asked him, sounding helpful rather than hostile.

'I am here to help clean,' Viktor said.

By then it was more a work area than a death scene and the smell of lye and detergent was comforting. Deaf Aunty took her place beside the other two aunties and got to work.

'Hey! What are you doing?' I was startled when Viktor's hands squeezed my waist, but I wasn't alarmed. Not because the aunties were present and gaping, though that did reassure me, but because I realised even as I cried out that Viktor wasn't groping me. He was checking that my *kris* dagger was still in its sheath under my dress.

Fair enough.

Still, I flicked my dirty cloth at him. 'You could have asked me to show it to you.'

'Do you want to hit me?' Viktor offered politely.

'No, thanks.'

'All right, then.' Viktor turned on the radio and fiddled with the tuning.

'There's a medium-wave radio here?' I hadn't realised.

'Boss Max didn't like to share,' Viktor said. He found a radio news broadcast.

Before the war, radio had been a big thing, thanks to the British-run Malaya Broadcasting Corporation. It had been broadcast from as far away as Penang, transmitted and retransmitted. Then, as the Japanese advanced south, one by one the radio stations had stopped broadcasting. I hadn't realised they had resumed. The Japanese had banned all radios, except for their specially modified sets that received only the Japanese propaganda programmes. If you had a radio on your premises, it was compulsory to keep it switched on, even though the announcements were also broadcast over loudspeakers.

Like many people I knew, I'd not listened to a radio since. Radios were, to me, associated with shouted threats, reports of public beheadings and ravings about the glories of Japan.

I know, don't shoot the messenger – or the messaging service. But it's hard to break associations. Maybe this temporary exile would heal the rift between us and the outside world. After all, it was the most modern form of universal communication.

A lot of the news was of the flooding and casualties. But most of it had to do with the upcoming wedding of Princess Elizabeth and the newly created Duke of Edinburgh, Philip Mountbatten.

There was mention of the suspected Nazi hunters and that the British Army was withdrawing troops from Palestine.

'What are you people doing in here?' Terry Cook appeared in the doorway.

'Cleaning,' Viktor said.

'Huh,' Terry said. 'Where's my wife got to?'

He looked around, but she wasn't in the room. Terry left, but he was back almost immediately, glass in hand. 'What's this piss?' He threw the glass at the nearest person, who happened

215

to be me. It glanced off my forehead (ow!), sloshing its contents on me and shattering on the floor.

'What's wrong with it?' I got to my feet, shaking off the liquid.

'There's no damn ice, you fool!'

'There hasn't been ice for days now,' I said. 'Everyone here knows that.'

That made him pause to look at me. 'How dare you talk to me like that? Who do you think you are? You're not – you're that– What the hell are you playing at?'

Viktor gave a roar of laughter, which didn't help matters.

'I'm not used to doing nothing,' I said, 'so I'm helping to clean.'

Terry Cook hadn't recognised me in my sweaty work clothes with my hair bundled up. He'd registered a servant and assumed the right to yell and assault me to vent his bad temper. In other words, he was throwing a tantrum. He had always been polite enough to me as Le Froy's wife, but I wasn't surprised. In fact, I preferred Daffy being rude to me to my face.

'You've no right to make a fool of yourself–'

'What's going on?' Le Froy asked.

'Nothing,' I said, meaning I would fill him in later. 'What did Harry Palin tell you?'

'Nothing,' he said, meaning exactly the same thing. 'Why are you all wet?'

I looked at Terry's aggressive, cowardly face. '*Pontianak*s,' I said. 'We were talking about *pontianak*s. I got excited and spilled this on myself.'

'What do you know about *pontianak*s?' Le Froy surprised me by asking.

'They're female vampires that have long fingernails they can use to take out your eyeballs. And long black hair that covers their faces so you can't see that their eyes are red.'

'Folk legends, used to frighten children? Not warnings to abusive men?'

I saw where he was going. 'Yes, I suppose so. That's why *pontianak*s tend to turn up after a woman has died in child-birth, or when someone's been raped and murdered. And *pontianak*s attack mostly men.'

'You're thinking Max killed Elfrida so she came back as a ghost and killed him?' It was Terry's turn to laugh. 'Le Froy, they weren't kidding when they said you'd gone native and crazy. Next you'll be saying that's how she got into the locked room!'

'As a human, she definitely couldn't have killed Max in his room because the door was locked and the windows were barred,' Le Froy said. 'Also, your wife and my wife were in the dining room the whole time. They would have seen anyone who went in or out.'

'Look, it was probably Japanese soldiers, hiding in the jungle, who don't believe that their country has surrendered and are picking us off one by one.' Terry said. 'If you're going to talk nonsense, I'm getting out of here.'

'We finish cleaning here,' Aunty Rakiah told me. 'You go with your husband.' With a sly smile she added, 'Don't forget about the healthy sons ...'

'What was that?' Le Froy asked.

'Nothing,' I said. This time I meant I didn't want to say any more about it to him until I'd thought about it or got more out of Aunty Salmah. 'Did Harry find out anything about the *kris* daggers?'

'What nasty daggers are you talking about?' I was startled to hear Daffy's voice. I hadn't noticed her come in. 'The one that killed poor Max? Oh, Le Froy, you've got to do something to help us, and find out where that terrible knife came from. We don't want to end up like poor Max.'

Kris Daggers

———◆———

'Kris daggers aren't nasty,' I told Daffy, 'and they're not just weapons.'

Even as I spoke I knew it was impossible to explain to someone like her the sentimental and symbolic value of a *kris*. Often they are passed down the generations as family heirlooms and are believed to offer the protection of the ancestors' spirits to the person carrying them.

Like the one that Ah Ma had given me. Even if I'd had some overwhelmingly compelling reason to kill Max Moreno, I wouldn't have done it with the *kris* that Ah Ma had given me. And, even more crazily impossible but for the sake of argument, if I had, I would never ever have left the *kris* behind.

But it was no use saying anything because none of these people would have understood.

Actually, I was wrong there. Viktor nodded. Of course the man who was wearing his *abuela*'s gaucho knife understood.

Le Froy noticed and looked curious. In all the excitement over the blue dress that had turned out not to be Elfrida's body, I'd forgotten to fill him in on everything that had happened earlier that day, but I would – once I had heard everything he'd learned from Harry Palin.

'I'm going back to my room now,' I said to Aunty Rakiah and Aunty Salmah, Deaf Aunty having slipped away unnoticed, as she usually did. 'Please will you empty my bucket for me?'

'Of course!'

'Thank you for your hard work.'

I slipped my hand through my husband's arm, detached the brassy hussy (Daffy Cook – I loved daring to think that) from his other and walked back to the Moonlight Lodge to hear what he had to say.

After all my cleaning efforts, I was in drastic need of the washbasin. Le Froy started telling me what Harry had learned as I washed.

'He says the local Communists can't have been responsible for killing the Walkers.'

'He's been saying that all along,' I said. 'People don't believe him because they don't want to.'

'The authorities think certain locals were responsible because the weapons found at the murder scene matched those that had been confiscated from Communist fighters,' Le Froy continued. 'But the thing is, it seems the weapons don't just match those weapons. According to the records, they are almost identical. What if they are the same weapons?'

'A lot of *kris* daggers look alike to Westerners,' I said. 'As we do. In fact, just this afternoon Terry Cook thought I was—'

'It's more than that,' Le Froy said. 'The *kris* daggers found at the site of the Walkers' murder match the knives in the Japanese collection confiscated after the British returned. The people in charge of the Japanese collection documented the *kris* daggers they acquired very carefully, even noting comparisons to their own *tantō* daggers, making the knives easy to identify. The Japanese claim that the *kris* daggers were legitimately confiscated from Communist fighters but Palin has statements with identifying characteristics from the families of several men murdered by the Japanese who owned these particular daggers. Palin was trying to arrange for their return when the whole collection went missing.'

'What?' I stopped drying myself to look at him. 'Then when you say the weapons found at the murder scene matched . . .'

Le Froy nodded.

'. . . you think the killers used the confiscated *kris* daggers to kill the Walkers and left them to be found at the estate? That's crazy! Why?'

'It seems there were calls for men willing to take on a risky but high-paying job. Palin said several of his clients were approached just after the rainy season started.'

That wasn't unusual. Once the monsoon rains start and the tapping stops, employers look for cheap, short-term labour.

'According to Palin, the job was confidential. All equipment would be supplied. They had to do some cleaning up and would be paid half before and the rest on completion of the job. After that they were on their own.'

'They seem to know a lot about it for men who didn't take the job,' I said, much as I wanted to believe Harry.

'His clients were telling him that from the start,' Le Froy

said. 'They say they believed the contractor was looking for men to force some local landowners to sell.'

'Has Harry spoken to anyone who did take the job? Can you track them down?'

'After news of the Walker murders came out, Palin said someone told him the men who went through with the job were angry because they hadn't been paid the money owed to them. They tried to claim it but the guys who commissioned them gave them the brush-off. The next he knew, they were all gone.'

'Gone? As in left Ipoh? Or the country?'

'Gone as in dead,' Le Froy said. 'Arrested on suspicion of murder and shot dead trying to escape.'

'You think Max hired killers to get rid of the Walkers? And the police shot the killers he hired? So why . . . Maybe the police didn't get all of them. And one tracked Max up here and killed him in revenge. Plus he had to use a *kris* to show it was revenge.'

It sounded far-fetched, I'll admit. But I managed not to suggest it was the angry ghosts of the dead unpaid hired murderers who had left the *kris* in Boss Max's chest in revenge.

'Why didn't Harry say something?' I demanded. 'If only he'd made a fuss about the *kris* daggers as soon as they went missing, Max might not have dared to give them to the men he hired to kill the Walkers.'

'I asked him,' Le Froy said. 'He said he couldn't be sure it wasn't just an administrative error. He didn't want his people worked up over what had happened during the war when he was trying to get them to build new lives. And most of the time he was following up on stories that the Walker men had been abusing local women.'

'Were they?' There might be angry husbands, brothers and fathers to take into consideration.

'They all do,' Le Froy said. 'Some just aren't as good at hiding their tracks. But I don't think that's the case here.'

I sensed Le Froy's frustration and how much he wanted to be in Ipoh or out on the plantation, hunting down evidence of what had happened. I felt the same. I wouldn't have been much good in Ipoh or on the plantation, but stranded up here in the Cameron Highlands I was no use at all. Cleaning up the mess left by the man who might have ordered the murders of his predecessors was a lot of work but solved nothing.

'There must be something... Bank records perhaps show what Boss Max paid people. And other records may tell us how he could have got hold of the daggers used in the murders.'

'Not likely,' Le Froy said. 'They were in the storage room adjacent to the police station. Anyone looking for lost property could walk in there.'

Of course he meant that any *white* person could have walked in. But I had too much to process to school my *white* husband on that.

'A local wouldn't have stolen someone else's *kris*,' I said. 'They might reclaim one that belonged to their family, that's all. Otherwise it would be dishonouring it.'

'What would you do if you were attacked suddenly?' Le Froy asked.

'What?'

'What if I were a stranger and burst in here and attacked you?'

'If that happened I would take my *kris* and ...' I slid it out of its sheath and mimed stabbing him with it.

'I would suggest a longer blade,' Le Froy said. 'But blood gushes out, you would be covered with it, and it would be hard to get away.'

'If you broke in here and attacked me, I wouldn't care. I wouldn't even wipe the blood off before I got dressed and went for help.'

'What if you were inside Boss Max's bedroom and he attacked you?'

If it had been anyone else, I might have suspected Le Froy of setting me up. But this was Le Froy, so . . .

'If I was inside Boss Max's bedroom and he attacked me, it would serve me right. Luckily I would still have my *kris* dagger with me. That doesn't mean I planned to kill him, just that I had it with me when he attacked me.'

'And after?'

'After what?'

'After the murder. Would you take the knife with you? Or leave it inside his chest?'

'I wouldn't have let go,' I said, picking up the *kris* again to demonstrate. 'You use this to stab or slash – it's not so good for slashing – but you don't let go. Of course I wouldn't leave it behind. The only time people leave a knife in a dead body is when white hunters stab hunting knives into animal carcasses to take photographs!'

Le Froy looked at me, 'Get dressed, then pack. We're leaving right now. Never mind the flooding.'

'What?' It was raining again. It had started when we were walking back to the Moonlight Lodge. 'How?'

'I'll speak to Viktor about borrowing the van.'

Le Froy turned to go, but stopped when our bedroom door opened and Captain Henry came in. 'What's that you've got there?' Captain Henry nodded towards my *kris*. Le Froy had picked it up after my little demonstration. 'I heard you were going on about these local knives. Sir, I must ask you to put down that weapon and come with me.'

Captain Henry turned to Jaimin, who had followed him in, 'Get that and bring it. Yes, the knife, you fool!'

Jaimin averted his eyes from me. I was in my singlet and knickers, so not entirely indecent, but I appreciated his trying to spare me additional embarrassment.

'What's this about?' Le Froy asked.

'After finding a weapon matching the murder weapon in your possession, it's my responsibility to make sure you don't harm anyone else,' Captain Henry said.

'You're crazy!' I said.

'Maybe I should be locking you up as well . . .'

'Sir,' Jaimin said, 'you already put Sergeant Prakesh in the cage. There is no more space, sir.'

'I'll come back to question you later,' Captain Henry said. 'Don't pull a disappearing act like Mrs Max unless you want your husband to end up dead like Max.'

I waited until he had taken Le Froy away before I pulled on a fresh dress. Then I forced myself to sit down and think about my options before I rushed after Le Froy and the captain.

Getting myself locked up as well wouldn't do either of us any good. What was happening here and what could I do about it? I didn't even have Ah Ma's *kris* dagger with me.

House Arrest

———◆———

'Make sure no one leaves without my say-so,' Captain Henry was saying to Jaimin, when I got to the security post. 'Take all their keys and keep them here.'

'You have no right to do this,' Prakesh said. 'You're private security, not police.' He was back in the tiger cage. At least Le Froy was sitting on one of the two chairs.

'Citizen's arrest for now. You'll be locked up properly after we get to town. I have every reason to suspect you after finding you with a murder weapon. I'm only doing my duty. You wouldn't understand duty, Le Froy. You're working for the locals and the Chinese Communists now, aren't you?'

'I consider it my duty to hold the British to the standards they impose on others,' Le Froy said.

'That's not the same thing at all,' Captain Henry said.

'Colonial racism harms the minds and souls of all involved,' Le Froy said.

'The people out here don't care about minds and souls. They don't have any! They're only concerned with spirits and ghosts and black magic.'

I thought Captain Henry was joking, but no one laughed.

'Please, sir,' Prakesh said. 'The best thing you can do is release Le Froy and let him investigate. That's what he does best. It's the best chance of finding out who killed Boss Max. And this ties in with the Walker murder he was sent to investigate.' He saw me and shook his head slightly. In other words, he didn't want me there, didn't want Captain Henry to notice me. But it was too late.

Captain Henry seemed happy to see me. 'Come to join the party? Plenty of room in there.'

'Don't be such a fool,' Prakesh said.

'Who do you think you are to call me a fool? I'm not the one locked up like an animal!'

I knew Prakesh. He was doing everything he could to draw Captain Henry's attention to him and away from Le Froy and me. Maybe he was a fool, but a sweet one.

'I know exactly who you are,' Captain Henry told me. 'Your family runs all the gangs and black-markets in Singapore. And now, thanks to him,' he jerked his head at Le Froy, 'you've got your claws into the Singapore police force too. But it's not going to help you. They'll thank us for getting rid of you.' He was grinning, barely suppressed excitement welling out of him, like a child looking forward to ice cream.

I drew myself up. Thanks to all my reading, I might see myself as Virginia Woolf's Clarissa Dalloway, maintaining a good façade and doing the flowers while keeping my thoughts to myself, but anyone else sees a Straits-born Chinese woman, crooked from polio, a misfit wherever she might be. Reading great literature might open your mind and make you aware of the world around you, but it also shows you that it doesn't affect how others see you.

Still, Captain Henry wasn't wrong about me. I was the daughter of Big Boss Chen and the granddaughter of Chen Tai. The only thing he'd got wrong was his underestimation of me.

'The *kris* dagger you took belongs to me, not to Le Froy,' I said. 'If you're going to put anyone under detention it should be me.'

Le Froy shut his eyes briefly in exasperation. Yes, I knew he wanted me to stay out of it. But my *kris* had got him detained.

'You know this has nothing to do with them,' Prakesh said. 'Whatever you're trying to do, you'll just end up looking stupid.'

'You're going down for this,' Captain Henry told Prakesh. 'You know what they'll do to you for killing a white planter? For being behind the deaths of all the others? Think about it. If you come to your senses and tell us where that woman went, maybe we can work something out. But otherwise you're cooked. All of you.' Generously, he included Le Froy and me in that last. 'I'll give you some time to think about it.'

'Keep them in here. Come and get me if he says anything,' Captain Henry told Jaimin, and headed out. Jaimin pulled the sliding gate across the floor runner, then chained and padlocked it. It was simple but effective. Those inside couldn't get out but anyone outside could see everything going on within.

I watched as Captain Henry crossed the centre of the roundabout under the rose apple tree, heading towards the

Emerald Lodge. I wondered who else he planned to detain. Viktor? Terry Cook?

'He's not good with power,' Le Froy said. 'Some men are like that.'

I hurried across to him and threw my arms around him. Le Froy held me to him hard, as though trying to cover me with protective energy. Then he started speaking very quietly and concisely into my ear. 'I want you to go down to the resort centre and telephone Harry Palin. Tell him to come and get you. And after you've made the phone call, I want you to stay in the shop. Keep out of sight until Harry comes or sends someone. Also ask him to get in touch with Brandon Sands and tell him what's happened. Tell him to send back-up here, that it concerns the Walker murders as well as Max Moreno. Keep leaving messages for Sands and Palin if you can't get through to Palin, but stay there and out of sight no matter what. If you can't get through to either Palin or Sands, call de Souza in Pahang. He's far away, but not as far as Singapore. All their numbers are in my notebook.'

'Anything else?' I tried not to let on that he was frightening me more than Captain Henry had.

'I love you,' he said. 'More than anything.'

I was still frightened, but that was nice to hear.

'He didn't tell you to lock Su Lin in, right?' Prakesh called to Jaimin. 'She's just here visiting the prisoners, right? You'll unlock the grating and let her out when she wants to go?'

Jaimin hesitated, then nodded. I guessed that Prakesh was giving his colleague a way to hang it on him if Captain Henry gave him trouble for letting me out.

'Palin's got his own problems,' Prakesh said. 'The other *ang mob*s think he's a traitor. They believe you and Palin are working to help the Communists. I don't know if he can get up here.'

'I know Harry's helping the Communists, but what's wrong with that?' I said. 'The Communists helped him, the British and all of us survive against the Japanese during the war. Now they're suddenly the enemy. What changed?'

'They haven't changed,' Le Froy said. 'They're still fighting for their lives and for independence. What's changed is they were fighting Japanese oppression but now they're fighting British interests that want to exploit natural resources without frightening off London-based insurance companies and investors.'

'It's not fair,' I said.

'Unfortunately for them, the Communists are too successful and too popular,' Le Froy said. 'The people love them for defending them against the Japanese. The Malayan Communist Party is going to win all Malayan elections wherever they stand. And the Communists want independence for Malaya, which makes them the enemy where the British are concerned.'

'Have they asked you to do something about it?'

Le Froy shook his head. 'MI6. They don't trust me.'

'That's to your credit, sir,' Prakesh said.

'I'm sure they don't trust you either,' Le Froy said.

'Thank you. I'm honoured you think so,'

We all laughed and even Jaimin smiled.

'How did you end up up here?' Le Froy asked Prakesh. 'Here in Perak?'

'I thought it was a beautiful place,' Prakesh said. 'No people. After the war trials and everything, I just wanted to get away. I took the furthest posting I could get. There wasn't even a police station on record anywhere near the Emerald Estate when I was posted there. It was more like Boss Max wanted full-time security guards he didn't have to pay for. So he called his important friends in the capital and pulled some strings. Talked about all the danger from rebels, Communists and gangs of vigilantes roaming the area and threatening the workers. I got here and found he wanted us to act like his own personal army. He was setting us against his own workers most of the time, told us to shoot them if they gave trouble. It was cheaper than firing them and paying their back wages. He swore he'd say that they'd attacked his wife and he'd shot them himself in self-defence.'

I could well imagine Boss Max saying that.

'What was all the trouble with his workers?' Le Froy asked. 'Why were they attacking him?'

'He refused to pay them for last season's work. They had been hired by the Walkers, not by him, so he refused to pay them, even though he was taking over the estate and all the latex and rubber they had collected and processed. No season's pay or bonus meant they couldn't take the boat home to see their families and it would be hard for them to survive until the next season's work started. They were foraging and trying to pick up any part-time work but it wasn't easy. Boss Max,' Prakesh shook his head, 'said it wasn't his problem. As far as he was concerned, he could import foreign labourers, work them to death and then import some more.'

'If Moreno hired you to work for him, why did he have it in for you?' Le Froy asked.

'I wrote down some stuff about what I thought,' Prakesh said. 'I decided if I got it out of my system I wouldn't say it, but then my notebooks disappeared. I'm guessing Boss Max or Terry Cook took them, so now they know what I think of all of them. Max especially. And of you.'

'What?' I said. 'What did you write?'

'Nothing,' Prakesh said. 'Anyway, he brought Captain Henry in after that. He couldn't fire me without reason, after he'd requested security. Captain Henry . . . His official response was "arrested for drunken behaviour, shot while trying to escape".'

'He wouldn't have had to pay dead workers,' I said. I felt sick.

'It's a new project for Max Moreno,' Le Froy said. 'He might not have had the cash flow to pay them.'

'He could have let them go on living in the plantation huts,' Prakesh said. 'When he and Cook took over the rubber plantations, they took over the smallholdings and homes on the estate as well. According to them, that meant the people living there – who had been there long before the Emerald Estate was formed – couldn't stay in their own homes during the off-season unless they paid rent to the estate. What were they supposed to pay with, if they didn't get their earnings for last season's work?'

'How do you know so much about them?' I asked. 'Are they still around? Did they have trouble with the Walkers too?'

'I don't know, but Jaimin is from the village around the plantation, right, Jai? Did you hear anything about that from them? Did they have trouble with anyone else – any of the previous *mat salleh*?'

'I don't know anything,' Jaimin said, from his station outside the entrance grating.

'We talked to them. They were all considered suspects, of course, after the murders, all the families that the plantations had belonged to before. We questioned them all but there aren't many left. Most families only have women now, mothers, grandmothers, daughters, because there are so few men left alive. There was an old father and an even older grandfather who said some stupid things and made wild threats, but they didn't have anything to do with it.'

'How can you be sure?' I asked. 'What kind of stupid things did they say?'

'Things like how the Walkers deserved to die and they would have killed them if they could, but it was better that the forest spirits struck them down.'

'The forest spirits?' I must have looked blank.

'The Walkers wanted to tap the rubber trees through the monsoon months. Yes, just like Max. They didn't care that it would weaken the young trees, maybe kill them before the next season. When the labourers refused to work they threatened to burn down their huts so that there would be nowhere for them to live.'

Mass murder was wrong, of course, but I was beginning to feel the Walkers might have had it coming.

'Jaimin, can you escort Su Lin back to her lodge?' Prakesh said. 'Take the umbrella. The rain is starting again.'

'Oh, wait,' I said.

'Go.' Le Froy passed me his notebook. If I managed to get down to use the telephone in the shop, I didn't know when I'd see him again.

'Of course, sir,' Jaimin said. He clearly wasn't happy, but he unlocked the padlock, unravelled the chain and slid open the barrier.

When Jaimin walked me back to the Moonlight Lodge. I was not really surprised to see Captain Henry and Viktor there, or that Le Froy's and my belongings had been searched.

'Did you find anything interesting?' I asked.

I could tell from Captain Henry's grumpiness that he wasn't happy with whatever they'd found.

'This was in your bag,' Viktor held up my gold bar. 'I will give it back to you now. I helped in the search. I can verify nothing was found that points to your husband's guilt.'

'Le Froy has Boss Max's notes, doesn't he?' Captain Henry said. 'Where did he hide them? Where's the blasted notebook he's always writing in?'

Boss Max's notes were hidden under the dried mushrooms basket in the shop at the resort centre. Le Froy's notes were tucked into my knickers – since the man had taken my waist sheath with my *kris*.

'I don't know what you're talking about,' I said, trying to look intimidated. 'Can you drive me to the resort centre?' I asked Viktor.

'No,' he said.

'Why not?'

'Captain Henry has the keys to my van. He has all the keys. I can only drive when he allows it.'

This cheered Captain Henry. 'Come on, let's go. Sleep tight, China girl.'

As they left, taking the umbrella Jaimin had used to shelter me, I called Jaimin back and handed him Le Froy's umbrella. 'Can you return it later?' I whispered. 'I need to talk to you. Please?'

Jaimin paused, then nodded.

What could he tell Captain Henry, if he was inclined to? That I'd loaned him an umbrella and wanted it returned?

And if Jaimin didn't report this to Captain Henry, maybe I had a chance of getting him to help me. How I didn't yet know.

Jaimin in the Night

◆

'You climbed down the ravine using ropes that day,' I said to Jaimin. 'Can you help me climb down to the resort centre?'

I'd watched Jaimin manage the slippery slopes in the rain as well as Prakesh. I wasn't sure if Jaimin didn't like the idea or whether it was me he didn't like. But at least he'd turned up with Le Froy's umbrella.

'It's too dangerous,' Jaimin said. 'You should go by the road.'

'It would take me much longer,' I said. 'And if they come to look for me, they'll find me. If I climb down the slope, I only have to cross the road three times.'

Jaimin frowned. 'It's too dangerous.'

'I know Captain Henry is your boss, but if you help me it will help Prakesh too. Don't you want to help Prakesh?'

'You don't understand anything,' Jaimin said. 'You don't know what you're talking about.'

'No, I don't,' I agreed. 'So explain to me.'

'Why ask me?'

'Because Prakesh trusts you. And Prakesh is my friend,' I said.

Jaimin accepted that, even if he didn't trust me yet.

'Somebody killed Boss Max and took Mrs Max away,' I said. 'Captain Henry wants to blame that on Prakesh and Le Froy, so that he isn't blamed. That's what's going to happen if we don't do anything, so we have to do something.'

Jaimin shrugged helplessly. We were sitting in my bedroom with the curtains drawn, so that anyone looking in wouldn't see he was with me.

'Is being alone here with me making you nervous?' I asked. 'I know Prakesh got into trouble with Boss Max for being too friendly with his wife.'

'That wasn't Prakesh's fault,' Jaimin said at once. 'When they first came to the plantation, Elfrida was spending a lot of time at the security post. She told us we must call her "Elfrida" not "Mrs Moreno" because that made her feel like an old woman. She said she was bored in the big house and she liked to practise her English with Prakesh. The other people at the big house, especially Mrs Cook, were always teasing her, saying she was in love with a local man.'

'Not him with her?' I asked. 'Wasn't he the one asking her to come and talk to him?'

Jaimin shook his head. 'Not at all. Prakesh was embarrassed because – well, because I think he did like her. But he always stayed away from her. Sometimes when Elfrida came to look for him, he would tell her to talk to me instead. Or the aunties.

But Elfrida always said he was the only one she trusted to find things out for her.'

'What kind of things?'

'Elfrida wanted to know how the rubber plantations were run in the old days. Prakesh didn't grow up in our area so he didn't know much, but he tried to find out. How old children were when they started to work and so on.'

It didn't sound very romantic to me. Of course, who was I to judge? I'd fallen in love with a man I'd spent most of my time discussing murder with.

'She got upset when she found out the imported workers weren't being paid. The plantation paid the agents to ship in the labourers they needed, and the labourers had to pay the agents to get passage here from India. So they weren't paid until they'd finished paying off all that.'

My grandmother would have been impressed by the system those agents had set up, I thought. Then again, she probably wouldn't have approved. Ah Ma believed it was good for your health to eat what was grown in your area by people you lived with. The same applied to hiring workers from your neighbourhood.

'Your family were from around there too? Did you work on the plantation before the war?'

'Yes, of course. The village had a smallholding and we all worked on it before and after school. During the season we helped to tap and collect latex and went to school in between. Off season we went to school for longer hours.'

'Did you like school?'

'It was not bad. The schoolhouse had one room divided in half for boys and girls to study religion and English language. In the school garden we all helped the teachers grow bananas and bitter gourd. Before the plantations took over the land, we could live off what we grew and what we got from the jungle.'

I knew what he meant. Since motor-cars had become popular in the West, thousands of acres of forest had been cleared for rubber growing.

'Anyway, I could join the police because I could speak English.'

I supposed that was a good way to pre-filter candidates. At least they would be able to understand their superior officers in a common language even if their mother tongues were all different. But ...

'You can't have been a police recruit before the war,' I said.

'Why not?' Jaimin's sudden aggression startled me. 'You think I'm not strong enough? Or you think I'm not smart enough? Why do you say I can't be a police recruit?'

Too late, I realised I had touched on a sore point to which I, of all people, should have been more sensitive. After all, I'd experienced a lifetime of being told I was too young, too weak, too female or too Chinese to take on responsibility for things I was already doing.

Jaimin looked healthy enough, but he was definitely on the small side, probably due to growing up in the war years.

'It's just that you look so young,' I said. 'I'm sorry. I didn't mean to offend you.'

'I'm older than I look,' Jaimin sounded a bit less put out. 'I speak English and I have my corporal certification papers.'

I nodded, not wanting to set him off him again. It was Jaimin who spoke first. 'Why do you want to go to the resort centre?'

'I want to telephone Harry Palin.'

'Oh!'

He clearly knew the name. 'What's wrong?'

'You mustn't tell Captain Henry.'

I shook my head, which might have meant 'No, I won't', as well as 'No, I can't agree to that.' And I know that wasn't a decent thing to do, but a good friend's freedom and maybe life were at stake.

'When the workers were unhappy about not being paid, Captain Prakesh told them to go and see Mr Henry Palin.'

That wouldn't have endeared Prakesh to Boss Max or Captain Henry.

'Prakesh is not a *mat salleh*'s policeman,' Jaimin said. *Mat salleh* was a colloquial – more descriptive than perjorative – term for white men. 'He doesn't bully people, tries to be fair to everybody. At first I joined the police so that I could stop people bullying my family by bullying them first. Prakesh told me the job is not about locking up hungry people for stealing food, but making sure everybody can work for food.'

I'd not seen that side of Prakesh. He had matured since leaving Singapore and I realised this young man might know him better than I did. But we both knew that.

'Prakesh didn't have anything to do with Elfrida disappearing or Boss Max's murder,' I said.

Jaimin nodded. Even if we didn't trust each other completely, we were agreed on that.

'Le Froy didn't have anything to do with that either,' I said.

Jaimin's nod to this was polite rather than convinced.

'Le Froy hadn't even arrived when Elfrida went missing,' I said. 'And he was down in the town centre with Viktor when Boss Max was stabbed.'

'Okay,' Jaimin said. 'But according to Prakesh, nobody could have stabbed Boss Max. You and Mrs Terry said nobody went into the room and killed him. He thinks Captain Henry suspects you and Mrs Terry, but can't prove it. Maybe that's why he accused Le Froy.'

'Then he should accuse Terry Cook too, to be fair,' I said.

But I understood the problem. It was a fact that Boss Max was dead. I had seen the *kris* in his chest. I was a witness to the fact that someone had got into his locked room, stabbed him to death, then disappeared from the room while I sat outside it, hearing and seeing nothing.

My rational Western-educated brain told me that a ghost or spirit could either pass through walls or stab a man to death but not both. My Eastern brain told me that spirits, vengeful or otherwise, cannot wield physical weapons. If they could, they wouldn't need to rely on haunting and scaring people to death.

But my superstitious self wanted to believe that Max had killed Elfrida and her ghost had returned and killed him. That would have tied things up so nicely.

'What do you think of the other planter bosses?' I asked Jaimin.

'Terry Cook and his wife don't like living out here. But they want the money Boss Max promised them for partnering with him. Viktor likes living out here. But I don't think he liked Boss Max. He liked Elfrida, though.'

'Oh? How did he feel about Elfrida spending time with Prakesh?'

Jaimin clammed up immediately. Sheesh. There was no predicting what would upset these young people. But it was late and now I wanted to be by myself so I could think over what to do. I had to find a way to get down to the telephone in the shop, but I didn't think I could manage it safely in the dark, even if I went by road. Also, I could hear the rain starting again.

'So, do you want to ask me anything?' I asked. I expected Jaimin to say, 'No,' and when he did, I would say, 'Good night, then,' and show him out, once more with the umbrella that had been his excuse to return.

To my surprise he did have a question. 'How did you know that Mr Le Froy was the man you should marry?' Jaimin asked. 'Was it because he was the most powerful man you knew?'

'No!' That wasn't the question I'd expected. But I'd said I would try to answer. 'We got along. And we talked – we talked a lot. That's how we were most comfortable, right from the start. Talking about problems and figuring out solutions. It was comfortable, but it wasn't romantic . . .'

'What do you mean by romantic?' Jaimin asked. 'Solving problems is romantic?'

'You know what I mean – just romantic.'

'No, I don't know.'

I saw he was serious. He really didn't know and wanted to. 'Romance is different depending on whom you fall in love with,' I said. 'Different girls find different things romantic. Like my best friend. When we were growing up she used to dream about falling in love with a man who brought her red roses and wrote her poetry, and she talked about how they would release white doves at their wedding...' I laughed, remembering Parshanti's girlish fantasies. 'I told her there would be bird droppings all over the wedding guests.'

'Did she fall in love with a man who gave her roses and birds?' Jaimin asked.

'She married the man she fell in love with when they were in the jungle together hiding from the Japanese,' I said. 'She says he saved her life. He says she saved his life. I think that's the most romantic story I ever heard.'

'Me too,' Jaimin said.

He looked so small and lost that I reached over and squeezed his hand, 'Don't worry,' I said. 'You're still young. There will be someone for you one day. And when that happens, you will know.'

'What if you've already met the person and they don't like you back?'

Ah. But thanks again to Parshanti Leask née Shankar, I had the answer to that one too. 'That just means she wasn't the right girl for you. My friend fell in love so many times before she met the man she committed to loving for the rest of her life. She said all the times before that were for her to learn what she didn't want.'

Jaimin nodded. I wondered who'd broken this young man's heart, but I wasn't going to risk a telling-off for asking too many questions again.

'So – no doves at your friend's wedding?'

'Oh, there were! Spotted doves and zebra doves and pink-necked pigeons...they had an outdoor wedding next to a quarry pond. There were birds above and bugs beneath and, yes, it wasn't anything like she'd dreamed of when she was a little girl, but it was so romantic.'

Jaimin nodded. I hoped I'd made him feel better. I found I was feeling better myself. Just saying encouraging words to someone else had lifted me out of my hopeless mood. Sometimes you need to hear yourself talk before you know what you should do – or what you want to do.

'I will help you get down to the telephone, I swear,' Jaimin said. 'But you mustn't tell anybody.'

Though he spoke softly the fierceness of his promise took me by surprise. But I got it.

'And I won't let anybody hurt you,' I said. I didn't know how I was going to keep such a promise, but I meant to try.

Jaimin nodded and then he was gone.

Women Must Stick Together

———◆———

'Come on, isn't it obvious?' Daffy said. 'This woman isn't dead. Clearly Frida set this whole thing up. She made us all think her husband had done something terrible to her, and tried to get him arrested for it. When that didn't work, she came back and murdered the poor man.'

I had girded my loins and gone over to the Emerald Lodge for breakfast as usual. And, also as usual, only the Cooks were in the dining room. Clearly, though, Captain Henry had already presented his version of what he'd done, because the first thing Daffy said to me was, 'Captain Henry says he's only doing his job. After he saw Le Froy with the knife, he knew he'd get the blame if something happened to one of us.'

Aunty Rakiah brought me coffee and I asked her if something could be carried over to the security post for Le Froy and Prakesh.

'Already taken them breakfast,' Aunty Rakiah told me very properly, but she patted my shoulder after putting down my coffee cup and I knew she meant it as comfort.

'The best thing you can do for your husband is to tell Captain Henry what he's planning,' Daffy said. 'Men can be so stupid and stubborn, and that gets them into trouble.' She gave her husband's arm a little squeeze.

'Excuse me,' Terry Cooke said, pushing her away. 'I'm eating.'

Daffy pouted. Then she took out a perfume bottle and dabbed some on her wrists and under her ears. 'It's by Avon,' she said. 'It's called Wishing and only launched recently. It's all the rage in places like London and New York and Paris. It's a lovely bottle, isn't it? Impossible to get hold of and very expensive.'

Could something be all the rage *and* impossible to get hold of? It was a squat little glass bottle, just over half full. I sniffed the wrist Daffy shoved under my nose but couldn't smell anything beyond the odour of stale sweat on clammy skin. I suppose fashionable scents are in the nose of the inhaler. 'Nice,' I said vaguely. 'I've heard of it, I think.'

'No, you haven't,' Daffy said. 'No way you'd come across something like this out here. It's very exclusive.'

I saw her struggle with the idea of giving me a dab of her perfume, but she couldn't bring herself to do so and put the bottle away.

'The best thing, really, dear – Susie Linda – is to help them. Captain Henry's only trying to make him see sense. Le Froy has been in touch with that awful Communist Palin fellow, hasn't he? You know he wants to take all our property and pack us into work camps like animals?'

'I don't know anything about that,' I said. 'Why don't you let me telephone Harry Palin and ask him what he and Le Froy have been talking about?' I thought that was quite brilliant. But it didn't work.

'Oh, no. No, no, no,' Daffy said. 'You can't talk to that terrible man. He'll try to turn you into a Communist too. And you've already got a tendency in that direction, haven't you? Being so brown?'

'Best stay away from Palin,' Terry said. 'Bad egg, that one. Not a team player.'

Well, I wasn't a team player either. I ate quietly. I was hoping to see Viktor so I could try to persuade him to take me to the telephone. I decided that if he refused again I would start walking. It was downhill all the way to the gully bridge and uphill after the fork in the road that went round to the other side of the golf course and the town.

I ought to be able to hear a vehicle before it reached me, and if I did, I would get off the road and hide in the shrubbery on the lower slope until it had passed. Anyone in a car could see only what was on the slope above them. As long as I stayed close to the edge, I could hide below them.

'You know,' Daffy said, 'have you thought about what you'll do if Le Froy goes to jail for this?'

'What? No. He's not going to jail for anything.'

'That's what we all hope, of course, but we can't tell what's going to happen and a girl has to watch out for herself. We're probably going to move to Australia or South America when we finally get clear of this place. If you're a sensible girl and help us work this out, you can come with us as my servant. I'll buy you some nice clothes and you can start a whole new life. Nobody need know about Le Froy or that you were married before. You don't have to be so loyal to the man. He doesn't deserve it. He's one of those woman haters. Even I can see that. They want women for their bodies, nothing else.'

'Oh.' I had a vague feeling Daffy had said the same thing to me before, if not about Le Froy. More importantly, I realised this was exactly what Elfrida had been offered – a whole new start in a place where no one knew anything about her previous life. Elfrida might even have been married before. Why hadn't we looked into that? A jealous or abandoned ex-husband in the picture might explain why Elfrida had disappeared and also why Boss Max had been murdered.

It made me think of that book by Agatha Christie – I couldn't remember the title. It starts with ten people stranded on a deserted island and ends with them all dead. At least that wasn't happening here (not yet, anyway), but I remembered that one of the first 'victims' had faked their death. Once safely dismissed as dead, they were then able to go around the island killing the others before killing themselves in the same manner as their faked death to fit in with the written accounts left by their victims.

Of course, that still didn't explain how Elfrida or her partner had managed to get into Boss Max's room, stab him and exit without being seen, or why they had used a *kris* that couldn't have belonged to either of them. And why had the *kris* been left behind?

'Do you know if Elfrida was married before?' I asked Daffy.

'Elfrida?' Daffy looked taken aback. 'What's Elfrida got to do with it?'

'She had more motive than anyone else here, given the way her husband treated her,' I said. 'And with everyone thinking she was dead, no one would suspect her of killing her husband. Have you read any of Agatha Christie's books?'

'Please focus, girl.' Daffy clearly wasn't a reader of mysteries. 'It's your future you should be concerned about. I'm trying to help you. We women have to stick together no matter what, don't you see?'

'It is my future I'm thinking about,' I said. 'If we find out that Elfrida's alive and killed Boss Max, there's no reason for Le Froy to be in prison.'

'There'll be another reason,' Daffy said. 'With his sort, there's always be another reason. His type is forever running around, sticking his nose into things, getting into trouble and dragging you down with him.'

I looked at Terry Cook, I couldn't help it. If you were comparing the quality of husbands I didn't think I'd done too badly. Daffy pursed her lips and looked sour. If we were to be friends or even polite company, we would have to pretend that that moment had never happened. But it had. And I had enjoyed it.

'Make more toast!' Terry called. 'This batch is stone cold! Hurry up!' When Aunty Salmah hurried out, he threw the toast rack with its three remaining slices after her.

'I'm going to look in on Le Froy,' I said.

Le Froy didn't find my morning exchange with Daffy as funny as I did, though Prakesh laughed.

'She's got a point. Look at me. An old cripple,' Le Froy said. 'It's not right. You have all your life ahead of you. You know better than I do how people look at local girls who go after the worst dregs of the empire that end up here. As though a white man is some kind of catch.'

I stared at him, then reached over and touched his neck – no fever. 'You *siao*?'

Siao means crazy, but the weird, nutty end rather than the weird, dangerous end of the crazy spectrum.

'I'm sorry. I know this is a bad time to come up with all this.'

I've heard about people losing their mind in the jungle. But usually they're talking about delirium induced by malaria. I didn't know what was causing this. Had he been bitten by anything? I didn't want to ask him to let me take his temperature just then but his eyes were over-bright, and he looked feverish.

'I would say I'll go away and never bother you again. But I can't exactly get away right now, so if you put up with me until the roads are cleared . . .'

'What suddenly brought this on?'

'It's not sudden. It's something that's always been a part of me. It just never came up before.'

'So why would it come up now?'

'It's a long story.'

'Well, you have until they clear the roads,' I said.

'It's easy to pretend when nobody knows you,' Le Froy said, 'but this is my true self. No hiding behind qualifications or the authority of the British Empire. Here in the jungle I'm just a useless old man with a game leg. I can't even take care of myself, let alone a wife.'

'We'll talk about it when we get out of here,' I said.

'You didn't manage to get Palin on the telephone, did you?'

'Not yet. But I will,' I said.

It was difficult to have much of a conversation because, in addition to Prakesh and Jaimin inside the security-post barrier with us, Daffy was walking up and down in front of it with her parasol as though waiting for me to get tired of talking with my husband.

'What is she trying to do?' Prakesh whispered.

'It's called intimidation,' Le Froy said.

'So what do we do?'

'Not be intimidated,' Le Froy said.

I couldn't tell if he was referring to Daffy or Viktor. Viktor was watching us in the security post too. He was standing further away with his back against his van, cleaning his teeth with his knife.

Mist Rings

———◆———

It was miserably cold outside when I asked Jaimin to unlock the security barrier and let me out. The mist from the last rains had risen from the forest canopy below and was hovering over the sodden lawn like cooking steam, but was neither warm nor fragrant.

I didn't want to go near any of the lodges where Daffy and her friendship might be waiting for me, so I walked to the edge of the slopes behind the buildings.

There was nowhere to sit, but my legs didn't want to go on standing so I squatted.

I could see my breath coming out of me like smoke and my energy was draining away. Why had I thought cold weather was romantic? Why had I dreamed of winters in England? This was nowhere near as cold as it would have been in England and I was already having trouble. Why indeed was I here? I was no help to Le Froy, and I was sure it was partly because of me and my family that he was in detention. Even if this was sorted out as soon as the roads cleared, my identity would always be hanging over him. I had never wanted—

'Cold,' Viktor commented. He squatted next to me, surprising me: most *ang mohs* had trouble with that stance.

'And wet,' Viktor added, when I didn't answer. 'If it was dry cold it would be all right. But this wet cold gets inside your bones.'

I thought Viktor meant to question me too, but he said nothing and we squatted in companionable silence for a while.

I was too tired to worry about whether he would proposition me again. If he tried, I might push him down the slope in front of us – or jump down it myself. Only it wasn't a steep enough drop to kill. I was more likely to tumble and roll down to the next trail, getting mud all over myself, just to make things a little worse than they were now. I grimaced at the thought.

'What?' Viktor caught the movement.

'Nothing.'

'I show you something.'

'No. Please don't,' I said.

But Viktor did anyway. He blew a mist-ring. It was like the smoke-rings Daffy was always trying to produce, but without smoke.

'How did you do that?' I was startled out of my low mood. 'Can you do it again?'

He pursed his lips, like a goat making a kissing face. And, like the goats did, he rolled his tongue and stuck it out and, with a quick pulse from his throat, there was a mist-ring. 'Try it,' Viktor said. 'Breathe in deep and hold it to get warm and damp.'

I tried. I didn't manage to produce a mist-ring, but I came close, producing mist balls.

I think it was the deep breaths and distraction that helped me more than anything else.

'Thank you,' I said.

'As long as you are alive, it is good to learn new things,' Viktor said. 'I showed Elfrida how to blow mist-rings. She was not as good as you the first time. But she got better until she was very good at it. Just not as good as I am. When she blows, she laughs too much.'

I hadn't started with a very good impression of the missing Elfrida. I'd thought her a bored, selfish woman who'd entertained herself by flirting – and maybe more, but there was no point thinking about that – with various men, including my good friend Prakesh and this man squatting beside me. Not a woman who'd laughed too much blowing mist-rings.

Viktor chuckled to himself.

'What?'

'Daffy. She came and said, "Does Max know you two are out here alone? What are you doing with him?" And Elfrida said, "He is teaching me to do things exciting things with my mouth and tongue!" Oh, the look on that woman's face!' Viktor pursed his lips and opened his eyes very wide. Imagining what Daffy must have thought, I had to laugh too.

'Elfrida sounds like she was fun.'

'She is very fun,' Viktor said.

'You don't believe Elfrida is dead?' I said.

'That is a stupid question,' Viktor said. 'If you say she is not dead, where do you say she is?'

'I don't know. That's why I'm asking you,' I said.

'I don't know,' Viktor said. 'It is not Viktor's business.'

'Whose business, then?'

Viktor shrugged. He blew another mist-ring. 'Sometimes I fear I have lived in the wrong way. The best thing is never to have been born. Next best is to do what we can.'

'Philosophy is all very well, but right now we're stuck here with a killer who can walk through walls or a vengeful ghost, and my husband is locked up as a suspect,' I said. 'I really need to use the phone. Please can you drive me to the town centre?'

'Captain Henry won't like that.' Viktor blew a mist-ring. He hadn't exactly said no. 'He will make things very difficult for you and for your husband. Remember, a ghost isn't a dead vengeful person. Sometimes it can be the echo of wrongs that have been done in a location that can't let go because the vibrations of evil are still around.'

'I don't believe in ghosts,' I said.

'Of course not,' Viktor said. 'Do you believe in God?'

'Well – yes?'

'Same thing,' Viktor said. 'You leave them alone, they leave you alone. But they are still there.'

'The aunties believe in ghosts,' I said.

'Prakesh is your friend. He is also Elfrida's friend. He showed her how to eat rose apples.' He winced a little. 'Sometimes they're too sour, but sour things can be good for your gut. He would loop the branches and pull them down so that she could pluck them. She liked them very much. Later, when she couldn't get out of her room, the *makciks* would bring fresh fruit and push it under the fence to her.'

'Oh?' I just managed to stop myself saying I'd thought Elfrida and the old women didn't get on.

Viktor looked surprised.

'That's very nice of them,' I said. 'I didn't know *ang mohs* know how to eat *jambu*.'

'Oh, Elfrida liked trying new things, including food,' Viktor said. 'The *makciks* said she liked it better than the *ros bif* and pork chop they learned to cook for the boss planters,'

'*Makciks*?' I was surprised to hear him use the respectful Malay term for older women, rather than the more common 'aunty'.

'*Makcik*, aunty, same thing,' Viktor said. Yes, they were, but only someone familiar with them would know that.

'You know the aunty – *makcik* – who doesn't talk? Is she deaf?'

'She doesn't talk much since her husband died,' Viktor said. 'Very sad.'

'I thought she was deaf,' I said.

'Maybe she's also deaf,' Viktor said.

If the cleaner-cook *makcik* aunties had been such good friends with Elfrida, why had she told Prakesh she hated having them around? If she'd deliberately misled him and Boss Max, wasn't it possible the old ladies had helped her to get away from her husband . . . or to kill him?

But how had they managed to get in and out of a locked room?

'One more thing. You speak German, don't you?'

'A little.' Viktor looked surprised. 'Why?'

I've always been better at being stubborn and working around orders than making decisions for myself. It was as though I didn't know what I wanted to do till I'd pushed away all the suggestions other people had made. I might have longed for the freedom to make my own decisions, but unlimited choice was almost as paralysing as no choice at all.

'Just try one thing,' I told myself, 'as if it's the only thing. If it works – good. If not – I'll try something else.'

Wasn't that how I'd lived most of my life up till now? And I was still alive, so something there had worked. I didn't want to see Captain Henry or anyone who suspected Le Froy.

I walked to the kitchen behind the Emerald Lodge. I could offer to help the aunties, talk to them and ask them to help me get down to the town to use the telephone.

But as I approached I saw the three aunties sitting around the table on which Viktor had laid Max's shrouded body, chatting as they worked on something.

The aunties looked at me expectantly when I stopped just beyond the sheltered area.

'Is that . . . Are you . . .?' I couldn't see what they were doing to the body.

'Do you need us to clean something for you?' Aunty Salmah had accepted that I knew she understood English. She pushed back her stool and stood up. 'Need broom or bucket?'

'*Wo wird das Brot aufbewahrt?*' I said politely. Where is the bread kept?

257

'*Es gibt kein Brot mehr. Ich kann dir Süßkartoffeln machen, wenn du magst,*' Aunty Salmah said. Or 'There is no more bread. I can make you sweet potatoes if you like.'

I'm not squeamish, but the thought of them fixing me a snack after whatever they were doing to a corpse on the table . . . As Aunty Rakiah also stood and turned to face me, I saw they'd been hand picking vegetables by yellow lamplight. 'Mr Viktor said better to put it in the hammock behind the tree.' She'd guessed what I was looking for.

'Thanks,' I said.

Deaf Aunty said nothing, but she smiled at me and pointed to a clay bowl on the table. I understood she was offering me tea. I was the one of the boss's friends who had to be served. How could I have thought I could just join them in the kitchen and fit in, as I would have if I were in my grandmother's house?

The war had been a great equaliser. Now we all knew what it was like to be hungry and dirty when each day might be our last. Like these people, I had lived on water that had to be carried from the pump in the dry season and plucked off leeches after wading through ankle-deep mud to rescue mired chickens.

Right now, the weather was an even greater leveller.

But I was still on the outside.

Growing up, I'd kept at a distance *ang moh*s who thought they were one of us. Now I felt as if I was on the other side. Except I wasn't, was I? I was on no side at all.

'Mrs Terry was intimate with Boss Max and Captain Henry,' Aunty Rakiah said. 'Some men are like dogs. They will take anything available.'

It was quite a bombshell to drop into a conversation, but it's hard to make small talk when you're surrounded by murder.

'Poor Elfrida!' I said.

'Oh, Mrs Max doesn't care,' Aunty Rakiah said.

Daffy doing it with Boss Max? And Captain Henry?

I couldn't imagine it. But why would Aunty Rakiah make up something like that? And that last thing she said: was it a minor error with tenses – or a major slip-up?

'Why don't you believe me?' Aunty Rakiah asked.

'Just look at Boss Max!'

'Look at Terry Cook,' Aunty Rakiah said.

'You've got a point,' I said.

I must have looked sad because Deaf Aunty handed me a tiny pink heart. It was made of the soft clay found abundantly in the Perak River that made Perak's *labu sayong* pottery famous. They were called *sayong* because the Sayong district of Kuala Kangsar was where they'd first been made. I knew this because, of course, my grandmother loved *labu sayong* clay pots.

I pressed the little heart into Le Froy's palm when I went to see if he needed anything from our luggage. He touched it to his lips, just as I'd touched it to mine before I passed it to him. But romance wasn't uppermost in my mind.

'Daffy told me you're a woman-hater. Why would she say something like that?'

Le Froy looked surprised. 'Well – she might have tried to seduce me.'

'What? Might have?'

'She did. No mistake about it. She was quite aggressive. I tried to deflect her gently, but ended up being quite rude because that woman doesn't seem to understand anything less.'

'You should have told me!'

Le Froy shook his head, still unwilling to discuss it.

'I'm your wife now! You're supposed to tell me things like that!'

'We'll never be married long enough for me to want to waste our time together talking about people like her,' Le Froy said.

'Look, no woman wants to hear about other women going after her husband, but it's a hundred thousand times better than being told her husband hates women.'

'She is her own problem, and nothing to do with us.'

'It might have something to do with what's happening here.'

I told him Daffy had said almost exactly the same thing about Viktor when we first met. How Viktor hated women and spent time with them only when he wanted to have intercourse.

'And now she's telling me the same things about you after you turned her down. Maybe it wasn't Viktor who propositioned her but the other way around, and this is just how she talks about men who reject her.'

'Maybe,' Le Froy said. 'But it's still not our problem.'

But did I smell the solution to our problem somewhere in there?

'Where would Daffy have got that bottle of exclusive perfume?' I asked. 'She hasn't the money or the connections.'

Le Froy didn't want to talk about Daffy, 'People give perfume to women.'

Not to all women. Women like Elfrida, maybe. But I certainly wasn't given perfume and I suspected Daffy Cook wasn't either.

'I think Daffy stole Elfrida's perfume,' I said. 'That was what Viktor meant when he said, "Captain Henry smells of Wishing." That's the name of the perfume. Viktor assumed Elfrida was sleeping with Captain Henry because he smelt her perfume on him, so to him that meant Elfrida didn't dislike the security people.'

Le Froy was listening now.

'If Daffy dared to take and use Elfrida's perfume even before she disappeared, she must have known that Elfrida meant to disappear.'

'Or she knew someone was planning to do something to Elfrida and she wouldn't be able to retaliate,' Le Froy said.

Jaimin and Prakesh's Room

———◆———

The servants' lodge was the least grand but most practical of the three on the Moonlight Plateau. It was built in traditional style, with a gap of about a foot between the top of the walls and the roof, so that there was a constant flow of air. The rain that had now started coming down again was shunted off by the attap roof that sloped over and beyond it for three feet, providing a sheltered walkway and storage area around the outside of the building.

The door was open to the room that Jaimin and Prakesh were sharing, just as Prakesh had said it would be. It was a single room with two narrow beds set against the walls at right angles to each other. In the other corner, there was a table with a cloth mat folded under it. Prakesh had clearly preferred to eat sitting on the floor.

I saw he had been using the space under one of the beds as a makeshift cupboard, and had crammed everything into a travel box.

I started shaking and folding some of his clothes to put them away as I chose something for him to change into that day. The rest I arranged into neat stacks and put away on top of some notebooks I had stuffed under the bottom lining of the box. It had come loose when I turned it upside down to shake out the dust.

I remembered when Prakesh started recording his tasks in notebooks like Le Froy did. I was glad he was keeping it up. When this was over, I would find a couple of nice notebooks to give him for Christmas. You can never have too many.

'What are you doing here?' It was Jaimin, looking hostile. 'How dare you touch my box?'

'I'm sorry!' I was startled. 'I thought it was Prakesh's. I came to get some clothes for him. He said I could take them from here. I wanted to collect the clothes he's wearing to wash. But...' I looked at the clothes I was holding '... these are Prakesh's clothes, aren't they? And those notebooks at the bottom of the box are his.'

'We share the box,' Jaimin said. 'If Prakesh wanted clothes he would have asked me. What are you really doing here?'

'What do you think I'm doing here? I brought Le Froy a change of clothes and asked Prakesh if I could do the same for him. He told me where to come and get them. I didn't know you two shared a box, but all I did was take these out for him,' I held up the shirt, shorts and underpants I'd chosen, 'as he asked me to, folded the rest and put them back. Why are you so angry?'

Actually I sensed Jaimin was acting angry because he wasn't sure how to react to finding a woman in his room. I suspected he believed I'd been flirting with Prakesh, even though I was married to Le Froy, and wasn't sure if I had been nice to him because I was trying to win him over too.

It didn't bother me. In fact I understood how Jaimin felt because I'd felt like that about some of the women Prakesh had fallen in love with and who had used him. Jaimin was just trying to be a good friend to him. I didn't want us to be at loggerheads. 'I only want to help Prakesh,' I said. 'I'm not trying to make trouble for him in any way. I know he had to leave the police force because of something that happened at his previous post, something about assaulting an English woman. If I could clear that up I would, because I know Prakesh and he would never ever—'

'Mrs Colwin,' Jaimin said. 'Her husband is a bully. He used to beat her. Her servants brought her to the police station. Mrs Colwin told us she wanted to buy a ticket for passage back to England. At the time Captain Prakesh was still running the police station. He told her she should get in touch with the local administrator who would be able to help her arrange passage back. But her husband found out. He came to the station to fetch her and take her home. She didn't want to go and he struck her in the face. That was when Captain Prakesh hit him.'

'In other words, she was leaving her husband,' I said, 'and went to the police for help. Prakesh was protecting her as a police officer. Why was he dismissed, then?'

'Major Colwin filed charges against Captain Prakesh for molesting his wife and assaulting him.'

He didn't have to say more. I knew how the 'justice' system worked.

'Major and Mrs Colwin are still living in Ipoh?' I wondered if some warped viciousness could have provoked Major Colwin to make trouble for Prakesh.

'No. Major Colwin beat up his servants. One died. After that the local administration posted them back home.'

'Was he charged with the death?'

'Accidental death.'

'So Prakesh was blamed and sacked for stopping a man hitting his wife, a man who later killed one of his servants?'

'We also resigned. Me and Henry. We were both sergeants under Captain Prakesh there. Then Captain Henry came and said he'd got a post to run security for the Emerald Estate plantation just after the murders happened, and the new owners were scared. Captain Henry said he would be in charge and offered to hire Prakesh and me. It seemed like a good idea.'

'They set up a police post just for the rubber plantation?'

'It's not a regular police post. It's a private security post, set up for the planters. I don't think they were really scared of murderers. They just wanted us to control their workers without having to pay for their own security.'

'After the previous planters and their families were murdered, I can understand they would be scared,' I said.

Jaimin nodded. 'That was terrible. Some people must have thought that if the Walkers were gone, they'd get their plantation lands back, but that didn't happen.'

'Sometimes people with good intentions make mistakes,' I said. 'Are you happy for me to take Prakesh's clothes to him?'

I'd listened to his story, and Jaimin seemed less suspicious of me. 'Yes. Why not?' he said.

We found Daffy lurking in front of the security post again. It was as if the inmates were animals on display at a travelling carnival in full view from the outside. They were even allowed to use the servants' outhouse behind the security lodge, just not at the same time.

Captain Henry's pendulum seemed to swing between 'highly suspicious' and 'just doing my job'. At that point he was tending towards just doing his job, which seemed to consist in letting Daffy tell him all the things she found inconvenient about having a missing friend with a murdered husband.

I couldn't hear what they were saying, but that meant they couldn't hear us either.

I talked to Le Froy as Jaimin escorted Prakesh to the outhouse to change, though Le Froy had been happy to switch clothes behind an open cupboard door. Prakesh was shy about his body, and my presence, as well as Daffy's just outside, made him uncomfortable.

'Tell him to go ahead,' Captain Henry said, when Jaimin asked permission. 'Where is he going to run away to?'

'Why do you think Elfrida didn't run away from her husband earlier?' I asked.

'Beg pardon?' Le Froy said absently. He made a quick notation before looking up at me.

'If you were a horrible husband and I was sick of you, I would run away from you when we were near the town. Then I could get a car to the coast and buy a ticket on the next liner. I wouldn't come up with you to an isolated resort with no way out and run away after learning that the floods and mudslides were making escape impossible.'

Le Froy lowered the eyebrows he'd raised at 'horrible husband'. 'She might have acted on impulse rather than after rational thought,' he said. 'Or having to come up here was the straw that broke the camel's back.'

'Then why would she wait until she got up here?' I asked. 'Once she knew Boss Max was planning this trip, she should just have run for it.'

'Maybe she didn't have enough advance warning.'

'She did.'

Quickly, while Prakesh and Jaimin were absent, I told him what Viktor had said about Elfrida getting along well with the aunties – meaning she'd led Prakesh on, making him believe she was afraid of them and that it was his fault Boss Max had included them on the Camerons trip.

'She was hiding something,' I said. 'Everybody knew she was unhappy. She stole the emeralds from her husband's safe. She manipulated Prakesh into getting the *makciks* on this trip with her. Then one day she just disappeared. Doesn't it make sense that she had a plan and executed it?

'Or she made several disconnected attempts to get away that didn't come together. And one fine day, being locked up in that prison room was too much for her. She snapped and walked off into the jungle. That's probably the best we can hope for.'

I could tell he didn't like the idea. Even if Elfrida had just walked away from her husband, what would a woman like her do alone in the jungle? How long could she survive?

'What's the alternative?'

'Her husband finally pushed her too hard. She wouldn't or couldn't tell him where those bloody emeralds are and he threw her body off the road into the ravine. If she's ever found, he could go with the she-just-ran-off story.'

'Then why is Boss Max dead too?'

Le Froy cleared his throat. 'Guilt creates its own ghosts. Maybe he killed himself. Set it up to look like a murder. Don't your mystery stories have cases like that? Fixing the *kris* then falling forward onto it . . .' Le Froy leaned forward onto his pen '. . . and stabbing himself through the heart?'

I took the pen away from him. It wasn't sharp, like a *kris*, but this was no time to add an accidental stabbing to the mix. 'Even if he managed to pull off a self-stabbing, he couldn't have leaned back in his chair afterwards and looked all relaxed, could he?' I remembered how – apart from the blood coming out of his chest – Boss Max had looked deeply asleep when we found him.

Exactly as we would have looked, if someone had come in and stabbed us in our sleep the night the aunties' tea had knocked us all out.

There was something I needed to think about, but not there. Jaimin and Prakesh had come back in and Viktor was shouting at Captain Henry, telling him that if he didn't go down to the town for charcoal and paraffin we wouldn't be getting anything but raw tapioca and cold mushrooms for dinner.

'Come to the garage next to the storeroom,' Jaimin said, as he trudged past me, not looking at me.

I was torn, not wanting to leave till I knew whether or not Viktor had managed to talk Captain Henry into giving him the keys to the van. But Captain Henry turned and saw me watching the exchange.

'No,' I heard Captain Henry say loudly. He might have been answering Viktor but he was talking at me. 'No one's leaving this place, you hear me? Especially not Mrs China Wife. I've had enough of women running off and leaving their menfolk.'

I continued walking away, around the building and out of sight . . .

'Get in here!' Jaimin hissed at me. 'Hurry up! Why did you take so long?'

I hadn't known there was any hurry. 'What—'

'Shut up and get in! Quickly!'

I climbed into the sack on the trolley. Was this how people got kidnapped? By willingly and stupidly climbing into sacks just because they're told to? Why didn't I just ask Jaimin what on earth—

But then I heard Viktor. He was talking loudly about fools who wanted to put you in prison just for driving to collect charcoal and tinned milk and Spam. I stayed put and kept quiet.

All the more so when I heard Captain Henry saying he had to check the van before he handed over the keys.

'Go to town yourself, then!' Viktor said.

There was a sudden heft and I was suspended across Viktor's back. He'd picked up the sack I was in and slung me over his shoulder as if I weighed nothing.

'Go ahead,' Captain Henry said. 'But you're going alone. I need Jaimin here.'

'With all these empty tins to return and the paraffin tins to fill?' The metal tins typically held four gallons each.

'What kind of milksop can't handle that?'

Viktor growled and I was dumped (gently) in the back of the van. I tried to spread out as though I were a heap of metal cans, but no one seemed to be paying attention to the sack in the back.

Terry Cook had turned up and seemed inclined to go for a ride to the shop. 'Daffy's off trying to get Le Froy's China doll to spill on him,' I heard, to my alarm. 'I may as well go for a drive to town.'

'I could use the help,' Viktor said. 'If we have to dig the van out of mud you'll be more useful than Jaimin.'

Terry changed his mind. I heard Captain Henry telling Jaimin to make sure I was in the lodge and stayed there. 'Don't just assume she's in the room. Get your eyes on her and make sure.'

Jaimin wasn't going into town with us, then.

I felt the rumble of the engine vibrate through the van and then we were off. I couldn't help wondering if this was how Elfrida was taken. And if the same thing was going to happen to me.

The Final Phone Call

———————

That was probably the worst – but also the best – drive I'd ever been on.

The suspension on the van wasn't great, but it was moving in the direction I wanted to go and any discomfort was worth putting up with.

I appreciated Viktor and Jaimin getting me into the back of the van, even if I didn't think the sack had been necessary. Still, I'd thank them if I got to the telephone. That was the only thing I needed to focus on at the moment. I got out of the sack, but kept it close to me in case Captain Henry raced down to stop us and demand to check the back. There's nothing wrong with being too careful if a crazy ex-police captain is out to get you.

All went well till the van stopped and Viktor pulled open the back doors to let in a blast of sunlight. I saw he'd stopped in front of the little shop that also served as the resort centre.

'Thanks,' I said, and headed inside.

I called the number in Le Froy's notebook and Harry picked up immediately. 'Su Lin? Is Le Froy all right?'

'For now, yes. Listen. He told me to tell you—' I stopped. I didn't want Harry to come and pick me up. I wanted him to help me decide how to get Le Froy out of the idiotic Captain Henry's stupid clutches.

'He needs you to send back-up. It's to do with the Walker murders as well as Max Moreno's. Can you reach Brandon Sands and tell him what's happened?'

'Consider it done. Where is Le Froy? Why couldn't he call himself?'

'It's crazy, but Captain Henry suspects Le Froy had something to do with Max Moreno's murder because he saw Le Froy holding my *kris* dagger. He said it was like the murder weapon and he had to lock him up. I don't think he believes it. He's just trying to cover himself in case Terry Cook or that wife of his complains he didn't do his job protecting them.'

'Terry Cook? I thought he and his wife left for Indonesia? They'd bought passage and everything.'

'No. They're here. They were Boss Max's partners in the Emerald Estate deal, but I don't think they'll carry on without him. They don't like the weather here.'

'Su, listen. Terry Cook is a crook. He and his wife were carrying out frauds all over England before and during the war, collecting for all these war bonds and running charity sales. Only, of course, now with the war over, people expected to see what they had been putting away . . . and the Cooks disappeared. They were Tommy and Daffodil Crown when they were in London. They would have got away with it, too, except they tried to set up a fraud here and someone found their travel documents had been forged. I thought they'd left already.'

'You can tell Brandon Sands they're up here too. But, really, a con-man and his wife aren't important at the moment. You've got to get hold of the real police and tell them to come and rescue Le Froy from Captain Henry.'

'Hold on. It's possible that Max found out about the Cooks' carryings-on and blackmailed them into working with him. They must have made off with a bundle of money. If he forced them to invest in his plantation and they couldn't say no, they would have had every reason to kill him.'

'True,' I said. 'But the same argument against that applies as it does against Elfrida running away from Boss Max on her own. Why did the Cooks come up to the Cameron Highlands with Boss Max? Why not just kill him on the plantation and save themselves the trip up? Wouldn't it be easier to get away with murder if there's some way of disappearing after you've done it?'

'Boss Max probably got them to see it as an investment. All good and profitable if not quite legal. They couldn't say no but they might get rich working with him. In that case, they would stick with it until they were sure it wouldn't pay off.'

'Or until Elfrida ran off with the emeralds that were part of the plan,' I said. If so, Elfrida had triggered her husband's murder.

'Listen, Su. I told Le Froy that the *kris* daggers used in the Walker murders were the ones, not just the same kind, that had been confiscated from the Japanese collection. Now there's more and more evidence that Max Moreno was behind the Walker murders. I've already reported it, but the police here don't pay much attention to what people like my clients say. They all mention that an *ang moh* man was hiring workers for a temporary job. And that at least two men who went to discuss it with him were among the five shot dead after trying to escape from the police.'

'An *ang moh* man doesn't necessarily mean it was Boss Max,' I said. 'It might have been Terry Cook. And if it was, he could have got someone to kill Boss Max when he couldn't produce the emeralds.'

It might also have been Viktor, but I didn't want to think about that. After all, I needed him to drive me back up to the Moonlight Plateau. Regardless of what Le Froy said, I wasn't going to hide behind a shop counter while Terry Cook hired thugs to finish off him and Prakesh.

'Max Moreno was blackmailing a lot of people, including the other planters,' Harry said. 'It was just his way of doing things. He didn't see himself as a blackmailer, just as somebody who was smart. And knew how to work the local conditions. And he always said that if you want to run a good ship, you need something to keep your people in order. He made a point of having something on everyone he worked with. Even Prakesh's colleagues. Captain Henry was involved in smuggling, and there's talk that he owed a lot of people money, so Boss Max might have put pressure on him for that. He might even have forced him to get the *kris* daggers out of the lock-up.'

'Did you tell Le Froy that?'

'Hah, it was Le Froy who suggested it and told me to look into it.'

Why hadn't Le Froy said anything to me about that? The man kept things to himself, even when I was with him. He wasn't trying to shut me out: rather, he had to give his thoughts time to ripen or, like mangoes picked too soon, they wouldn't have the taste of tree-ripened fruit. But sometimes that meant someone else pilfered your fruit before you had time to pluck it.

'I think Boss Max meant to use you against Le Froy,' Harry said.

'What? Say that again?'

'Nothing,' Harry said. 'I didn't mean it. Look, Su, you're in Resort Central where Le Froy said he was phoning from, right? Is anyone with you? Never mind. I think you should stay where you are till I get someone up there to collect you. I'll even come myself if I can't get anyone else, but promise me you'll stay there. I'm sure Le Froy would agree with me.'

Le Froy and he thought along the same lines, clearly. But I didn't.

'I have to go!' I shouted. 'My lift's leaving. Send help, okay?' I put down the receiver even though my coins hadn't run out.

Viktor didn't look surprised when he saw me come out of the shop. He was loading cans of paraffin. 'Not good for you to sit in the back with this,' he said. 'You'll ride in the front with me?'

'Of course,' I said. After all, why would someone who was set against me leaving have anything against me coming back? I climbed into the front seat. It wasn't a luxury ride but better than a sack in the back.

'Did you get hold of who you wanted to talk to on the telephone?' Viktor asked. 'Are you sure you want to go back up?'

'Was Boss Max blackmailing you to make you work with him?' I asked. 'What was he blackmailing you with?' If it was anything less serious than murder I might have a chance of talking him into helping me to keep Le Froy and Prakesh alive until Harry's reinforcements came.

'In my previous life I did all manner of disreputable things. But that old self is dead,' Viktor said. 'I am continuing here for the same reason as you are.'

'Really?' I felt doubtful.

'Because the life of someone I value more than my own is at stake.'

Maybe he got it.

Daffy Accuses Jaimin

I was a little nervous when we rounded the final turn after crossing the bridge over the gully. But there was enough going on that the arrival of the little van was barely noticed.

I'd wondered whether I ought to hide in the back again for the return trip, but Viktor dismissed the suggestion. 'What's Captain Henry going to do if he sees you coming back? He might as well learn now that even if women are always leaving their men some of them come back.'

The sliding bars to the security post were open. Daffy and Captain Henry were inside with Le Froy, Prakesh and Jaimin. It was a little crowded in there, but not so crowded that Daffy had to be pressed in as close to Le Froy as she was. Was she trying to seduce my husband again? This time in broad daylight in front of an audience?

I heard her as I climbed down from the van and storm-limped across.

'Frida was sick of Max and had been planning to leave him for some time,' Daffy was saying. 'I'm sure she's far away by now. Women have ways of persuading men to help them.' She smiled at Le Froy. 'You know what it's like, don't you? I'm sure there are loads of women after you.' She probably thought she was being seductive, leaning against him like that.

'Hello, Daffy,' I said.

'White women, I mean.' She smiled at me, challenging me to be jealous or intimidated. 'You can have your fun. I know these local girls will let you do anything to them for a bit of money, but you have to think long-term. You'd be much better off with a wife who fits in with your kind, don't you think?'

Was it wrong that I suddenly wanted to laugh? I should have been furious, but Daffy was being ridiculous. Had her seduction methods ever worked?

But maybe I wasn't angry because I could see Le Froy's reaction. He didn't have to say anything: the soft, sticky flab of her freckled arm was making him hot and uncomfortable.

'Women are always going after poor Le Froy,' I said brightly. 'Especially the older ones – married or not it doesn't make a difference. They can be totally shameless, the way they throw themselves at him.'

Daffy's smile wavered a little. 'You can't blame me for pointing out—'

'Oh, I don't blame you at all, Daffy. You're far from the worst.' I turned to Le Froy. 'Remember Mrs Lawrence? How she thought she was madly in love with you?'

'Mrs Lawrence.' Le Froy shook his head in mock-horror and used it as an excuse to move away from Daffy.

'I don't know any Mrs Lawrence,' Daffy said. She turned to reach for Le Froy again, 'Anyway, as I was saying, this man is just too—'

Le Froy moved to my side and gave me a quick hug, 'Phone?'

I nodded. He squeezed my shoulder, a gesture that managed to say 'Glad you're here,' but also 'You shouldn't have come back.'

I smiled at Daffy. 'Mrs Lawrence is a white woman – English like you. About your height but a lot thinner. Also like you, she's about fifteen years older than Le Froy. She's been pursuing him rather aggressively for some time now.'

'Pursuing?' Daffy said.

'Aggressively.' I nodded. 'At first we thought she wanted him for one of her three daughters or her widowed sister, but she made it quite clear she was trying to get him for herself. Even though her husband was around and she was living on his money while she was telling Le Froy he needed a woman, like her, by his side, someone respectable people, like her, would accept.'

'It's just a little fling,' Daffy said. 'A little flirtation. So what? You've no right to judge me.'

'I'm not judging,' I said. Though I was. But who was she to judge me for judging?

'And I'm not fifteen years older than he is. I don't know how you can even say something like that.'

At least she'd moved away from Le Froy.

'She's just trying to make Captain Henry jealous,' Prakesh whispered, more loudly than he usually spoke. 'Don't worry, she's not really after Le Froy.'

Daffy glared at him, then glanced at Captain Henry, who shrugged. 'We're just friends,' she said, 'and he comes to talk to me when I'm bored. Especially when Max was sending Terry all over the place to chase after forms they needed to apply for provisional licences. I even suspected Max was working something behind Terry's back and I needed Captain Henry to look into it for me. You know that man of mine's a few sandwiches short of a picnic. So I got to know Captain Henry a bit better, and things just happened. We're really close – but just friends.'

'This was before you all moved into the Emerald Estate?' Le Froy asked. Daffy would probably have jumped on me if I'd asked, but Le Froy got away with it. Maybe she was just so keen to get him talking to her that she would have answered any question he put to her.

Captain Henry looked interested too. Maybe she'd succeeded in making him a little jealous.

'Oh, yes,' Daffy said. 'At that time they were supposedly talking about taking over some plantation in East Malaya. But since the admin people already had Terry's details and references on record when the Walkers were killed, they didn't need to hold the auction. All their paperwork was ready. They couldn't have timed it better. Lucky break, that.'

It was a very lucky break, almost as though Boss Max had anticipated what was going to happen to the Walker family.

'Not with Captain Henry.' Viktor looked shocked. I'd been so focused on getting Le Froy away from Daffy I'd not registered him. 'You,' he said to Daffy, 'and Captain Henry?'

'Why are you so shocked? It's not as though you would ever be faithful to any one woman,' Daffy snapped. 'Hurts your feelings, doesn't it, when someone gives you a taste of your own medicine?'

So Viktor had propositioned Daffy, probably much as he'd propositioned me, and had been accepted.

'Oh, no,' Viktor said. 'My feelings are not hurt. I'm just surprised. But now I see why you had that smell.'

'I don't smell of anything!' Daffy howled at him. 'I am a white woman, you ignorant lout. I'm not like those animals you pick up everywhere. And you can't even see the difference.'

Daffy was more offended by Viktor saying she smelt than my calling her old. I stored that up as a nugget of interesting information in case I ever needed to provoke a woman quickly.

'I think she's still likes you,' I said to Viktor.

'I don't like her.' Viktor was grinning. He caught my eye and winked, as though I'd finally got the joke.

Le Froy and I had been right, then. 'You've been having an affair with Captain Henry,' I said.

'Don't talk nonsense,' Daffy said.

'Yes,' Viktor said, at the same time. 'Yes! It was Elfrida's perfume but you took it from her. You wanted to smell like her.' He turned to Captain Henry and sniffed. 'Citrus, moss and musk. And jasmine – same perfume but not as strong – mixed with the smell of her sweat.' He nodded towards Daffy.

'Oh, you horrible, horrible men!' Daffy howled. 'I know you fell hook, line and sinker for Frigid Friddy! All you stupid men did. She was playing you fools all along. The way you looked at her with your tongues hanging out, thinking, Poor thing, she's so pretty, so sweet and clever. Well, she wasn't! I showed her who was smart!'

'Daffy – Mrs Cook–' Captain Henry tried to interrupt, but the brakes had failed on the Daffy steam engine and she rattled on.

'When I started being friendly with Max, just to make sure he didn't cheat my Terry on their partnership, he bought me a few nice things. Frida came and told me she'd found out that her husband was doing "a terrible thing" and she was going to run away from him. It was such a joke! Foolish Frida suspected her man was having an affair so she ran to the woman he was carrying on with. Of course I told Max what she'd said. That was when he got all controlling and started locking her in and taking away her shoes. I got her that time!'

'You might have got her killed,' I said.

Slowly, Daffy realised everyone was staring at her. Captain Henry was shaking his head, but it was Viktor she turned to. His mouth was open. When he closed it, his eyes were hard.

'Max killed his wife after a fight, then tried to escape downhill. Body never found,' Captain Henry said. 'It could have been so simple. Everybody goes home happy. Why did you have to come along and stir up all this trouble? What am I going to do with you all?'

Daffy looked at him, then at Le Froy. Then, 'He assaulted me,' she said suddenly.

'No, I never!' Prakesh said automatically.

'Not you – him!' Daffy pointed at Jaimin.

Jaimin stared, mouth open. Daffy screamed, as she launched herself at him, 'Help! Shoot him! Get him off me! Shoot him!' It looked to me as though *she* was attacking *him*.

Captain Henry already had his gun raised and pointed at Jaimin. 'Get away from her!'

'You know the boy is harmless,' Le Froy said. 'The woman's mad!'

'I have to listen to all accusations.' Captain Henry didn't lower the gun.

'Who do you think they'll believe? A white woman or that little brown worm?' Daffy said. 'Listen, Mr Holier Than Thou, I'll have this boy lynched if you don't find the emeralds and hand them over to us. Max thought you could find them. I think that, with enough pressure, you can. I just want to get out of here. That's what we all want, isn't it? So do something about it. Get out there and find them. The boy stays in here until you hand them over. Simple as that.'

Jaimin was trying to prise Daffy's fingernails off his arm. 'Prakesh! Inspector Le Froy, I didn't do anything!'

'After all, Jaimin was from one of the dispossessed families. He could have been in with them all along. You find the emeralds like she says, Le Froy,' Captain Henry ordered. I didn't like how tightly he was gripping his pistol, or his focus on Jaimin. 'You shouldn't have come up here interfering, but since you're here you might as well make yourself useful.'

'His Indian friend can help him find them,' Daffy said. 'They won't dare do anything as long as you have the China girl and the brown boy locked up.'

'What's happening?' Terry Cook appeared and rushed over to his wife.

'This boy molested your wife.' Captain Henry indicated Jaimin with the barrel of his gun.

'How dare you touch my wife? I'll kill you, boy!' Terry said. He turned on Jaimin – it was either foolish or brave to step in front of a man pointing an armed weapon but he did. I hoped there was enough British conditioning in Captain Henry not to shoot an unarmed man in the back.

'Put that down before you hurt someone!' Le Froy barked, as Captain Henry rushed forward to pull Terry off Jaimin. For a moment, I thought Captain Henry was going to shoot him. He looked mad enough. But he lowered his gun.

'He went crazy! He attacked me!' Daffy bleated. 'He raped me. Captain Henry, you have to make sure he doesn't attack anyone else!'

'Yah,' Captain Henry said. It seemed to take him a while to process everything Daffy was saying. You could almost see him working through her points one by one.

'I'm not his first victim, you know. He attacked Elfrida too. She told me. He used to go to her house when Max was on the plantation and he would take advantage of her. And – and she was going to have a baby. She couldn't bear the thought of it and wanted to go into the jungle to kill herself. Max had to lock her up to keep her safe. But they got her away and killed her. Those two!' She pointed at Prakesh and Jaimin. 'They were abusing all the white women here. We were living in terror. Please, Captain, you have to do whatever you can to make sure they never hurt another.'

'So you want me to shoot them?' Captain Henry asked.

Daffy looked so exasperated I thought she was about to smack him, 'I want you to do your duty, man,' she said. 'How can I sleep at night knowing that monsters like them are loose? I want you to lock them up in here and free Le Froy to find whatever evidence he can that will prove them innocent before we turn them in to the authorities.'

'No,' Terry said. 'Forget your authorities. If that bastard raped Elfrida we're stringing him up right now.'

He started for Jaimin but I pushed Le Froy aside and got there first, 'Daffy's lying. Jaimin never raped anyone. She's a girl!'

I stopped and looked at Jaimin. I was relieved to see a small nod.

'You were living as a boy during the Japanese time, weren't you?' I said. A lot of girls had been disguised as boys to escape violation by Japanese soldiers. 'I'm guessing you used your brother's corporal qualifications to get work when the police post was set up after the Japanese surrender.'

'My brother was killed,' Jaimin said. 'I had no choice. Before the war I had three older brothers, but they're all gone now. But I still have two sisters-in-law, their children, my mother and aunts and I am trying to look after all of them.'

Everyone was shocked, Daffy, Captain Henry ... but I could see they believed me once they had looked properly at Jaimin. Only Prakesh couldn't look at her.

Sometimes Prakesh was so useless. He was just looking at Jaimin as though he'd never seen her before. Which was true, in a way.

'How did you know?' Jaimin said.

'You smell like a girl.'

Viktor would know what I meant, even if no one else did.

Jaimin and Prakesh Romance?

———◆———

The drawback, of course, was that if Jaimin came from one of the families dispossessed by Boss Max's grand plantation, she had one of the strongest motives for wanting to murder him.

I didn't believe that, and I don't think any of the others did, but she would have been an ideal scapegoat for Captain Henry if we didn't manage to sort things out.

As the rain started coming down again, Captain Henry locked us in while he and the Cooks went back to their lodge to discuss what they would do next.

Prakesh was still resolutely not looking at Jaimin.

'I thought you two were such good friends,' I said.

Prakesh shrugged. 'I've never talked to anybody like I talk to you until . . .' He tilted his head at Jaimin without looking at her.

Jaimin smiled awkwardly, but didn't turn away. I could tell how difficult she found this rejection. 'You helped me so

287

much, Prakesh,' she said. 'I didn't know how to do anything
when I first came to the police post and you were so patient
with me. I wouldn't have made it this far without you. I owe you
so much.'

'Please, Prakesh,' I said.

'I can never look at him – her – again,' Prakesh said.

Is it possible to be a good, smart person at the same time
as a total idiot? Yes, it is, because that was how my friend
Prakesh Pillay was behaving. He had the best heart in the world
and would do anything for his friends but was totally useless
once he fell in love with someone – which he did fairly
regularly, usually with people he barely knew.

This was different, of course. He knew Jaimin. He'd worked
with, trusted and been close to Jaimin. I'd noticed how much
they cared about each other and it had bothered me, especially
as they had seemed blissfully ignorant of the connection
between them.

At least it wasn't a case of one leading the other on.

'Jaimin was only doing what she had to to survive,' I said.
'She didn't set out to deceive you. You can't hold that against her.'

Jaimin nodded, but said nothing. Prakesh, refusing to look
in her direction, wouldn't have seen it. I felt sorry for
matchmakers who had to deal with this kind of thing all the time
– people who were clearly perfect for each other but too stubborn
to see it. 'You must have known at some level. How could you
not?' I asked. 'You were sharing a room, for goodness' sake.'

'Only while we were up here in the Camerons. And one of
us was always on duty in the security area so we were never in

the room together. Not at night – I mean, not for sleeping. I don't know what I mean.'

Prakesh started to crawl back into the cage but I grabbed his arm and stopped him.

'Let me go.'

'Prakesh, stop. If you don't turn around and talk to her now, I swear I'll never talk to you again. You'll lose two of the people who love you most in the world. Is that what you want?'

I knew I was being unfair, but it was for his own good. I also knew I was lying, but – same excuse.

Slowly I let go of him. He didn't bolt. A good sign, I thought.

'You can be angry she deceived you,' I said. 'But she had no choice.'

'I'm so sorry,' Jaimin said. 'I never wanted to hurt you in any way.'

'I'm not angry with you,' Prakesh said, to the far wall.

'What is it, then?' I asked.

'I–' He shook his head. 'I undressed. In front of her. She saw – everything.'

There was a bark of laughter from across the room where Le Froy was sitting. He quashed it, then it burst out again. I couldn't help it. I had to laugh too. After the briefest struggle, Jaimin also started to laugh. Prakesh spun around, looking like he couldn't decide whether to be furious or horrified.

'Why are you – how could you–?'

Jaimin closed the distance between them before he finished speaking. She put her arms around him and rested her face against his shoulder. Prakesh's eyes met mine over the top of her head as his arms moved around her. Tears were running down his face, but we were both smiling.

'Of course you found it hard to look at her,' I said. 'Because you're in love with her, aren't you?'

'Hey, hey, hey,' Prakesh said, 'you can't go around saying things like that.'

'Yes,' Jaimin said. 'Yes. I love you. For so long I couldn't say anything. You were so good to me. I didn't want to spoil it all by telling you I had lied to you. Before Captain Henry was brought in to replace you, I thought of telling you the truth many times, but we were getting along so well as colleagues, I was afraid of spoiling it.'

I knew exactly what she meant.

'Close your mouth, Prakesh.' Le Froy had stopped laughing, but he was smiling.

'Tell me I'm not dreaming this,' Prakesh said. Despite all he'd been through lately, and despite all the years I'd known him, I had never seen Prakesh Pillay look so happy.

Maybe if I didn't make it as a reporter I could take up matchmaking.

'You can't trust him,' Viktor said, from outside the barred grate. 'Prakesh Pillay assaulted Elfrida.'

'Boss Max made that up,' I said. 'It's their favourite story. Any local man they want to get rid of, they tell a white woman to claim he molested her. The woman can't be questioned because it would upset her too much and the man is found guilty without proof and taken away. We just saw Daffy try it on Jaimin.'

'I have proof Prakesh Pillay assaulted Elfrida. I witnessed it myself,' Viktor said. 'I heard Elfrida cry out. She said, "Go away, leave me alone." Words like that, but the meaning was clear.'

I hadn't expected this from Viktor of all people. 'Why should anyone believe you? You propositioned Elfrida yourself, didn't you? She turned you down and you're just saying this out of jealousy, aren't you?'

'No – it's true he heard that,' Prakesh said. 'But it's not how it sounds. Elfrida didn't scream at me to leave her alone. She wanted me to get away from her bloody *jambu*.'

'Her what?' Viktor asked.

'Rose apples,' Prakesh replied. 'I was only going to throw out the rotten ones she had on the table. They go bad so fast and there's so much more fruit on the tree. Even the *jambu* doves wouldn't eat fruit so decayed. I just wanted to clean up the room a bit. Her husband said he was keeping her in there for her own safety, but he was treating her like a prisoner.'

'The three rotten rose apples on the ledge outside the toilet?' I asked.

Prakesh shrugged, 'I don't know. Two? Three? They were inside her room and already rotten when I saw them. But she went crazy and screamed at me not to touch them, get out, go away, and leave her alone. That must have been what Max heard. I don't blame him for thinking I was attacking her. I thought she'd gone crazy. I was going to leave, but then Boss Max came in – I didn't see you,' he said to Viktor.

'Men don't notice Viktor,' Viktor agreed. 'Not as much as women notice Viktor.'

'Why didn't you just tell Boss Max what happened?' I said. 'Why didn't she?'

'I don't think she knew why Boss Max dragged me out of there. She was already so upset. And I felt guilty.'

'Why guilty?'

'I knew it was partly – maybe mostly – my fault she was having such a hard time up here,' Prakesh said.

'You two weren't really—'

'Of course not! Su! How can you even think—'

I don't know which of us was more horrified. At least we could still follow each other's thoughts.

'Captain Henry is certain Prakesh and Jaimin arranged Boss Max's murder between them,' Viktor said. I couldn't tell if he'd come especially to tell us this or was just making small-talk.

'Why?' Prakesh demanded. 'And if he thinks we killed him, how does he think we did it?'

'He said you must be Indian snake charmers with a flying snake.'

'Crazy!' Prakesh laughed, as I snorted.

'I am just telling you what Captain Henry said.' Viktor didn't seem offended. 'And Captain Henry is the authority.'

There are flying snakes around here, like twin-barred gliders with red 'saddles' on their backs. While their venom might paralyse a bird or rodent, they would never be able to kill a man – far less stick a *kris* into him.

But something else bugged me. 'Is Captain Henry still trying to blame all this on Prakesh?'

Viktor smiled. 'I did not say that,' he said. 'He needs a suspect, to show he is doing his job well, so that they don't send more people to investigate what happened. He doesn't want outsiders upsetting how things are run here. It has to be Prakesh because Jaimin is too young and the rest of the staff are female.'

The two females present made sounds suggesting they might have changed Captain Henry's mind if he had been present.

'Captain Henry intends to say Prakesh Pillay was working with the Indian workers who attacked the Walker family. He stole the *kris* daggers for them from the police storage area. Boss Max found out, so Prakesh killed him to shut him up. When Captain Henry heard that, Prakesh tried to kill him too, but Captain Henry shot him first.'

'No!' I said.

'Yes. That's what I was told,' Viktor said.

'But if they let Captain Henry get away with this kind of behaviour, he'll just go on doing it,' I said. 'Come on, Prakesh. You're always saying that if we don't do something to change things, nothing will ever change. We've got to do something!'

'Yes,' Prakesh said. 'I know I used to say that. Look, in Singapore we complained about how badly people treated us. We complained about the taxes, about everything. We didn't realise how good we had it. In Singapore, the *ang mohs* think they are superior but they at least pretend to follow the laws they set up. Here they don't see themselves as superior human beings. They think they are gods.'

He was sitting with his arm around Jaimin. I worried that requited love had got into his brain and made it go soft.

'I think Elfrida's dead,' Prakesh said. 'I think she tried to run away from Boss Max and he caught her and killed her. Look at the jungle around here. There are tigers, wild boar, great apes . . . Nobody will ever find her body.'

'I don't think so,' I said. 'At least I don't think Boss Max killed her.'

'You don't think he was capable of doing such a thing?'

'I think he would have behaved differently if he'd done it.' I thought back to what I had seen of Boss Max's behaviour. 'When we arrived, he was really worried.'

'Of course he was worried,' Prakash said. 'He was worried people would find out what he'd done to her.'

'More than that,' I said. 'The man was in a panic, frantic for information. You see that in desperate animals on the verge of starvation. They will try to eat anything in the hope that something will work. That was how Boss Max had been when he was searching for Elfrida.'

'She was nice,' Prakesh said.

'Very nice,' Viktor agreed, from outside the barred gate.

'Unless you tried to touch her rose apples,' Prakesh said.

'Can you get Captain Henry to let me out of here?' I asked Viktor. 'Tell him I need to use the WC or something.'

Viktor headed off to look for Captain Henry.

'What are you up to?' Le Froy asked.

'Just an idea,' I said. 'I'm not sure, but there's just a chance Elfrida told Prakesh where she hid the emeralds.'

Fire Emeralds

◆

The three rotting rose apples were on the cement block by the side of the *jamban* where I'd last seen them. Rose apples deteriorate very fast. By now I'd expect the fruit I'd seen earlier to have deteriorated into a mushy puddle that even the ants wouldn't consider worth collecting. Instead the three rotting rose apples looked like . . . three rotting rose apples.

I saw now they hadn't been tossed there and forgotten. Rather, they'd been carefully arranged in a row, like offerings at a shrine. When I picked one up, it was light but solid, like a clay model. I realised its ugly brown splotches didn't cover the soft rottenness of decay but had been painted on as a deliberate decoy, like the ragged robes worn by Buddhas.

I don't think of myself as Buddhist but I bowed before removing them. They had been placed there reverently and there was no point in offending any lurking spirits, whether

Buddhist, Taoist or left by an unhappy wife trying to escape her marriage.

Elfrida had made these beautifully modelled rose apples with Ipoh clay, and painted them, just as she'd painted the clay bowls and models she'd made. And, like all art, they had captured their subject at a particular moment. Anything truly alive was constantly moving towards death.

Without the fragrance of fruit, the clay models didn't attract birds and bugs, and because they looked like samples of the rotting fruit scattered all around the compound, they didn't attract the attention of people either.

It was brilliant. So many people had searched Elfrida and her things in her rooms. The bowls and pots in Elfrida's room hadn't been smashed in anger or from spite: someone had guessed Elfrida would try to hide her precious stones in her clay models. They had been right, but they had only searched – and destroyed – her beautiful little bowls and models. They would have seen the rotting fruit, but dismissed it, as I had.

It just shows that when you don't want to attract the wrong kind of attention, it can pay to look shabby.

'Look,' I said. I passed the three little rose apples to Le Froy through the bars of the sliding gate.

'What?' Le Froy's eyes widened in surprise as he took the rose apples from me and felt their weight and texture. 'Elfrida made these?'

'I think so. Remember all the bowls and models of birds she made?'

We had seen only the crushed remnants. Boss Max or one of the other searchers had obviously suspected her of concealing the gemstones in her work, but they'd underestimated her ingenuity.

The three little 'rose apples' Le Froy was holding had been crafted with the soft red clay found so abundantly on the Ipoh riverbanks. Elfrida had deliberately moulded the pear-shaped rose apples unevenly and painted brown and black patches over pink to simulate the look of rotting fruit. A touch was enough to reveal them as counterfeit. But no one had bothered to pay attention to a pile of decaying fruit.

Le Froy dug into one with a fingernail. 'There's definitely something hard in here,' He looked around, but Captain Henry had not left them with anything that could have been used as a weapon.

Prakesh held out his hand and Le Froy hesitated only a moment before handing them over. Prakesh put one on the cement floor and ground his boot into it, smashing it. He plucked out the largest fragment and handed it to Le Froy. 'Is that an emerald?'

'A trapiche emerald,' Le Froy carefully scraped away the clay to reveal a grimy green stone. 'The rarest emerald. You can see the star-shaped pattern, due to impurities in the emerald's crystal junction. Interesting how some impurities make emeralds more desirable.'

'You can tell that just by looking at it?' I asked.

'I read the brief on the family emeralds Elfrida's father took out of Germany.'

'How much is it worth?' Prakesh asked.

'This?' He hefted it lightly in his palm. 'I would say it's over fifty carats and would be worth much more than a diamond of double its size.'

'And there's two more,' Prakesh said. 'Whew. I may have joined the wrong side.'

'I'll take those,' Captain Henry unlocked the padlock. He was holding his gun and he gestured for me to go inside before taking the emerald and the other two clay rose apples.

Then the framework of sliding metal rods turned the security post into a holding cell.

'Now that Captain Henry has the emeralds he should let you go, right?' Jaimin said.

'He'll probably leave us locked up here and drive off,' Prakesh said. 'But we'll get him.'

Even if Captain Henry took Daffy and Terry Cook with him, sooner or later the aunties or Viktor would find and release us. My main concern was that I wouldn't need the WC too desperately before we got out. Even if no one turned up, the sliding barrier didn't look very sturdy. We could probably break it down and get out without much trouble. But that could wait till Captain Henry and his gun were safely out of the way.

Although I was tired and frustrated at being locked into that uncomfortable space with Elfrida's fate still unknown, I felt the worst was over. I'd told the others Harry Palin was rounding up help and the troops would be arriving soon. All we could do now was wait.

Even if we hadn't worked out who had murdered the Walkers or Boss Max, we would soon be leaving the Highlands for home and the south. And I was married to Thomas Le Froy. I was glad we were married.

I smiled at Le Froy, but he and and Prakesh were poring over a record book, muttering to each other, and he didn't notice.

'How do you know,' Jaimin said softly, 'whether you are just good at working with somebody or if you are actually friends?' She looked at Prakesh and Le Froy. Both men were right there but far away.

'I've wondered that too,' I said, 'often, and for a very long time.'

'So how do you tell? What if everything he's feeling now is just from shock and excitement? And when we're not working together, what if he doesn't even want to be friends?'

'It doesn't have to be either friendship or love,' I said. 'If you're lucky, it's both.'

I didn't want to discourage a young woman who'd already gone through so much. I was impressed by how she'd stood by Prakesh, even if he hadn't been aware of it. And I knew all about falling in love with someone you work with, only gradually discovering how you feel. Not to mention the dreadful uncertainty over the other person's feelings.

'Sometimes you have to take the risk,' I said. 'True love and true friendship aren't all that different, but men can be stubborn and stupid, so don't say too much too soon.'

I'd been talking more about my experience than hers, but Jaimin nodded. 'What if there's nothing and it was only the work?'

'Then at least you'll know. Believe me, it's always worse never knowing.'

Jaimin nodded.

Prakesh caught the movement. 'What are you two whispering about?'

'Le Froy,' Jaimin said. 'Look at him, he's so *kacak*. How can you trust him around other women?'

Kacak usually described a man so handsome that girls fainted at the sight of him. Jaimin was showing a side of herself she'd hidden while acting as Prakesh's male colleague.

Le Froy snorted, but I saw him smile. Prakesh looked uncomfortable.

'He's the same man as he was when I first saw him,' I said.

'Minus one foot,' Le Froy said.

'He's still the thirty-year-old who came out east to make his fortune so that he could return home to marry the woman he loved. Only she died. And, like Queen Victoria, he resolved to mourn her for the rest of his life. And he mourned her for fifteen years until we got together. I trust him to be as loyal to me.'

Prakesh's eyes widened. He was making a valiant effort to maintain a neutral expression, but was losing the struggle as the thrill of learning stoic Thomas Le Froy's secret danced in his eyes.

'It must have been very difficult for you, sir.' Prakesh's voice was pitched slightly higher than normal.

'This will be written off as a natural disaster. So many of them around right now,' Captain Henry shouted. 'Emergency services are overwhelmed. Nobody will come up here for weeks!'

He was hefting a can and sloshing something into our prison space. It had a pungent, oily smell – paraffin! It had to be the paraffin Viktor had brought up from the shop.

'You got your emeralds!' Le Froy shouted. 'That was the deal! Don't make things worse for yourself!'

'You're not as smart as people think you are,' Captain Henry said. 'You shouldn't believe everything they say.'

I certainly wasn't very smart. I didn't understand what he meant to do until he stepped back, struck a match and threw it. It bounced off one of the bars instead of passing through, but that tiny flare was enough to flame up into a wall of fire in seconds.

The building was made of wood and attap roofing. And, despite the wet weather we had been having, it was burning fast. We could have got out – except that we were still locked in. The rolling bars across the front of the security post remained locked in position and would certainly hold us in for a while . . . or for ever.

Through the flames I could see Captain Henry watching and laughing.

'Viktor!' I shouted. 'Daffy! Help us!'

'Viktor's dead to the world!' Captain Henry shouted back. 'That stupid chump and those two old busybody bitches. Daffy's tea did them in! Again! You'd think they'd have learned something but *noooo*! Hah!'

Daffy's tea? Again? Of course. Just because a woman is loud and stupid doesn't mean she can't also be evil and sly.

'If Viktor, Aunty Rakiah and Aunty Salmah are unconscious in the servants' lodge, the fire will kill them too,' I said. 'And why only them? What did he do with Deaf Aunty?'

'They're going to live longer than we are, most likely!' Le Froy pulled Prakesh back from trying to get through the flames to the bars. 'It's no use. Don't kill yourself before you have to.'

Jaimin held Prakesh away from the worst of the fire and Le Froy left her to it. He helped me towards the back of the room, furthest from the blazing entrance.

'Damn,' Le Froy said. 'I promised Leask I wouldn't try to get out of being godfather to his firstborn. But this time it's really not my fault!'

'Godfather?' I said. 'There's going to be a baby? You didn't say anything. Why didn't you tell me? Why didn't Parshanti tell me? When is it coming?'

'Well, you didn't tell her you were getting married without her, so I think it evens things out.'

'I hadn't expected "till death us do part" to come quite so soon,' I managed to say, before we were all coughing.

'Don't talk.' Le Froy pressed his handkerchief over my mouth and nose. 'Don't inhale more smoke than you have to.'

I wanted to say the same to him, but that would have used precious oxygen, so I would save it for later.

'Shut up!' Prakesh growled. I saw he was holding Jaimin with her face pressed into his chest. 'I love you too, but keep your mouth shut.' They say it's never too late to say the words, but those two were cutting it pretty close.

The thought struck me that if we didn't find a way out of there, no one at home would know what had happened to us. All my family knew was that we had come to Ipoh for Le Froy to follow up on a murder case. My grandmother, uncle and Little Ling would never know what had happened to me.

We experience death only once in a lifetime. I decided I would face the experience rather than panic. Seeming to read my mind, Le Froy took my hands in his. Staying married till death did us part wasn't as difficult as others had made it out to be.

I hoped the aunties were safe, even as I knew it was wishful thinking. This fire would likely move on to the staff lodge behind us, where they were deep in their drugged sleep.

But what did I see through the thick, stinking smoke? Someone pulling another away from the servants' lodge, past the rose apple tree onto the far side of the driveway.

At the moment of death, some relive their past; others see their afterlife. In that moment, I saw who Elfrida was – because I'd just seen where she was.

I had nothing to lose.

'Elfrida!' I shouted. 'Elfrida! Help us! We're in here! Locked in here!'

Elfrida

Through the thick smoke, something like a huge maggot was moving towards us. As it came closer I realised it looked like a worm because a white sheet was clinging to it – a sheet soaked in water against the fire. But it moved past the blazing entrance of the security post and out of sight as part of the front overhang crashed down, making me scream as we were pelted by soot and hot debris.

Le Froy put his arms around me and pressed us against the wooden back wall of the room so I couldn't see anything more. It was purely animal instinct. The flimsy wooden wall against my back would go up in flames too, but might give us a few more seconds. Then I felt a blow shudder through the wall against my shoulder blades. I was startled and tried to jerk away from it. Le Froy pressed me back against the wooden planks even as I fought to move from the spot. He must have thought I was panicking and delirious from smoke.

'Move!' I yelled at him. 'Let me go! Move away!'

Le Froy let me go just in time. A split second after that, the plank that had been just behind my left shoulder splintered and the blade of an axe broke through, sending splinters flying.

I started trying to pull apart the shattered wood, Le Froy and Prakesh joining me now that they understood.

'Move!' the woman outside shouted. Another blow crashed through more of the wall.

There was just enough of a gap for Prakesh to stick his arm through and grab the handle of the axe. He was much stronger and continued attacking the wall from the inside. Even as the gap in the wall grew, though, it let in air that drew the flames towards us faster.

My lungs burned with every shallow breath, even through the wadded fabric of my dress, which I was holding over my face. Decency be damned. I could taste thick, acrid smoke with every dry swallow. I closed my eyes, not just against the smoke but from the haze blurring out the edges of my awareness.

While I could still hear the thuds against splintering wood, they didn't seem to have anything to do with me. I didn't care any more. As my legs buckled, I felt as if the smoke was wrapping me in blessed oblivion and carrying me out...

Only I was actually being carried out, and not to oblivion. I gasped, coughing violently, and found myself under the rose apple tree on the verge of the slope down to the golf course. My head and shoulders were on Le Froy's lap. Next to us I saw Prakesh and Jaimin.

'You shouldn't have risked yourself coming back,' Prakesh said. 'It was a stupid thing to do. You could have been killed!'

'It's a more stupid thing to stay locked inside a cell with a fire burning outside,' Elfrida said.

I recognised her from the photograph, even with her hair cropped short. It was Elfrida, the missing (presumed murdered) wife of the murdered Boss Max.

No wonder we had been unable to find her body in the jungle – Elfrida had been here in the resort all along. And she had come to rescue us. She was looking at me now. 'Are you all right? How did you know I was there?'

'I didn't,' I said. 'But Captain Henry said Daffy's tea took care of two aunties and Viktor, and I knew they weren't the only ones in the servants' quarters.'

'He didn't make it for Viktor either,' Elfrida said. 'Viktor rushed in and helped me to get Aunty Rakiah and Aunty Salmah out before the fire reached us. Then he rushed away again. I don't know where he went. We only saw the fire and didn't know there was anybody inside.'

I tried to see what was going on, but Le Froy made me lie down and close my eyes – just for a moment, I thought. But when I woke it was two hours later and the fire was already dying down. As I learned later, Le Froy and Prakesh had draped wet curtains on the side of the servants' lodge to prevent flames spreading there from the security post. Best of all, it was starting to rain. I swore I would never ever complain about wet weather again.

Yet the remnants of the front wall of the police shack were still smouldering.

Still smouldering?

'Paraffin?' I said. 'Viktor bought cans of paraffin from the shop just now.' Could he have been in on this? Even if he'd helped Aunty Rakiah and Aunty Salmah to safety, why had he chosen to leave with Captain Henry and the Cooks?

'Somebody took all our cooking paraffin,' Aunty Rakiah was struggling to sit up. 'Such a waste to burn it like that. Cost us almost nine hundred and fifty banana notes.'

'We told Viktor he must go and buy some more paraffin or else no more food, no more hot water.'

They didn't seem very upset. In fact, the atmosphere around us was of relief and release. And why not? We were alive. Elfrida was alive and not hiding any more. And if Captain Henry and the Cooks were gone, I for one wouldn't miss them.

There would be time to worry later about justice. Le Froy and I were happy to be sitting there, grimy and ash-streaked, catching our breath. I could see Prakesh and Jaimin sitting side by side, eyes closed, gripping each other's hands.

'What happened to you?' Le Froy asked. 'We haven't been introduced. I'm—'

'I know who you are,' Elfrida said. She came to sit closer to us. 'I saw you in the big house.' She smiled at me. 'You were nice to me. You were nice to all the servants.'

'Why did you run away?' Prakesh moved over to join the conversation, Jaimin with him. 'Do you know how worried people were? How could you let everybody think you had run away or been kidnapped or killed? How could you make us all worry like that?' He was really angry now.

'Max brought me up to the Camerons to make me a prisoner,' Elfrida said. 'On the estate, there were too many people around and it was too near to the town. He knew you, Le Froy, were being sent to investigate the Walker killings, but he thought the weather and flooding would delay you until he'd got what he wanted.'

'What did he want?' Le Froy asked.

'He wanted me to give him the emeralds,' Elfrida said. 'My emeralds.'

'I heard you took them from his safe,' Le Froy said. His fingers twitched for his notebook, but he'd passed it to me and I'd lost it somewhere in the conflagration.

'Max and Terry killed the planters who owned the Emerald Estate before them because they wouldn't sell for the price they wanted – those poor people. And their poor wives.'

'Are you sure?' Prakesh said. 'There were so many rumours going around . . .'

'I heard Terry and Max talking one night. Daffy found out Max had paid to have the Walker brothers killed – the two brothers and their wives – and threatened to report him if he didn't sell up and give her and Terry enough money to get out of Malaya and settle somewhere else. Daffy hated living here. She swore she'd die rather than stay, regardless of how much money Max promised them he would make for them. Terry knew about the last three emeralds. He wanted Max to sell them, split the money with him and get out. Max agreed, but said if that was what they wanted, they had to leave without telling anyone they were going and then sell them.'

'Why?'

'That's what Terry wanted to know. Max said they were owed to the person who had taken care of getting the Walkers out. The agreement was that he would pay after the Emerald Estate had been in production for a year, if no one came after him before then.'

Le Froy caught my eye and gave me a tiny nod. Harry Palin had been right, after all. The local Communists hadn't turned on the white planters, however angry they might have been. And Le Froy's arrival to look into the plantation murders had made things worse.

'Why didn't you leave Max the emeralds and run away?' Prakesh asked. 'If he'd had them, he might have let you go.'

'I didn't want to think of him using my grandmother's emeralds to pay for a murder.'

'Why didn't you leave once you'd got them out of Max's safe?' Le Froy asked. 'You could have gone to the police and asked for protection.'

Elfrida glanced at Prakesh and Jaimin who admittedly didn't look very capable of protecting anyone.

'I tried – but I didn't know where to go and I left it too late. I was stupid enough to ask Daffy to help me. I thought she would be as shocked as I was by what our husbands were up to. And I didn't think Max would suspect me right away. I mean, anyone could have come in and taken them. Then I was drugged one night and I knew someone had come into my room and searched it. But I had already hidden the emeralds. Then, because he heard Le Froy was coming to investigate the murders at the plantation, Max said we were all coming to the Cameron Highlands till you gave up and left.'

'Brandon Sands saw through that,' Le Froy said, with a small smile.

'Max kept saying he only wanted the emeralds back but I knew he would kill me once he had them.'

'How did you get the aunties to help you?' I asked.

'They knew. Even before we left the plantation they saw how Max treated me. And Aunty Salmah spoke German and English, so I could talk to them. But I had to pretend I didn't like them or Max would have fired them.'

'Yes, indeed,' Prakesh said.

'I'm sorry,' Elfrida said. 'I didn't want you to get into trouble with him. You are nice. You were trying to help me. But I knew that if you helped me, Max would kill you. I warned Aunty Salmah and Aunty Rakiah, but they said they had to die anyway so they might as well get me out and die together. They were great actors. Max told them to watch me and search my things and promised them a reward if they found what I had stolen from him so they pretended to be stupid and on his side. But Aunty Salmah heard him tell Captain Henry that, whether or not he found the emeralds, he was going to get rid of me up here. And he wasn't going to pay any of the servants, just leave them here to get home on their own.

'Until then I actually thought it might be better to stay in my safe prison, that things might improve. But Aunty Salmah told me I had to get out. She told me to go behind the WC. It was the best spot because Max and the other men always avoided that area.

'The two aunties cut through sections of the bamboo sticks behind the toilet. But they didn't cut the vine leaves, just slid the poles out. I was so thin by then, I could squeeze out. Then they slid the bamboo pieces back so the vines held the bamboo in place and tied the vines back and no one noticed.'

It was true. Even I hadn't seen through the thick covering of creeper fig. I understood now why Aunty Rakiah and Aunty Salmah hadn't wanted me to examine the vines too closely.

'I almost found the emeralds that day you stopped me,' I said.

'Yes,' Elfrida said. She smiled. 'I stopped you just in time.'

'I saw you with the lighter Daffy lost,' I said. 'I almost told her you were a thief.'

'Daffy was stealing from me. That Princess Ronson lighter was mine,' Elfrida said. 'Daffy took it from me, so I stole it back.'

'Even before the murders Max Moreno hired thugs to intimidate the previous landowners,' Le Froy said. 'That was how he pulled the Emerald Estate together. They threatened anyone who wanted to buy any of the smallholdings, threatened and beat them up if they didn't back off. Did you know about that?'

'He said everybody did it,' Elfrida said in a low voice. 'He said that was how people did things here. I didn't know he hired someone to murder the Walkers until later. I don't think he meant to. He thought they would just threaten and frighten them off, like he did back in South America. But Captain Henry killed them. He said it was easier than paying them off. And then he killed the killers and charged Max extra for the cleaning up.'

'I found your valentines,' I said. 'From your grandmother, I think.'

'Thank you,' Elfrida said simply. 'They were important to me. Her letters helped me to stay strong. Max said he would burn them. He didn't understand that I already had them inside here,' she touched her chest, 'where he could not damage them. My *oma* always said that even if a woman cannot choose whom she marries, she can choose to live the best life she can. She had an unhappy marriage.'

I saw her pause. Almost as though she was trying to decide whether or not to add 'like me'. She didn't, and I respected her for that.

'Oma always said that in her day you had to marry who your parents chose for you. She hoped I would have more freedom to choose for myself. To marry for love, and to find more happiness than she had. But, of course, during the war there was little hope, and even less choice. Oma always said that for her everything was worth it because she had a granddaughter – me – whom she loved so much. And so she could regret nothing in her life. She told me to remember that. Sometimes you find great love out of great misery. And she left me all her property. All that is gone now. And all her jewellery. This is all that is left of the family fortune. That's why I hid the last of my emeralds from him. After all my father had done, I couldn't let my husband use my family jewels to pay for murder.'

'Lucky for me I came back.'

I'd thought Captain Henry was long gone.

But he was back. Not in Boss Max's car but on foot, which was why none of us had noticed him. But there he was, gun in hand, Daffy and Terry plodding up the road behind him.

'I hate leaving a job without everything cleared up,' he said.

The Murder of Max

———◆———

'Why did you come back?' I asked.

'The damned gully bridge is down.' It was Terry Cook who answered. 'There's a pile of stone and rotten wood on the other side and just a gap. It looks like it was blown up. Maybe something triggered ammunition planted by the Japanese. We're cut off.'

'How are you going to explain things when you're found up here with us?' Le Froy asked.

'I won't have to say anything if I'm forced to shoot you to prevent your escape,' Captain Henry said smugly. He raised his pistol and pointed it at my husband.

'Better make sure you have enough bullets first,' I said. 'There's a lot of us here, you know. More than the men you shot after they killed the Walkers for you.'

That was a guess, but I suspected Captain Henry wouldn't have hired more workers than he'd had to, even if he had no intention of paying them.

Captain Henry looked around and, for the first time, registered Elfrida, who had been sitting next to the still drowsy Aunty Rakiah and Aunty Salmah. 'Elfrida?'

'It's Elfrida!' Daffy shouted. 'Max wasn't lying – he truly didn't kill her. Where were you hiding all this time?' She switched gears without waiting for an answer. 'Look, Elfrida, now you're around to verify the sale, we'll get much more for the emeralds than if we have to hock them on the black-market. Everything divided between the four of us. Do you understand? That's enough to get you out of this hellish country and set you up for life.'

'You were sleeping with Max,' Elfrida said to Daffy.

'What's that got to do with anything?'

'I trusted you. I believed you when you said we were friends,' Elfrida said. 'Instead you betrayed me.'

'Is that why you did it, Cook?' Le Froy asked. 'You found out Max was sleeping with your wife. Is that why you killed him?'

It was a dramatic (even logical) accusation, but if it was meant to shock a confession out of Terry Cook it failed miserably.

'Daffy?' Terry Cook stuttered. 'Daffy and Max? My Daffy?'

I might have been a petty crook, but I couldn't see him as a murderer. Neither could Daffy, apparently.

'I'm fed up of you being so useless!' his Daffy told him. 'Same with Viktor. He was nice in bed but too dumb to be useful. You're the one who's been deceiving us all.'

'I didn't deceive everyone. Viktor knew,' Elfrida smiled gently into the darkness beyond the rose apple tree. 'The others didn't even notice whether there were three servants or two.'

'Yes.' Viktor stepped forward. 'I smelt you. I never said anything.'

'You could've told me,' Terry Cook said to Viktor. 'You could have told Max where his wife was. Especially with everyone suspecting him of doing away with her.'

'You're such a stupid oaf!' Daffy said. 'If you'd just handed over the emeralds we wouldn't be stuck here and Max might still be alive.'

'But Elfrida might not,' Viktor said. 'That is why she had to leave. Because of the danger to her.'

'Anyway,' Daffy said, 'Elfrida, you'll be strung up for murdering your husband unless you decide to be reasonable and sell the emeralds for us. A good legitimate sale and you walk away with enough to start a new life.'

I was surprised Captain Henry was letting this go on. He still had his gun pointed at Prakesh, but he was frowning. 'How much less on the black-market?' he asked.

I could tell that whatever Elfrida decided to do the rest of us would be dead. And so would she, once they got what they wanted from her.

'Of course people will believe only Elfrida could kill her husband in a locked room,' I said.

'Of course.' Le Froy picked up immediately. 'Elfrida's the most intelligent woman here – apart from you, my dear.'

Daffy wavered. I could almost see her sense of self-preservation fighting with the desire to show how much cleverer she was than anyone else. 'And she managed to disappear without being found,' I said. 'Daffy didn't have a clue.'

'Quite brilliant.' Le Froy nodded. 'And very beautiful too.'

That was the last straw. 'Elfrida's a fool! She doesn't know anything!' Daffy screeched. 'She wanted to be a good wife to that man and she didn't realise he'd dump her as soon as he got his hands on her emeralds. He was going to double-cross her all along, same as he was going to double-cross us all! Well, he didn't get a chance, did he?'

'Be quiet, woman!' Captain Henry said. 'Don't say anything—'

'Don't talk to my wife like that,' Terry Cook interrupted.

'Shut up, you fool!' Daffy said.

'But, Daffy, you told me that you heard—' Terry stopped.

And suddenly, 'I know how you killed Boss Max!' I said. 'Yes! I know how you must have done it!'

They all (and Captain Henry's gun) swung round to me, but I was too caught up with finessing the details to care. I turned to Le Froy. 'Remember the morning we got married, my grandmother and uncle rushing to the Waterloo Street temple to get Kuan Yin blessings and buy food for a feast? They meant well and it was a lovely surprise in the end, but until I found out, I was miserable, believing they were so angry they wouldn't even see me?'

'Surprises are always a bad idea,' Le Froy said. 'What's the point?'

'I would have sworn they were in their rooms, that I heard Ah Ma telling me to go away when she was in town. I believed I heard it myself, even though it was my cousin telling me what she said.'

'Because your cousin was in on it.' We turned to look at Daffy. 'Daffy was in on it.'

'You didn't hear Max inside his room the day he died, did you?' Le Froy asked.

Daffy looked flustered. 'I thought – I was sure – but I could have been mistaken—'

'She could have stabbed Max the night before, when no one was looking,' Prakesh said, 'and locked the room. Then pretended to hear him.'

'No. The blood was red, not brown,' I said. 'Fresh blood. Max Moreno wasn't stabbed the night before. And the door was locked. Not just with the lock but the door latch hook was on until Captain Henry broke it.'

Le Froy nodded, 'I heard Max hook it when he locked himself in that night.'

'I think Daffy put her sleeping powders in his whisky,' I said. 'When Boss Max woke and felt bad he would very likely have drunk more. But he was alert enough to be aware that something was wrong, and sit up with his gun.'

Just as Le Froy had done that night when Daffy dosed us.

'Max was drugged, like we were. Daffy pretended to talk to him through the door, and I believed her. I heard him too. Then Captain Henry came and broke down the door, barged in to where Max was slumped in his chair covered with vomit and told us that Max was already dead even as he stabbed him with the *kris* dagger he'd brought in with him. He had me and Daffy as witnesses and Daffy's hysterics kept me from seeing the body till Max was truly dead. Leaving that *kris* in his chest was your biggest mistake,' I told Captain Henry. 'You wanted to tie the murders to the locals you framed for killing the Walkers. But if a local owned a *kris* like that, he would never have left it in the body.

'And you got the dagger from the station, didn't you? Is it one they found in the bodies of the murdered planters? One of those confiscated from the Japanese collection that you took from the storage unit? I thought you and Max were partners. Why did you do it? Were you really that much in love with Daffy that you had to have her all to yourself?'

'Daffy?' Terry Cook said. 'Daffy and Max – and Captain Henry? Daffy?'

'Look, this is just a waste of time. I meant for Max to overdose,' Daffy said. 'Easiest way for him to go. And I wanted you around to find him dead with me. Only he wasn't dead and Henry had to stab him. That wasn't meant to happen.'

'Luckily I think fast,' Captain Henry said. 'Anyway, he asked for it. Daffy told me Max was selling me out to get out of paying me. I stuck my neck out for that bastard. Got the coolies to get rid of the Walkers and made sure those fellas disappeared. Not only does he not pay me, I heard he was setting up to hang the whole damn thing on me! Oh, no, not on my watch.'

'Actually, Boss Max was planning to pin it on Harry Palin,' Le Froy said. 'He had a grudge against him and thought he could use the murders to get rid of him.'

'What?' Captain Henry looked at Daffy.

'Maybe I got Harry and Henry mixed up. So what?' Daffy said. 'What difference does it make who he was going to frame? We've got the emeralds so it's all good.'

'The emeralds belong to Elfrida. They are not yours.'

Captain Henry turned his gun on Viktor. Viktor looked back at him calmly. Captain Henry wouldn't hesitate to shoot an unarmed man but Viktor was a really large unarmed man.

If you're ever faced with a really large wild boar, it's good to remember you're unlikely to kill it with a single shot. And that one shot will enrage the pig so you'll likely end up dead as its dinner. In fact, this is true of even a medium-sized wild boar. I suspect that's what was going through Captain Henry's mind as he gazed at Viktor.

'You can't blame Daffy for all of this,' Terry Cook cut in. 'Max was behind everything. It was his idea. He said all these rubber plantations confiscated from the Japanese were being handed out for free practically. All you needed was a Briton to sign for the grant. and Americans would be fighting to pay top dollar for all the rubber you could produce to make tyres for their motor-cars. Workers cost less than slaves, Max added, because you don't have to feed them, and he had a man who understood rubber. He could handle the factory processing and shipping and we wouldn't have to do a thing.'

Viktor held up a hand. 'He is referring to me. I understand rubber. From the growing of trees to the processing of latex. I also understand the growing of strawberries, but I have yet to master the processing process.'

'Unfortunately Max's so-called rubber expert turned out to be this crazy guy without any funds to buy the fancy processing equipment he was talking about. He wouldn't even let the workers collect rubber when it rains. Like they're going to melt?'

'Again he is referring to me,' Viktor said. 'To present my case fairly, my value is in my knowledge. I know you should not tap during the rains when the trees are growing, or the next season you will get a poor product.'

'Next season? What next season? Thanks to your nonsense, we didn't even make it through the first. I should have done this a long time ago—'

Terry Cook raised his rifle over his shoulder and brought it down on the side of Viktor's head. At least, that was the idea, but Viktor caught the descending barrel and raised it higher, forcing the shorter man onto his toes as he tried to wrestle it back.

'Damn you, you big fool!' Daffy jumped in and grabbed at Viktor's arm. 'Let go of his gun!'

'I should have done this a long time ago,' Viktor agreed. He let go of the gun and punched Terry Cook in the face.

'How dare you?' Daffy screamed. 'Nobody hits Terry but me!'

'Dammit, Daffy,' Captain Henry said, 'shut your mouth and let me think!'

'How dare you talk to me like that? I'm not going to shut up and I'm not going to listen to you any more. You're as much of a fool as my husband. Why don't you do something useful for once, instead of—'

The blast that momentarily deafened us all came as a relief after her grating voice.

Daffy looked surprised. Her mouth was open and so was the dark red hole blooming in her chest. 'You shot me.' She collapsed in a heap.

'She wouldn't shut up,' Captain Henry said. He looked at us. I suspected he was calculating how far his remaining bullets would go.

'No,' Terry Cook said. 'Not Daffy.'

I didn't know if it was her betrayal or her death that he had trouble believing.

'How are you going to explain all our bodies?' Le Froy sounded as though he was trying to work out the official report.

'Must have been a bomb left behind by the Japanese. Maybe you discovered it with your great detective powers but you died without telling anyone where it was. Really tragic loss. A great man before the war et cetera,' Captain Henry said.

'Put your gun down in the next five seconds,' Viktor said, in a very calm, very hard voice, 'or I will kill you.'

'I'm the one with the gun, stupid!' Captain Henry laughed. As he moved his gun towards Viktor, Le Froy launched sideways and pushed me to the floor. At the same time, Viktor yanked Elfrida behind him with one arm so his bulk shielded her from Captain Henry. With his other hand he seized the compact knife from around his neck and threw it with unerring accuracy into Captain Henry's neck.

'Nice throw,' Le Froy said.

'A strike in the eye would be more certain,' Viktor said, 'but there are women here and women don't like that.'

I didn't want to know how he'd come to realise that.

Prakesh and Jaimin had moved to flank Terry Cook, but he wasn't a threat. The man was crouched over Daffy's body, saying, 'What happened? I don't understand. What happened?' over and over.

Viktor kicked Captain Henry's weapon aside and searched him till he found a leather pouch containing the emeralds.

'These are yours.' He handed it to Elfrida. 'You can afford to get away from here now.'

'Where would I go?'

'You can afford to go wherever you wish,' Viktor said.

'I would like to stay and learn more about producing and processing rubber,' Elfrida said. 'But I don't know much about rubber trees.'

'I am an expert,' Viktor said modestly. 'I can help you. But you need to buy processing equipment.'

'I will sell the emeralds now,' Elfrida said, 'not to pay for murder, but to buy equipment and to improve life for the people living on the estate. In particular, reinforcing the canals and digging wells so that there's enough water in the dry season and no flooding when it rains.'

I remembered the pit latrine in her prison room. It made sense that Elfrida wanted to use her money to build sanitation and water filters for the people who would live on her plantation.

They had been through a lot, but I thought they would be all right.

Life and Love Go On

◆

'What do we do now?' I asked Le Froy. 'Harry won't be able to get up here and we won't be able to get off the Moonlight Plateau now the gully bridge is down – unless . . . Do you think Harry blew up the bridge?'

'I blew up the bridge,' Viktor said. 'It was the only way to stop them getting away. It was the only solution.'

'It was a good solution,' Le Froy said. Then, to me, 'Now we wait. No one is missing, nothing is missing, everything's all right.'

'Not really,' I said. 'It's starting to rain again.'

At least the rain woke Aunty Rakiah and Aunty Salmah. Once they got over their nausea they were happy to find Elfrida was herself again and eager to share stories of how clumsy and inept she had been when she started in her servant role.

'We used to have amateur theatricals at home, so I loved acting and pretending,' Elfrida said. 'But doing real housework is much harder than acting a servant.'

* * *

When Harry's reinforcements came, they took the gully in their stride and set up a rope bridge. Thick hemp ropes were anchored on both sides and they created a makeshift walkway by tying small planks together, then additional ropes to serve as handrails. They got us out of there in a few hours, even carrying over most of our belongings.

I didn't see what they did with the bodies. Some things I'm happy to leave to the authorities.

Something else I didn't know was how things would work out between Jaimin and Prakesh. Jaimin wanted to stay close to her mother and sisters, but there was no way she could continue working on her late brother's qualifications. Prakesh wanted her to accompany him to the city, starting with Kuala Lumpur and maybe going on to Singapore. However that went, as long as there's life there's hope, right.

And, of course, the best part of all was getting home.

I'd never appreciated my family and Chen Mansion as much as when I'd thought I might never go back.

'You had your honeymoon in the Cameron Highlands? That's so romantic. You're so lucky, Su!'

When we got back my best friend Parshanti was at Chen Mansion with her parents and husband. She ran out to hug me, thrilled to hear we'd been to the Cameron Highlands.

'Not fair!' she said. 'Oh, you must have had such a wonderful honeymoon, Mrs Le Froy. I'm so sorry to have missed your wedding, but you're going to tell me all about it.'

'Well . . .' There had been much more going on than just a honeymoon and our wedding seemed so long ago I couldn't think where to start.

'You are happy, aren't you?' Parshanti asked. 'Happily married?' She looked so alarmed I couldn't help smiling.

'Thank you, Mrs Leask,' I said. 'Yes, I am happily married. And there's something you haven't told me about, isn't there?'

Even if Le Froy hadn't told me I could feel the rounding of her belly. 'You're happy too, aren't you?'

'I feel horrible sometimes but, yes, I've never been happier.'

I moved out of Chen Mansion . . . into the house on the adjoining allotment. I made sure to have a rose apple tree transplanted outside to remind me of hidden treasures we shouldn't overlook. And, thanks to Elfrida, the shelves in the back of the little kitchen were already stacked full of Ipoh clay cookware. There were single-serving clay pots, just right for a child to spoon braised chicken cubes and sticky rice from. And then there were the giant clay pots that took two people to lift and could hold five chickens, as well as enough rice and Chinese sausage to feed up to twenty people.

I would never be able to reproduce Ah Ma's claypot fish head, vinegar-ginger pigs' trotters and chicken feet with clams, but I would enjoy trying . . . the cooking as well as the other stuff.

If Elfrida could take on a rubber plantation for Viktor and improve the lives of the workers there, I could take on helping my family business for my grandmother. To my surprise, Le Froy wasn't against the idea, despite his having resumed his position in the Straits Police Force.

'She did what was needed. When the police weren't enabled to act, Chen Tai brought order to the chaos,' Le Froy said. 'The clans, gangs and *tongs* fighting for territory would have been a lot worse if she hadn't taken charge.'

'You told your bosses in the force that my grandmother made the bad guys more efficient?'

'Order out of chaos,' Le Froy said. 'Any kind of order is better than chaos. But don't worry, there'll always be chaos.'

Not too much, I hoped. I went to the temple to light incense sticks to give thanks for our safe return home and wish the aunties and Harry Palin well. This might have caused some confusion, because the goddess Bixia is usually thanked for fertility and children.

So, yes, I lit an extra joss stick in thanks for that too.

Epilogue

———◆———

Unfortunately, these were only the start of the plantation killings.

When the British turned (subtly at first) on their former Communist allies, an MI6 operative, Denis Emerson-Elliott, infiltrated the increasingly popular Malayan Communist Party, inciting members to target rubber plantations from the surrounding jungle. After Emerson-Elliott rented the Cameron Highlands Moonlight Bungalow to Chin Peng, leader of the MCP, it was the site of terrible killings.

This was the start of the Emergency period.

Acknowledgements

I must thank all the people who made this book possible. First of all, my wonderful agent, Priya Doraswamy, who started me on this path and is still guiding me.

Thank you also Hazel Orme, whose sharp editorial eye and good sense made this a better book than it would otherwise be, for her support and friendship.

Thank you, Charlotte Stroomer, for the beautiful cover design.

Thank you, also, to Amanda Keats, for holding my hand and walking me step by step (and email by email) through the publishing process.

And thank you, thank you, thank you to the whole team at Constable/Little, Brown who worked on this book with me.

And my special thanks to Krystyna Green for the last time: thank you so much, Krystyna!